MAN
ON
ICE

Humphrey Hawksley is a foreign correspondent for the BBC, a regular speaker and panellist at Intelligence Squared and the Royal Geographical Society, and many literary festivals. Hawksley's writing has appeared in the *Guardian*, *The Times*, *Financial Times*, *International Herald Tribune* and *Yale Global*. Hawksley's television documentaries include *The Curse of Gold* and *Bitter Sweet*, *Aid Under Scrutiny*, *Old Man Atom* and *Danger: Democracy at Work*.

@hwhawksley humphreyhawksley.com

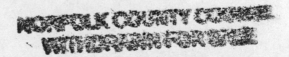

ALSO BY HUMPHREY HAWKSLEY

The Kat Polinski Series
Security Breach
Home Run
Friends and Enemies

The Future History Series
Dragon Strike
Dragon Fire
The Third World War

MAN ON ICE

HUMPHREY HAWKSLEY

BLACKTHORN

First published in Great Britain, the USA and Canada in 2019
by Black Thorn, an imprint of Canongate Books Ltd,
14 High Street, Edinburgh EH1 1TE

Distributed in the USA by Publishers Group West and in Canada by
Publishers Group Canada

First published in 2018 by Severn House Publishers Ltd,
Eardley House, 4 Uxbridge Street, London W8 7SY

blackthornbooks.com

1

British Library Cataloguing-in-Publication Data
A catalogue record for this book is available on request
from the British Library

ISBN 978 1 78689 494 6

Typeset in Dante MT Std by Palimpsest Book Production Ltd, Falkirk,
Stirlingshire, Scotland

Printed and bound in Great Britain by Clays Ltd, Elcograf S.p.A.

To all families and nations divided by politics

THE FOLLOWING TAKES PLACE IN THE TWO DAYS
BEFORE THE AMERICAN PRESIDENTIAL
INAUGURATION ON JANUARY 20th

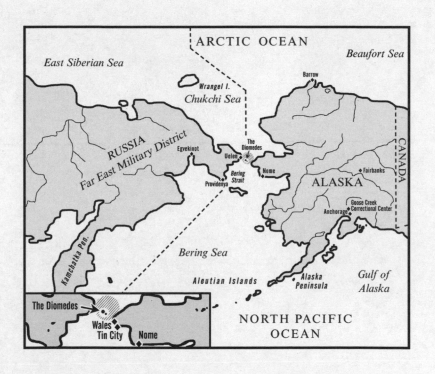

ONE

Little Diomede, Alaska, USA

Thick mist hung over the frozen Bering Sea and inside the helicopter cabin a familiar voice broke through the static of Rake Ozenna's headset. 'We have an emergency evacuation,' said his adoptive father, in a tone that was calm but edged with urgency. 'How far out are you?'

'On the ground in about five minutes, Henry,' said the pilot.

Rake's fiancée unwrapped her arm from his shoulder and pressed the talk button on her headset cable. 'This is Dr Carrie Walker,' she said. 'I'm with Rake Ozenna. I'm a trauma surgeon. What exactly is the patient's condition?'

A woman's voice answered. 'This is Joan, district nurse. Akna's waters have broken.'

Joan was Henry's wife. Rake had told Carrie about them and his home island many times. Even so, he had been apprehensive about bringing her here and the past minute was proving him right. He tried to catch her eye, but she was concentrating, at work a hundred percent on her new patient. 'Thank you, Joan,' she said. 'Do you know how many weeks into the pregnancy?'

'We think thirty-five weeks.'

1

'And how old is she?'

'Fifteen.'

Carrie showed no reaction to the young age. She had seen far worse, so had Rake. She snapped open her bag to check her medicines. 'Does she have a fever?'

'A hundred and two.'

'Thank you. Keep Akna comfortable—'

The pilot cut in. 'We're three minutes out. Henry, I need you on the helipad. The wind is everywhere.'

Carrie tapped her finger across packets of antibiotics and said confidently, 'Reassure Akna that help is on the way. We'll get her safely to hospital in Nome in a couple of hours.'

Rake wasn't so sure, but he stayed quiet. It depended on exactly where Akna was. It could take half an hour to get her stretchered safely down to the helipad. In January, this far north, the sun barely broke above the horizon. Its dim light merged with the moon and stars to create a glow of daytime winter darkness, and now it was coming up to midday, but it could have been midnight. The way clouds were scudding meant frozen fog could move in at any time.

An hour earlier they had left Nome to fly over a flat white Alaskan emptiness until fog almost forced them to turn back. The pilot managed to climb above it and for a long time they could only see the top of a shimmering low cloud bank. When they descended again, two islands appeared, solid and dark, like guards keeping vigil on the ice-covered expanse. Rake pointed to the longer, flatter island on their left. 'That's Big Diomede,' he said to Carrie, tapping the window. 'They call it Ratmonova. See, along the top, Russian military observation posts.'

'Oh, my God!' Carrie looked in fascination and turned to see out the other side. 'And you grew up over there?'

The helicopter shook as the pilot turned them into the wind at a mid-point between the islands, exactly where Russia and America met. The international dateline ran along the sea border. A few meters to their west, and they would drift into another day and another country.

As the smaller island on their right became more visible, Carrie hooked back her blonde hair and cupped her hand against the window. Light from outside the helicopter silhouetted her strong face, high cheekbones, and prominent jaw. An orange windsock on the helipad gave a splash of color against the grayness of the settlement, a pallid cluster of small buildings, dwarfed by the steep island hillside rising directly behind.

Carrie's home could not have been more different to his. She was half Estonian, half Russian, and was raised as a Brooklyn Catholic, from a family of successful doctors. He was a native Eskimo from the Diomede Islands, which lay at the very edge of American territory and where 'family' held a looser meaning. Her father was a top cardiologist, her mother a gynecologist, and Carrie became a trauma surgeon. Rake had no idea where his mother or father were, could barely remember their faces. He had been raised by Joan and Henry Ahkvaluk, his father's cousins. As soon as Rake was old enough, he had joined the Alaska Army National Guard. From the lowest rank of private, he broke through to reach captain in the 207th Infantry Group based at Fort Richardson outside of Anchorage, better known as the elite unit of Eskimo Scouts, perfect for deployment to mountain winters in Afghanistan, which was where a sensible girl from Brooklyn fell in love with a wild boy from the Diomedes, at least that was how they told it to friends. Carrie and Rake met over a car bomb in Kabul.

It was more than ten years since Rake's last visit to Little Diomede. Jumbled images came to him of this place he knew so well and wished he could understand. Since then there had been Iraq, Afghanistan, the Philippines, Iraq again, Afghanistan again. And now he had Carrie, who had settled him.

Drab clapboard homes stood on layers of walkways, one above the other, up the steep slope. The helipad, a rough concrete square, jutted out from a coastline of huge boulders. To the left stood Rake's old school, its green walls and snow-covered roof shimmering under clear moonlight. Three steel dinghy boats were pulled up on the iced shingle of a tiny bay. Rake spotted the one belonging to Henry. In front, half a dozen snowmobiles stood on the sea ice and further along was the old, abandoned one, that Rake had ridden the night a polar bear had threatened the village. In the wildlife magazines, polar bears were made to look majestic. Close up, they were dirty, dangerous, eating machines. Henry rode out on the snowmobile with his two surrogate sons, Rake and Don Ondola, and showed them how to track and kill the animal. That morning, the whole village had walked across the ice to carve off meat and store it for winter. Don got the hide because he was two years older. He had been like a brother to Rake. But now he had gone mad and was serving time for murder, which was why the emergency radio call was so troubling. Akna was his daughter.

Carrie knew some of this, but not all. Rake had told her about the hunting of walrus, seal, and polar bear; the isolation, the winter darkness, the summer light; how the Eskimos had lost their language because the school only taught in English; how men away hunting had asked friends to look after their wives in their own beds in a practice called wife-sharing which is why Eskimos weren't so good at doing the mom, pop, and three kids nuclear-family thing; how missionaries had tried to change them but without much success, and had given up and were now gone from the island. That had made Carrie laugh.

He told her about the sacred ancestral graves on the hillside and how he could read the weather by the way the birds flew around the island. Carrie loved all that, but she was no fool. She would figure out the whole picture for herself once they got there. He hadn't reckoned on her starting even before they landed.

From the helicopter window, he saw Henry step out from a hut next to the old wooden church on a higher walkway. It used to be Don's house. Rake didn't know who lived there now. Henry was more than sixty years old, but skilled with his boots on the ice, faster than many men half his age. He started down the walkway to meet them.

The helicopter shuddered against a brutal surge of wind. She was a Bell 214ST, an old military transport warhorse, probably from Iraq, maybe even Vietnam. There were straps and buckles to lock in a stretcher, two if needs be. Carrie would insist on flying with Akna to Nome. She wouldn't have it any other way, which meant Rake would go too, so ten minutes on the ground. They would come back tomorrow, weather permitting.

Carrie tucked the ankles of her jeans into her heavy-duty hiking boots, then lifted her headset, pushed her hair under the

hood of her green parka, and zipped it up to her chin in prepa-
ration for the freezing weather outside. She held her medical
pack on her lap. She turned her engagement ring towards him,
green and blue, jade and sapphire, from an old gem shop in
Kabul. She smiled quickly at him, as the ring vanished into her
red Gore-Tex glove.

Rake pulled up his sleeve to remind her of the tattoo of his
O-negative blood group on the inside of his right forearm. She
had made him get it as a condition of her marrying him. He
pulled his woolen hat over his ears and secured his green military
Arctic warfare jacket as Carrie had hers. She was an inch taller
than him, and would never let him forget it.

Akna's emergency was returning them to a familiar, professional place. Carrie was leading, Rake watching their backs, and,
at that moment, a new unfamiliar voice came across the radio,
nervous, tense. 'This is Wales. Mike, are you out there? We've
got a man through the ice. Anyone from Erickson?'

Mike was the pilot, Erickson the helicopter company. Wales,
twenty-five miles away, was the closest mainland settlement.

'This is Mike. I'm landing at Little Diomede now. What's
happened?'

A disjointed reply came with the ebb and flow of static. One
of the elders of the settlement had been cutting through sea ice
to catch crabs. The ice had broken, and he had fallen through.
With climate change it was becoming impossible for even the
most experienced to judge the thickness of the ice. Underneath,
the water temperature wouldn't be much above freezing, which
meant hypothermia setting in fast. They had gotten him out in
time. But now he had suffered a heart attack.

'I'm twenty-five minutes out from you.' Mike turned the aircraft side on and brought it in over the boats on the shingle until they were a few feet above the helipad.

Carrie flashed a worried look. 'Is a doctor there?'

The skids settled on the frozen helipad. The engine noise dropped, the rotor blades slowing. Mike turned to speak directly to Carrie. 'Yes, ma'am. They do have a doctor.'

'Best if we stay here,' said Rake. 'Mike goes to Wales and comes back. It'll be forty minutes' round trip. It'll take that time to get Akna down.'

That was it. The triage. The call on which casualty got treated first. They had done it together a dozen times. They wouldn't know about Akna's condition until Carrie had examined her. Rake and Mike knew this environment. Carrie nodded her agreement.

Henry pulled open the door, his weathered face clouded by his heavy breathing. Little in his craggy features had changed over the ten years. His marksman's eyes were as sharp as ever and he didn't look a day older. A gust of freezing air hit them, stinging their faces. Rake got down, wind roaring all around, and helped Carrie out.

'Fog's coming. We need to be quick,' said Henry. He embraced Rake, and firmly gripped Carrie's hand. He had raised a dozen children like Rake, their parents vanished or useless through drugs and drink. Rake and Henry were like father and son.

As Mike took the helicopter up again, they crouched, shielding luggage from the down draught. The sound of the throbbing rotor blades faded, leaving a sudden quiet. Carrie took in the island's desolation.

'I'll bring you both up,' said Henry.

Carrie hoisted her pack onto her back. 'Are Akna's parents with her?' she asked.

Without answering, Henry set off. That was enough to confirm to Rake what he had suspected. 'They're not,' he said, taking Carrie's arm to steady her on the slippery ground.

'Can they find them?'

'I don't know.'

'She's a child. She'll need her mom with her.'

Rake wasn't sure what to say. Akna's father, Don Ondola, adopted son to Henry and adoptive brother and best friend to Rake, had murdered her mother in a drug-crazed rage. He was also the father of his daughter's unborn child.

TWO

Little Diomede, Alaska, USA

Carrie held her patient's feverish hand. Soaked in sweat, Akna stared up at this stranger. She lay on sheets on a lumpy black sofa in a hut built into the hillside next to the Catholic church that had fallen derelict when the missionaries left. She had a rounded face with a dimple on her left cheek. Her skin was creased and dried from synthetic dope smuggled onto the island. Her eyes carried an emptiness Rake had seen so often when the human spirit just gives up. Akna had shaved her head halfway up the skull leaving a neat ridge of black hair on the top. She wore a red T-shirt, with a silver heart on the front. She was a kid, like millions of teenagers who experimented with fashion and hairstyles as they grew up. Somewhere, in what he saw, was the little girl whom Rake used to put on the slide in the school playground. Akna was five when he last saw her, laughing and full of excitement. She was about to give birth or die but it was as if neither one meant anything to her. Her waters had broken thirty-six hours earlier, but she had told no one and infection had brought her temperature dangerously high. Now she was barely conscious.

'We need to sit you up, Akna, to change you,' said Carrie softly. The room was warm and Carrie worked, jacket off, in a red denim shirt, sleeves rolled up and hair held back with a rubber band. In an adjoining room, Henry and three other men prepared a stretcher to carry Akna down.

'A helicopter is taking you to Nome. You'll be fine, Akna. Just fine,' said Joan, laying a towel wet with sterilized cold water on Akna's brow. She wore one-piece blue dungarees and was a thin sinewy woman, with short black hair and wide concentrating eyes.

Rake's phone lit with a message from the helicopter pilot.

Nome then back you.

That was bad. It should have been forty minutes. Now, Rake calculated an hour from Wales to Nome, fifteen minutes at the hospital, maybe another fifteen minutes for refueling, then an hour and a half back to Little Diomede. Maybe more. He touched Carrie's shoulder. She followed him to the next room where Henry was. He spoke quietly. 'Mike messaged me. There'll be a delay.'

'How long?' asked Carrie.

'A couple of hours at least.'

'It's too long, Rake. We need to get another helicopter.'

'I'll try.'

Carrie returned to Akna.

'We'll take her down to the school anyway,' said Henry. 'Get her close to the helipad.'

The National Guard in Nome kept a Black Hawk on standby, and Rake punched in the number and spoke to a duty officer who said they were handling a civilian emergency call a hundred miles north where bad weather had come down. Rake dialed his military unit at the Elmendorf-Richardson base outside of Anchorage. 'We might be able to lay our hands on a Black Hawk that's coming out of service,' said the sergeant who answered.

'Use my name, Captain Raymond Ozenna, and put us top to the list, sergeant,' instructed Rake, knowing that the chances of getting anything within a couple of hours was slim.

'Understood, sir.'

The hut shook as a wind gusted through the east side of the island. Rake pulled back a torn curtain and pushed open an ice-covered window to gauge the weather. The way clouds scudded across the property, snow was coming. A couple of hours and Little Diomede could be wrapped in fog or howling blizzard. Henry was right. Temperatures and conditions could change in minutes

'They'll get back to me about a helicopter,' he told Carrie. 'We need to get Akna down to the school.'

'We can't move her, Rake.' said Carrie. 'She could die.'

'We have to risk it, Dr Walker.' Joan wrung out a towel and soaked it in fresh warm water. 'If she worsens here we can't even get her to the helipad.'

'There are signs of internal hemorrhage.'

'Henry and the men will take her. He's done this before.'

Akna's eyes rolled; she was close to going into shock. 'Akna, are you there?' Carrie whispered, saying anything to keep the girl conscious. 'Stay with us, Akna. Tell me the name of your favorite song?'

Akna didn't respond.

Carrie checked the small front-room and kitchen. Dirty plates lay around and there was a smell of drains and rotting food. She rolled in her lips, glanced at Rake, and moved her gaze quickly away. He had seen that look before, in a mess of a house in Kabul. But then they had shared their astonishment at the muddle and filth. This was different because it was part of the man she was about to marry.

Rake's phone lit. *Sorry. Fog.*

'Mike can't make it from Nome back until the fog lifts.' He kept his tone measured, but a thousand bits of anger tumbled through his mind. Why was there no helicopter? Why had this happened to Akna? Why was this Carrie's first encounter with his island? However much you love a person some things are best left unseen.

'Snow will be in by then,' said Henry with a look of genuine alarm.

'How long?' Carrie, like Rake, was keeping her frustration in check.

'Impossible to say.'

'We have to get her to hospital, Rake. We need to make it happen.'

Sometimes weather and technical problems cut Little Diomede off for weeks on end. The islanders were meant to get flights every Monday and Wednesday. It rarely happened like that. Rake called back the desk sergeant at Elmendorf-Richardson and heard how they were already doing a medical emergency evacuation up at the Goose Creek Correctional Center, the big prison, and there were a couple of others that placed Akna's pregnancy way down the list of priorities.

Carrie read Rake's stressed expression. 'Let me talk to them.'

They stepped out of Akna's earshot. Rake put the call on open speaker. 'This is Dr Carrie Walker, sergeant—'

'Captain Ozenna has briefed me, ma'am.'

'I'm the doctor. You need to understand – if you do not airlift this teenager to hospital now, she will die.'

THIS WAS EXACTLY THE Dr Carrie Walker whom Rake had first laid eyes on outside Kabul airport when clearing the area after a suicide bombing. She had insisted on staying with a young soldier lying half out of a mangled and charred vehicle. Flames licked around the bodywork. It was only a matter of minutes before they would reach the fuel tank. An old minivan close by might be a second bomb. Anyone among the gathering crowd could have had a gun or grenade. Rake was no doctor, but knew that someone who had had both legs torn off in an explosion in Afghanistan had the slimmest chance of survival. If any. Period.

'Ma'am, you need to leave.'

'Take his arm,' she instructed.

'Ma'am. Leave. NOW!'

'I'm a doctor and this is my patient. Help me!'

Sirens filled the air. Gunshots erupted as police moved people away. This attack wasn't over. Everyone apart from Carrie, it seemed, expected something else to go down. Straight away he saw stubborn determination, the most difficult for a soldier to handle. But with her blonde hair tied back, and wearing a white medical smock, she made herself a ripe target for killing or kidnap. There was no time for debate. He slung his M-16 carbine behind his back, lifted her onto his shoulders, and ran towards the airport gate. She yelled, but she didn't fight back.

The fuel tank blew, sending flames and metal shards into the air. Seconds later, the minivan went up in a much bigger explosion that sent a fireball down the road, engulfing people and market stalls. He ran into the airport compound until the heat faded and he felt winter cold on his face again. He lowered her to the ground. He expected her to be grateful or angry, but she was neither. She told him later that she thought she was being kidnapped and that he was an Afghan because of his Asiatic features.

'Are you OK, ma'am?'

She checked herself, quickly, professionally, patting herself down, running her hands up and down her arms and legs, testing vision, touching her nose, her ears, all in less than ten seconds. 'I'm fine. Your men?'

At least one was dead, John Tikaani, a twenty-year-old private from Nome, the one Carrie had been trying to save. 'We have casualties.'

As he turned to go, she saw that Rake's sleeve was torn and soaked with blood where something had ripped through.

'Wait.' She started cleaning it up. 'You need to get this treated.'

'Next time, when a soldier says go, you need to go,' he said gently.

'I won't. Not while a patient is alive.'

She had said she fell for him because he made her feel safe without suffocating her. Carrie was neither an easy nor a settled person, and out there amid the heat and bombs, you didn't go for a man because of the cut of his suit or because he made you laugh. She admitted she never really understood Rake, but he satisfied her longing for the unusual because he came from a remote Alaskan island that sounded contradictory, stark and romantic like a poem, and because Rake himself was smart and rough.

After their first night together, she told him he was not like any previous lover, mostly doctors who knew the human body too well to enjoy it. Rake had not been over-eager to please nor selfishly fast. He was unrefined. He hadn't read manuals and worked from instinct. He was generous, but knew what he wanted. Carrie said she had never had sex like it before. It might have been the best ever; impossible to say because it was so different.

One evening, when things had quietened, they had dinner and he found she spoke fairly good Russian, much better than the Russian he had learned with the Eskimo Scouts. He asked where she was from.

'Brooklyn, to be quick,' she answered, but with her eyes wide open, alive with mischief.

'And if you want to be slower?' he said. 'If the person asking is curious?'

'Like you?'

'Could be.'

'And if I liked them?' She kept her expression straight, her eyes still dancing.

'Yes.'

'I'm half Estonian, half Russian. My parents married as young medics at the huge Soviet submarine base in Estonia. They were Soviet citizens. That collapsed, and those historical hatreds erupted. The Estonians hated the Russians as occupiers worse than the Nazis. The marriage became strained and they saved it by moving to work in a private hospital in Calcutta, India, where I was born and raised until I was eight. I saw my first corpse when I was five. And my first firefight when I was seven. We were out in the countryside when an insurgent gang attacked. I learned to do bandages and morphine injections. My mother said she had never seen a steadier hand with a syringe. It should have repelled me. But it didn't, and that was when I knew I wanted to be a trauma doctor and that's why I stick with my patient until they are dead or safe.'

'So that's why you did what you did back at the airport.'

She stopped playing him with her eyes. 'That's what I am, Rake. I work for an international hospital group which has sent me to Malaysia, Bangladesh, Kenya, Iraq, and Afghanistan. It's based in Brooklyn, where I have an apartment next door to my younger sister. She's a doctor too, except she doesn't remember much about India, so she's not like me and by this stage I would expect most people to say this is all too much information.'

'I would say not enough.'

'I've never told anyone like this before, all at once, like in a stream of consciousness.'

He laughed, and that made her laugh, a kind of belly laugh that lifted the coiled tension of months in Afghanistan.

'So where are you from?' she asked.

'That's what they say as soon as you step into an army camp,' he said.

'What do you tell them?'

'Alaska.'

'That's it?'

'Or if I want a game, I tell them China or Korea. A lot of people don't like Eskimos.'

'I thought Eskimo was a derogatory term.'

He explained that Eskimos were Alaskan and Russian, Inuit were from Canada and Greenland. It was about language, tribe, disputed history, and they were all family. Then just a few minutes after the laughter and he was telling her this, his phone had rung. Seconds later, hers rang too. Another bomb. Familiar territory.

RAKE LISTENED AS CARRIE, in her medical-crisis voice, challenged every reason the duty sergeant gave for not sending a helicopter for Akna.

'There's weather all over the state, Dr Walker,' he said. 'We will get to you as fast as possible.'

'When?'

'You need to allow twelve hours.'

Carrie no longer held back her exasperation. 'In twelve hours, you'll be airlifting out a corpse.'

'Your patient is fortunate that she has you with her.'

'She is dying.'

'You have my word, ma'am. We'll be as fast as we can.'

'Make it faster.'

Henry brought in the stretcher and laid it by the sofa. He and Joan quietly prepared for the journey down to the school.

They waited until the wind dropped. Rake opened the door to check. The island glimmered in pale daylight. A line of low-lying fog spread across the shoreline. 'Let's go,' he said.

'Akna. Can you hear me? Look at me, Akna,' Carrie said.

'What's happening?' Akna hadn't spoken before. Pain creased across her face.

'Your baby is coming early. We're taking you to the school to wait for the helicopter.'

Akna grimaced. They wrapped her in woolen blankets, lifted her onto the stretcher, laid a seal skin on top and then another blanket. Henry made sure her face was covered, no skin exposed, and secured a rubber tube to her mouth for breathing. The temperature outside was minus 15 Celsius with a wind ferocity to double that. If they made a mistake, Akna could die on the short journey to the school. Henry and the three other men carried her.

Carrie took the rear, her medical pack slung over her shoulder. Joan walked alongside Akna. Rake led.

At the end of the walkway, he took them down steps past an old military observation post, abandoned by the National Guard nearly thirty years earlier. There had been no government presence on the island since. Step by treacherous step, he guided them past the front doors of homes marked by drying seal skins, tied meat, and the skulls of walrus and polar bears.

Rake kicked a fallen ice block off the next walkway, testing the surface underneath, and brought them off the hillside to rocky ground wide enough for Carrie to join Joan and check on the patient. On one side was a shop called the Native Store and on the other an old wooden building that housed a laundry and a clinic where Henry got the stretcher from.

Rake crossed the small playground, testing the safest way through the red swing and the yellow and blue slide and on to the ramp to the school, the sturdiest building in the village, warm, with stocks of food and hot water.

Wild birds flew out of the hillside and Rake caught their smell in the air. They swept back and forth, shadowing through the dim daylight, but seemingly going nowhere. They had distinct styles of flight to mark the weather. Henry had taught him how they flew one way as the hunting season approached and another during the summer weeks of the midnight sun. They had a way of flight with fog, early snowfalls, full moons, and the seasons. Now they were different again. This was how they flew when a helicopter was approaching. You saw the birds long before you heard the engine.

The birds went into a frenzy. Then he heard an engine.

'There's a chopper,' he said, wedging open the door for Akna to be carried into the school. But how? Maybe one of the private companies had taken the risk, maybe not from Nome, but from Wales or Teller, the closer mainland settlements.

Carrie's eyes brightened. 'Well done, Rake!' She looked around. 'Where?'

'From the north. See the birds?'

'Amazing. You can tell from them.' She followed her patient into the warmth inside to get her ready.

A balcony wrapped around the school. Rake ran onto it, checking his phone on the way. There was no message from Nome or Anchorage, no missed calls. To the south and north, he saw nothing. He looked back up the hillside. Nothing.

The noise became louder. Then, straight ahead, he worked out what was happening. The helicopter had been impossible to detect with the naked eye because it was camouflaged against the dark ridge of Big Diomede. Now it rose up – a Russian two-engine 38, lit like a beacon with the Red Cross of a medical aircraft illuminated clearly on its sides.

It took a second for him to absorb what was before him. What he was seeing was unbelievable. But it was there, real and close.

Navigating the icy rocks on the pathway, he ran down to the unlit helipad to guide the aircraft in. He prayed that fog and wind would keep away. He held up his flashlight with both hands, flashing the traditional SOS Morse Code emergency signal. The helicopter snapped on a search lamp that caught him full in the face. He turned against the imminent down-draught of the rotor blades, looking back towards Russia.

His tongue suddenly dried in his mouth as he sifted through what was happening. Rapidly, he processed what he saw and it didn't make sense. It was an incredible sight, a terrifying one, and he had no idea what it meant.

Spread right across the ridgeline, seven more helicopters ascended from behind the larger island. He recognized three as troop carriers and four as new Russian attack helicopters, two on each flank, flying low and heading straight for his island.

THREE

British Ambassador's residence, Washington, DC

Stephanie Lucas, British Ambassador to Washington, DC and daughter of a London used-car salesman, walked briskly past a statue of Winston Churchill, right arm raised in his famous two-fingered victory salute, his left leaning on a cane. The statue stood outside her residence, a magnificent red-brick country-style mansion that – the way things were going – might not be home for much longer.

She was hosting a small dinner for the world's two newest leaders, America's brash President-elect who was two days away from moving into the White House and Britain's socialist Prime Minister who had been in office less than two weeks. Stephanie had made herself late by a few minutes to give Prime Minister Kevin Slater and President-elect Bob Holland time to gauge each other. Inexperienced, ambitious, and unafraid to speak their minds, they stood at opposite ends of the political spectrum.

Diplomatic protocol dictated that Holland and outgoing President Christopher Swain should not be invited to the same event. Even though Trump had torn up the rule book on presidential transition, Stephanie had stuck to it. Holland detested

Swain and, despite winning with a clear mandate, had made the presidential transition as acrimonious as if he were still on the campaign trail.

But Stephanie had succeeded in coaxing along Swain's Chief of Staff, Matt Prusak, on the grounds that they were old friends. She had met Swain and Prusak when they were all preppy law students, and a quarter-century later she had worked with Prusak to persuade Swain to run for the presidency.

For this evening, she had also called in a favor from the flamboyant Roy Carrol, Chairman of the Federal Reserve and one of Washington's most sought-after dinner guests. His premium had risen higher since his divorce. Carrol happened to be hosting the new reformist head of Russia's Central Bank, whom Stephanie insisted he bring along. Slater had asked her to seek out an old trade union friend, Jeff Walsh, who had taken some persuading given that Holland would be there. Stephanie anticipated lively, punchy conversation.

Inside the spacious entrance hall, she stopped by a gold-framed wall mirror to smooth down her dark-blue business suit and check her shoulder-length black hair. From the softly furnished drawing room, she heard a fast, hostile exchange led by Holland's raised baritone voice that had captured the nation and catapulted him towards the White House. She brushed her hair back from her forehead and stepped inside.

'I'm giving it to you straight, Mr Prime Minister,' Holland was saying. 'Honor your NATO defense spending, stop this question about your nuclear capability, and we'll get along just fine.'

'The democratic process must take its course.' Slater smiled, exaggerating his north of England accent. He wore a light red shirt with no tie. His brown sports jacket looked ten years old and his suede shoes were scuffed. Holland wore an immaculate pinstripe suit with a blue shirt, tie pin, and gold cufflinks. They stood on either end of the tall mantelpiece. Holland was a big, chunky man with little grace, his eyes skipping around the room like a cat. Slater was tall and as lean as a cane with a military-style buzz-cut that gave an appearance of part athlete and part bulldog. He concentrated his gaze on Holland.

'There's no democratic process when it comes to national security,' countered Holland. 'Winston Churchill described Britain as an elected dictatorship and you, Mr Prime Minister, are its current dictator.'

Stephanie made her presence known. 'Gentlemen, good evening. Prime Minister, Mr President-elect. Sorry for being late. Inauguration preparations are gridlocking traffic.'

'I've been enjoying a lively conversation with your new Prime Minister,' said Holland.

'Then I must not interrupt. You know what they say: The root of the British-American special relationship is that neither of us could speak French.' Both men laughed, and her attempt at a joke was enough to take her further across the room where a barrel-chested man, examining snow-covered grounds through a large window, turned to greet her. 'Jeff Walsh, ma'am. President of the International Longshoremen's Union.'

'I recognize you, of course, Mr Walsh. It's a privilege to meet you in person.'

'Thank you for asking me, ma'am. Your Prime Minister and I go back a long way.'

'No need to ma'am me, Jeff. This is a very informal evening.'

'The 1980s, ma'am.' Walsh grinned amiably. 'OK. Sorry. What the hell do I call you?'

'Steph. Or if that's too much, go for Mrs Lucas.'

'Right, Steph, I went across to England to support Kevin with your miners' strike in the early 80s. He came over here when we tried to take on Reagan. So, he and I are two old-time union fighters.'

A shadow fell on the door, created by the arrival of Matt Prusak. Unlike Swain, the slight and bookish White House Chief of Staff had succeeded in forging a working relationship with Holland.

'Come, Jeff, let's go mix it up a bit.' Stephanie waved at Prusak as she ushered Walsh towards the center of the room.

'Don't expect American body bags to be coming out of that continent when you mess it up again,' Holland was saying.

'It's more than seventy years since an American soldier died on a European battlefield,' said Slater. 'Since then our lads and lasses have been getting killed in your pointless Middle East wars.'

Stephanie caught Prusak's eye and suppressed a smile. If the conversation weren't so dangerous, it could be funny. 'Ambassador Lucas and I go back to our campus days at Georgetown University,' said Prusak urbanely as Stephanie introduced him to Slater. 'I am here as a friend and not as—'

'Even so,' interrupted Holland. 'How is the White House in your final days?'

'The packers are in, sir, and the property awaits you.'

Stephanie's attention shifted again to the door where the

Federal Reserve chairman, Roy Carrol, was ushering in Karl Opokin, a Russian entrepreneur turned Chairman of the Central Bank. Stephanie knew Opokin from her days in Russia, where she had fled on advice of her father. 'Go read those books and get yourself to university so no one controls your life but you,' he had told her after she begged him teach her how to rig mileage, fix oil leaks, and forge documents in the used-car trade. She had.

Stephanie learned Russian and studied East European history at the London School of Economics, then headed for Moscow. With communism fractured, it was a place of half organized crime and half crumbling authority with barely a line between the two, not that different from her father's edgy south London motor trade. Opokin had been on the fringes of her crowd of bright young friends who taught her how to buy favors and forge alliances. Opokin focused on oil and gas deals in Russia's Far East. Stephanie headed for technology companies in Moscow and St Petersburg and had made her first million before she was twenty-five. Her business partner, who was briefly her lover, made many times that. He had argued that he needed ten to her one just to stay alive, and Stephanie let it go. It had worked for both of them. Sergey Grizlov was now Chairman of the Russian parliament. Stephanie's previous post had been as ambassador to Moscow. And Opokin, her dinner guest, was being hailed as the modern post-Putin face of Russia. Carrol had been showing him around the Fed's magnificent ice-white 1930s building on Constitution Avenue.

Carrol pecked Stephanie on both cheeks. 'Good to see you, Steph.' Carrol's tailored suit, cufflinks, and polka-dotted bow tie far outclassed Opokin's regular dark pinstripe suit, which could have passed him off as any mid-ranking, mid-forties Wall Street banker. Holland eyed him with surprise as if expecting the traditional bling and glitter of a Russian oligarch.

'Thank you for having me, Madam Ambassador,' Opokin spoke softly while taking her hand.

'Very, very good to meet you again, Karl.' She introduced him.

'Prime Minister, Mr President-elect, congratulations on your election victories. I am indeed privileged to be here,' said Opokin.

'You need to tell your President Lagutov from me to stop messing around with Europe,' said Holland. 'We don't want to have to make an enemy out of you. The last I heard—'

'Hush, hush, Senator,' Carrol broke in, touching Holland's arm to correct himself. 'Not Senator. Mr President-elect. I do apologize; I should stick to calling you one of my oldest and closest friends. Karl is a new breed, a money man, like me. We live, dream, and plan money, and it drives our friends to despair.'

'You keep your side of the border in Europe, and you'll do well by us,' said Holland to Opokin.

Stephanie allowed more small talk. Opokin softened Holland. Walsh congratulated Slater on getting the top job. She took Carrol to one side to ask about his ex-wife.

'Divorce has gone through, and we're still talking,' said Carrol.

'Well done.'

'And Harry?'

'Better. Thanks for asking. We keep in touch.' Harry was Stephanie's soldier of an ex-husband. Briefly part of the Georgetown gang, he had cut out to the Iraq war, been wounded and decorated. He had just lost his seat in Congress where he had sat on several defense committees. Carrol and his then wife Lucy had been pillars of support when Stephanie's marriage disintegrated.

Stephanie guided her guests to a compact informal dining room with a table laid for six. 'They say the British Ambassador's residence is a three-dimensional piece of art, the greatest diplomatic home of any country in any capital city,' she said. 'So, this room I keep for family, close friends, and colleagues and we're having plain old pumpkin soup to start.'

She gestured for them to take their seats. It was then, as waiters ladled soup from silver tureens, that a Secret Service agent stepped in straight across to Prusak. His face taut, he leant down, whispering but loud enough for her to hear: 'I'm sorry, sir. You're needed back at the White House.'

Stephanie opened a message on her phone and a chill shivered through her. The others looked at their phones. Prusak pushed back his chair and stood up. 'We have a problem in Alaska.'

FOUR

Little Diomede, Alaska, USA

Seven Russian helicopters stretched between the two islands like dark insects. The lone medical helicopter was coming down directly above the landing pad. Standing on the edge, flashlight in hand, guiding the pilot, Rake struggled to determine if they were here to help or attack. They might have intercepted the phone calls between Carrie and the desk sergeant at Elmendorf-Richardson. They would certainly have heard the radio traffic on Akna's evacuation. They would know that her life was at risk, she was only fifteen, she was pregnant, her waters had broken, and that a helicopter wasn't coming back any time soon. From the eight watchtowers along the ridge of the Russian island, they would have tracked them taking Akna down to the school. Behind that northern corner of the island, there was a small old cold war helicopter base. The commander couldn't have authorized a rescue. But he would have kicked it upstairs and somewhere between the Bering Strait and Moscow a green light would have been given.

Rake had been on plenty of similar operations. If one guy needed to be airlifted out, they would send in a fleet of aircraft to make sure everyone's back was covered. All of that checked out. But what didn't was the big question – why didn't he know? Why wasn't his phone ringing? Why had Moscow not told Washington what was going on? Or had it, and the messages got lost in a sea of bureaucracy?

Glaring off the ice, Russian flood lamps lit the helipad. Rake used his flashlight to indicate the exact spot where the helicopter should land. The pilot came down slowly, then stopped the descent, keeping ten feet off the ground. He turned to an angle with the northerly wind, a smart move given that a gust could skew the down flap of the rotor blades. As the skids settled on the icy concrete, the draught scattered shoreline debris and tore ice off nearby buildings.

Four soldiers jumped out and took positions either side of the door. They wore medical Red Cross armbands and carried weapons. Two paramedics followed, each with green packs also marked with a Red Cross. A stretcher was passed out to them. A doctor jumped down. The other helicopters stayed right on the unmarked maritime border.

No conversation was possible against the noise. Rake pointed towards the school. He led them through the playground. The school door opened, and Carrie stepped out, a smile across her face. Akna lay, conscious and warm, on two tables pushed together in the small dining room just inside the door.

'Do you speak English?' she asked as the Russian medical team swept in.

'We do.' The doctor stripped back his face scarf. He was about thirty with a buzz cut and a hard face.

'Preterm premature rupture of the membrane. The mother

is fifteen years old. Pregnancy thirty-five weeks.' Carrie reeled off a list of drugs that Akna needed. 'It's not too late to induce the birth. Or carry out a Caesarean section.'

The doctor shone a pencil light into Akna's eye and checked her pulse. 'We need to be quick,' he said.

'I'm coming with you.'

'It is very basic over there. But as you wish.'

The paramedics skillfully wrapped Akna, lifted her onto the stretcher, and carried her out. Carrie moved to the door to follow, but Rake stepped into her path. 'No, Carrie,' he said gently. 'You've done all you can.'

'She's my patient, Rake. She needs me.'

'You cannot go.'

'I'm going. She needs me. I know Russians. They don't care about life.'

Watched by villagers and the Russian medical team, Rake had a few seconds to convince Carrie to do something totally against her professional beliefs, to abandon her patient. He could not let her go onto the Russian side.

Since the cold war, this had been a closed border. Before that Eskimo families ignored the frontier, crossing back and forth as they had done for centuries. They had completely ignored the Alaska Purchase back in 1867 when America bought Alaska from a cash-strapped Tsarist Russia. Henry used to crack jokes about which country would be buying them next, whether they would all become Japanese.

Rake glanced at Henry, whose expression reflected his own thoughts. Little Diomede had been through emergencies like this before and never once had America asked for help. Nor had

Russia offered. Akna needed to be saved, but something wasn't right. As an American army officer, he couldn't go with the military of a possible adversary and, as his fiancée, Carrie couldn't either.

'You need to stay here,' he whispered.

'She's my patient.'

'No!' he countered sharply. 'She's now his patient. That's what trauma doctors do, they save lives. They pass their patients on.'

'We'll go.' Joan stepped forward with Henry. 'She knows us. It will be better.'

That would work, thought Rake. Akna needed someone with her and, as Eskimos, the Russian would barely notice them. Carrie considered the proposition for a moment and agreed.

'You got a radio?' Rake asked Henry.

'Channel 7. Then 5,' said Henry.

'Let us know if it's a boy or a girl.' Rake managed a smile. They embraced. Henry was firm and sure of himself. Rake felt uneasy, like he was putting his uncle in harm's way. But if anyone was to go, it should be Henry and Joan.

As the paramedics carried Akna down, Rake led Carrie onto the terrace to watch them load her into the helicopter. They were interrupted by a command from behind them in bad English. 'Inside, now!'

Carrie went white, gripping the railing with her glove as if to say I'm not moving. Rake surged with helpless anger. Every-thing in the young soldier's voice and expression told him that his instinct had been right. This wasn't just a medical evacuation. That was why his phone had stayed quiet. America had not been told.

'What the fuck, Rake!' Carrie pointed behind them to where troops were herding villagers towards the school.

'I said inside.' The soldier levelled his weapon at them, flipping the barrel towards the door. He was nervous. Rake could take him easily. But then what? He didn't have the numbers to achieve much except get himself killed. Carrie too. By doing what the Russians instructed, he could at least protect her.

Down on the helipad, a soldier stopped Henry, frisked him, and took the radio.

FIVE

British Ambassador's residence, Washington, DC

'Never trust those fucking Russians!' shouted Holland.

'Whoa there!' cautioned Prusak, heading for the door.

'I told Swain about that border and he wouldn't listen.'

'Let's try and keep a lid on things, Mr President-elect.'

Stephanie was on her feet, trying to read her Prime Minister. Kevin Slater stayed poker-faced, not a trace of reaction; impossible to tell if he was a rabbit caught in headlights or playing cards close to his chest. The news coming through might be nothing or it might be that the next few hours would define Slater's place in history.

'I will return to my embassy, Madam Ambassador. This must be a misunderstanding,' said Opokin, turning to address Holland directly. 'I know the Chukotka region and the Bering Strait well. I can assure you we do not have the resources to invade the United States from there. Nor would we fucking Russians want to.'

Holland glared at him. Carrol said, 'I'll give you a ride, Karl. I'm heading over to the Eccles Building.' He folded his napkin and spoke to Prusak. 'Matt, tell the President I'll call a crisis meeting of the Fed for the early morning, just in case. Let's hope we have nothing to talk about.'

'I need to be with the President.' Holland stood up.

Prusak glanced across sharply. 'I'll check, sir. I'm sure he'll brief—'

'Not brief, Matt. In the Situation Room, sharing the decisions. This is going to spill into my term.'

'That might not work.'

'Have Swain decide if he wants me by his side or wants to cut me out. If you don't ask him, I'll ask through the news networks.'

'Matt, a moment.' Stephanie touched Prusak's elbow to guide him into the corridor and out of earshot. 'I can help with Holland.'

'Stay out of it, Steph. This is the presidential transition. We get sensitive.'

'You don't want Holland blasting all over the networks about the lame duck and the President doesn't want this crisis as his legacy.'

'Correct.' Prusak scrolled his phone.

'And you could help me, too.'

'How so?'

'Kevin Slater's untested as Prime Minister. There's a risk he'll shoot from the hip. We can temper that by getting him to the White House, the center of power. Take Slater, myself, and Holland there. Stick us in the Roosevelt Room or some-where.'

She had Prusak's attention. 'Not the Oval Office. Not the Situation Room,' he said.

'Exactly. Slater's presence dilutes transition protocol. He and Holland can say they are being consulted, and Kevin can help you deliver European support.'

'I should have married you when I had the chance,' Prusak smiled. 'We would have made the power couple to beat all others.'

Crises were routine to Prusak. In all the time she had known him, she had never heard him raise his voice or seen a line of tension in his face. 'You know Russia better than most, Steph. Any idea what's going on?'

'Has this ever happened before – a Russian medical evacuation from Little Diomede?'

'Never, that I know of.'

'I'll hit the phones.' Stephanie sifted scenarios through her mind. Was she reading too much into it? Was it a straightforward humanitarian act? If so, why did they not inform the United States? But if it were an invasion, as the hawkish networks were claiming, what was the point? Who cared about an Eskimo village on a remote Alaskan island? Strategically, it didn't add up. What did make sense, though, was that a potential adversary, like Russia, would test America on the eve of a new presidency. That was a given, and happened around every transition. But that didn't mean this was what Russia was doing now. How could it have gotten its timing so precise? To think it had conspired to have a fifteen-year-old girl's waters break on the eve of the inauguration was in the realms of magical thinking.

But if not that, what?

After the tension of the Putin years, shortly after Stephanie's move to Washington, the Russians had put a low-key, relatively unknown academic into the Kremlin. Viktor Lagutov was a quietly-spoken economist, and some had hailed his election as a return to reform and democracy. Stephanie didn't buy it. She had kept in touch with old friends there, including her old business partner and lover, Sergey Grizlov. He hadn't bought it either. Lagutov was a stopgap, a time to draw breath after Ukraine, Crimea, and Putin.

'The Russian soul remains angry, unsettled, and searching for dignity,' Grizlov had told her.

Back in 2007, Russian divers had planted a meter-high titanium national flag on the seabed beneath the North Pole. Sure, it was to lay claim to billions of dollars of oil and gas reserves, but it was also a statement of dignity and power, like an eighteenth-century land grab. There were energy reserves in the Bering Strait too, but hostilities there meant no one could get them out. So, what would be the point?

Which brought her back to Lagutov. Had he authorized it? If not, who? And was it a challenge to his presidency, American territory being used as a foil for a Russian coup? How many Russians would cheer to see their flag flying on territory that once belonged to the Empire, land lost in the ill-fated Alaska Purchase, when Russia was conned and America had paid a pittance? How many would hail the man who put it there as a hero? Putin had fudged, messing around in Ukraine but never having the real steel needed to restore Russian dignity. He complained but didn't act. But here was a man confident enough to take on America face to face, the type of leader that Russia needed. If she were halfway on the right track, then the Little Diomede operation could not be happening without the involvement of Russia's Far East Military District. Which is when it came to her. Of course – why was she being so slow? One name stood out like a razor.

'A thought, Matt,' she said. 'They'll be doing it anyway, but check out an Admiral Alexander Vitruk, appointed as military commander of Russia's Far East two years ago. He made his name in the Chechen wars, and by all accounts is a very nasty piece of work. A Russian helicopter crossing into American territory would have to have his authorization.'

PRUSAK WENT AHEAD TO the White House with his Secret Service detail. Stephanie and Slater rode with Holland who sprawled across the back seat dwarfing and ignoring Slater while looking at his phone. Stephanie sat on a jump seat across from him. She thought more about Vitruk. Would he be acting alone, or with Lagutov's support? If so, where was the end game? Russia's policy had been to keep this frontier with America low profile, the exact opposite to its fractious policy in Europe. Neither side wanted to face the other down across a shared border. Apart from the North Pole flag, Russia had been working cooperatively as a member of the Arctic Council, carrying out joint search and rescue, even military exercises. What, then, had been the catalyst of this operation?

Snow slid onto the darkened windows and quickly melted against the flashing beams of the convoy's blue lights.

'Exactly where is this place?' asked Slater.

Stephanie pulled a map onto her phone and held it in her palm so both Slater and Holland could see.

'The islands are here, about midway between each country's mainland.' She zoomed in on two green specks on a screen of blue sea. 'Russia here,' she said, pointing. 'America here. The border here. Unmarked, and less than three miles between, about the distance we're driving now to the White House.'

'The American people have no idea we're so damn close to them.' Holland angrily drummed his fingers on the arm-rest.

'It may be nothing more than saving the life of a mother and child,' said Slater.

'The networks are calling it an invasion,' said Holland. 'One thing you'll learn about leadership, Prime Minister, is that if the media says something, people will believe it and you have to react to it even if it's false.'

'I don't react to untruths and I've been leading working men and women all my life.'

Stephanie's thoughts remained fixated on Admiral Alexander Vitruk. They needed to check his war record, his relationship with Lagutov, and with Putin.

'If Russian troops are on American soil without our permission we need to get them out now, and we'll be looking for Britain's support in that,' said Holland.

'I would be happy to call President Lagutov to mediate a settlement.'

'You don't get it, do you? Swain doesn't either. It's not mediation that's needed. Lagutov cannot get away with this. We can fix it the hard way or the easy way, but for sure we fix it.' Holland sucked in his cheeks and looked out the window as they crossed H Street and slowed to go into the White House.

'It might not be Lagutov,' said Stephanie as the limousine drew up at the front door.

'He's the Russian President,' said Holland. 'The buck stops with him.'

Secret Service agents took them through to the windowless Roosevelt Room, which lay at the center of the West Wing of the White House. With a long rectangular conference table, it was used for meetings into which the President could drop by from the Oval Office across the corridor. Prusak was waiting for them and was about to speak when Holland said, 'I'm uncomfortable with them being here.' He deliberately used the third person. 'You cannot bundle me up with some foreign leader and an ambassador. That border is under joint US-Canadian command. It does not involve Europe.'

'Europe may be intrinsic to anything that occurs, sir,' said Prusak. 'Whatever is happening out there, the possibility of a mistake or miscalculation is very real.'

Holland jabbed his thumb towards Stephanie. 'And she wouldn't have the clearance for what's going on.'

Prusak betrayed only a flicker of impatience in his eyes. 'The President has asked that both Prime Minister Slater and Ambassador Lucas be here. She worked with us closely in Moscow. As you know, sir, her ex-husband is Harry Lucas, former Chair of the House Intelligence Committee, and she was given an extra level of clearance for that.'

'I need to see the President alone,' persisted Holland.

'In fact, the President has asked you all to join him in the Oval Office. I know it's unusual, but this is an unusual evening. He is about to speak to President Lagutov in the Kremlin.'

SIX

Big Diomede, Chukotka, Russian Far East

Admiral Alexander Vitruk secured his hat, earflaps down, and encased his face in a sealskin and wool scarf. The helicopter door opened, and he jumped to the ground into a strong wind that howled across the small military base on the island of Ratmonova that the Americans called Big Diomede. A rectangle of low-rise buildings dating back to the 1940s stood in a tiny natural harbor protected by high granite cliffs. There was no runway for fixed-wing aircraft, just a concrete helipad ringed by lights which were piercingly visible then darkened by a swirling blizzard that blinded the eyes and turned the air so cold a man could get frostbite in seconds.

He waved thanks to the pilots and clapped the shoulder of the waiting Colonel Ruslan Yumatov. The wind's roar made conversation impossible. Yumatov pointed through the blizzard towards the main base building whose front double doors were lit by two overhead lamps. There was urgency in the young colonel's expression. They stepped into the warmth, stamping snow off their boots.

'It's a go, sir,' Yumatov said, shaking his hat and scarf. 'You asked I didn't contact you while airborne. We have one medical M-8 on the island.'

'With paramedics?'

'And a midwife and a doctor. We had intercepts on their phones and radios. A native girl, aged fifteen. Akna Ondola. Pregnant. Her life is in danger. Two M-8s and four KA-52s are airborne at the border, waiting your orders.'

The KA-52s were Russia's most advanced attack helicopters and the M-8 a workhorse troop carrier. Three, in relay, would deliver seventy-two men to the island in a few minutes. Vitruk had flown two thousand miles from his headquarters in Khabarovsk to the closest airbase at Egvekinot and from there by helicopter to the island. Its small helicopter base had never been designed for such activity. More than fifty years old, the buildings celebrated Stalinist military pragmatism, weather-beaten concrete blocks, overheated inside, with a smell of polish and disinfectant and ceilings stained dirty brown by decades of cigarette smoke. Flickering fluorescent lighting strained the eyes. Given time, Vitruk could have pulled it all down and rebuilt. Instead, he had imported a military mobile base with quarters for the extra troops, hangars for helicopters, and a field hospital with a sanitized operating theater.

The old mess room to his left was now the command and control center, facing north-west to the Russian mainland and not across the border. To his right was the base's main reception room, underused, its design unchanged from Soviet times, with a faded portrait of Nikita Khrushchev on the wall. Vitruk stepped in, hung up his coat, and poured coffee from a table urn, one for him and one for his colonel.

'Well done, Colonel,' he said, handing Yumatov the cup. 'Fast and good work.'

There was a moment of quiet between them. Yumatov at six three was a good half-foot taller than his commanding officer, wiry with a thin sharp face and the physique of a long-distance runner. Vitruk was short for a soldier, stumpy with wide shoulders and hard, unsettled features. Yumatov, not yet forty, had been named as among the most talented officers of his generation. His home, wife, and two children were at the other end of Russia in St Petersburg, and he had to be cautious because he was still building the foundations of his career. Vitruk, on the other hand, at fifty-eight, was divorced and his only daughter had died many years ago. Without family, he craved risk and high stakes and he needed a younger, bright officer like Yumatov at his side against whom he could test his ideas.

Even though Vitruk was in command, they knew that if this operation went wrong they would both be finished, while success would make them national heroes and deliver Vitruk to the Kremlin. Vitruk detected a hesitancy as Yumatov turned his gaze away. 'Are you with me? Say it now, Ruslan, and leave without consequence. Stay and you will be glued to me and follow my every order or I will gun you down with my own pistol. Is that understood?'

THE DAY AFTER THE American presidential election, Vitruk had flown to Moscow to meet President Viktor Lagutov. Thoughtful, balanced, fair, uninterested in money, Lagutov was not the decisive and over-reaching figure Vladimir Putin had been. He was a Putin antidote, delivered by the Moscow establishment to give Russia a period of calm. Lagutov knew he wouldn't last. Nor did he want to. He was Russia's breathing space until it craved another strongman.

Lagutov was also Vitruk's patron, and Vitruk his protégé. Lagutov had spotted Vitruk's talent when he gave an economics lecture at a college in Khabarovsk, the military city in the region Vitruk now commanded. Vitruk was a Siberian peasant from a broken family. His father was riddled with drink, and the military became his lifeblood. Lagutov later told him that he had identified three qualities – high intelligence, determination, and ruthlessness. But that was a quarter-century ago, and there would always be a moment in the protégé–patron relationship when power shifted.

Lagutov could have met him in the yellow triangular Senate Building, the Russian President's everyday office, or, worse, the drab Building Fourteen from where the faction-ridden administration ran its monopoly on power. But no – Vitruk was led to the high-domed Vladimirsky Hall in the Kremlin's Grand Palace, whose opulence underlined Russia's sophistication and its sense of destiny. In the late tenth century, the Grand Prince Vladimir I had unified a weak Russia with Orthodox Christianity and expanded and secured its borders. Vitruk was escorted along the deep maroon carpet of the palatial hall while above him, written into the stucco patterns of the magnificent dome, was the insignia that was fitting to his plan. Benefit. Honor. Glory. Dignified and tasteful, with its unfolding sense of space, its marble, arches, and columns, this hall was the nucleus of the whole of Russia. It was a fitting venue for the meeting.

From behind an elegant wooden desk where dignitaries were received and treaties were signed, his mentor, the President of the Russian Federation, got to his feet to greet him. Huge crow's claws spread from Lagutov's sharp blue eyes. His lined face was framed with a head of thick gray hair. He was not a tall man, nor physically strong. But he was confident and casual. His dark suit jacket hung on the back of his chair. He wore a light-blue shirt with no tie, a relaxed leader in a lavish setting.

'Ah! Admiral!' Lagutov's voice bounced around the vast room. 'Thank you for coming so far. Your idea, this idea you sent me, will it work?'

'Yes, sir. It will.' Vitruk spoke softly. The glow of lamps on the huge chandelier of gilded bronze offset the night darkness that was visible through the skylight. Lagutov indicated that Vitruk should take a seat to the side of the desk.

'I like it. I respect your impatience,' he said, as they both sat down. 'But tell me, Alex: After Larisa, have you found anybody. Do you have family?'

'Russia is my family, sir,' he said. 'That has not changed since the day we met.' But the question took Vitruk by surprise. It was more than twenty years since, tanked up with vodka, he had driven a snowmobile into a tree. He was thrown clear onto soft snow. His eight-year-old daughter, Larisa, was crushed and killed. Katerina, his wife, never uttered another word to him. Vitruk cast himself into Russia's wars, aimlessly at first, until Lagutov had offered him a lifeline.

'All those years ago,' said Lagutov, 'when I saw you, restless and angry, at that dreadful military college, I knew you were special. Fearless. Intelligent. Nothing to lose. Russia's greatness has been forged on such qualities and war has tutored you well. I ask you now about Larisa because such a mission needs motivation that cannot be personal, and I know how badly you took the loss.'

'My motivation is only for the Motherland, sir.' Coiled inside, Vitruk spoke with assured calm.

'Then convince me, Alex. I need to see in your eyes planning, not revenge, pragmatism, not hatred.'

'We have an opportunity that will not arise for eight, possibly twelve or sixteen years. The antagonism between the American President and his successor has created a leadership vacuum of historical proportions.'

'An opportunity for what exactly? We need America. Even if we could weaken it, what would that achieve? And this island? What is to be gained from taking it?'

'It will force the Americans to reassess Russia. Under the Tsars we were savagely misruled. Under communism, America contained us. After communism, it exploited us and turned us into a Mafia state. Under Putin, it made us its enemy again. Russia has never been free to grow and live in the world with dignity.'

'And how will raising our flag on an unknown American island change this?'

'The Stars and Stripes has flown illegally in so many countries, sir. It is a symbol of oppression and war. Should a hostile foreign flag now fly over America territory, the world will applaud us. It will show American weakness and Russian courage. For too long, we have used the buffer of Europe as an excuse not to confront. This time we will break that hallowed border between America and Russia and begin to write a new world order.'

Lagutov was quiet for a long moment. Aware that many in Moscow wished him ill, Vitruk wondered if he had said too much. His enemies saw him as a Siberian peasant boy who had risen way above his station. But Stalin had done just that, and if he, the Georgian son of a cobbler and a housemaid, could make it to the top, so could Alexander Vitruk, the son of a loyal communist engineer whose roads and bridges had forged Russia's Far East. That was until his father became too drunk to build them and found solace in the beds of Eskimo women, just as his grandfather had before him. Through the contours of his low forehead and slight cheekbones Vitruk thought he might even be carrying native Eskimo blood.

He was living by a promise made to his late mother when he was ten years old and his father's vodka-poisoned body was dumped on the snow-covered doorstep of their miserable apartment block in the Chukotka capital of Anadyr. Eskimos had found him as a frozen corpse in the forest. They wrapped his body in a bearskin to allow dignity, and delivered it by dog sled.

The Eskimos rang the apartment-block bell and rolled the corpse out of the bearskin, which they took back. His mother saw the body from the window and screamed. She tore a blanket from her bed, grabbed his hand, and they ran down to the street. She covered the body and held her son tight. 'Don't die like this, Alex. Please. Don't be like he was. Ever. Promise me.' They shivered together in the cold, warming each other.

'Yes, Mama.'

'Be a big man, when you grow up, the biggest in the world.'

'I will. I promise.'

Vitruk had shed no tears, nor did his mother. His father left her with three children and a paltry pension. But Viktor had honored his pledge. He had smashed through ceilings and was now a few steps away from being anointed President of the Russian Federation. He didn't intend to lose the moment. Fogged in fast cars, yachts, and champagne, the Moscow fools had no concept that the future lay in the Far East, the Pacific and Asia. But Lagutov did and that was why Vitruk was with him now.

'How will it work, Alex, with this island?' said Lagutov.

'The island is vulnerable, sir. For the Americans to have allowed it to remain so was strategic madness. They could have requisitioned it, resettled the native villagers, and set up defenses like we did with Ratmonova. They have been arrogant. Some eighty Eskimos live there. The weather often cuts them off from the mainland. We monitor their radios and cellphones. The health of the islanders is not good. They have problems with narcotics, domestic abuse—'

'Which we have, too.'

'My plan is that the next time they make an emergency call for help and their helicopters cannot get to them we go, because we can get there in a matter of minutes.'

Lagutov eyed Vitruk with the skepticism of an academic. 'I don't understand. You go on a medical mission and raise our national flag?'

'Yes. We treat the patient either there or at a field hospital on Ratmonova. We also take the opportunity to offer the islanders health checks. We know from our own Eskimos that their health is not good – bad diet, diabetes, heart and dental disease, that sort of thing. We accuse the Americans of neglecting their own citizens and we take control of the island on humanitarian grounds.'

'Which they will reject.'

'President Holland does not come to office for more than two months. After that he will take more months to settle. America will be at its weakest. Holland will have to decide how to handle it. He will bluster. But will he risk war over this unknown island?'

'And Russia? What do I say when the American President calls me?'

'You have the finest analytical mind of anyone I know, sir, and you will judge. I will open the door for Russia and you can support me or you can abandon me as a rogue officer. I will follow your command.'

Lagutov took off his spectacles and gave Vitruk a genial look. 'I am merely a technocrat, an economics professor keeping the seat warm for my protégé. You are my muscle, Alex. You are what our country needs. If you fail, of course, Russia will destroy you, but I will do all within my declining power to help you succeed.'

And it was then, as Vitruk was expressing his thanks, that Lagutov surprised him. Through a doorway to the left came a beast of a political figure whom Vitruk knew only from his compelling appearances on television and whom he detested because of his sycophantic pandering to the West. Sergey Grizlov, the elegantly tall Chairman of the State Duma, wearing an expensive dark pinstriped suit that would have been hand-tailored in London or Rome, walked briskly across carrying a black leather briefcase.

He greeted Lagutov with a huge smile, but without a word, then clasped Vitruk's hand with both of his. 'What a privilege to meet you, Admiral. Your reputation dwarfs us all. I have heard some of your plan and am very excited.'

'We will need our elected representatives with us, Alex,' said Lagutov with a self-effacing frown. 'These are not the days of President Putin.'

'If you can take and hold this island for twenty-four hours, I can deliver the voice of the Russian people,' said Grizlov. 'The current border was approved in 1990 by Gorbachev, an arrangement between the United States and the Soviet Union, a country which no longer exists. America forced it through when we were at our weakest. The new Russia has no agreed border with America, and the Duma has never ratified the Soviet one. I also have documents disputing the Alaska Purchase of 1867. Again, Russia was vulnerable and America exploited us.' Grizlov unlocked the briefcase and spread documents on the table. 'So, this is what I propose.'

As the three men worked through details, Vitruk understood how Lagutov was playing him. Grizlov's political plan was as solid as Vitruk's military one. For either one to win, both had to work together. If Vitruk took the presidency, it would be on the image of raising the Russian flag on American territory, of his rejection of the West and his vision of building a strong Russian friendship with a rising Asia. If Grizlov took it, it would be through his skill in political persuasion and his horse-trading with world leaders. But Russia would again be controlled again by the West, weakened, humiliated, and stripped of self-esteem.

Over the next two months, Vitruk had put measures in place

to ensure that didn't happen. Lagutov, his patron, Grizlov, his enemy, and Yumatov, his protégé, knew barely half of what he had planned. Only the winner could take the presidential throne. Sixty-seven days after that meeting, with a high-risk teenage pregnancy, both men got their chance.

SEVEN

Big Diomede, Chukotka, Russian Far East

'The mission is completely understood, sir,' said Yumatov in response to Vitruk's threatening question. He turned on a television wall screen that showed a helicopter taking off from Little Diomede. 'This is a live video feed. The pregnant girl is on board and will be here in five minutes, sir. Eight men remain on the island. I need your orders now to send in the others and complete the occupation.'

A jolt of exhilaration ran through Vitruk as his eyes scanned the screen of snow swirling around rotor blades. Lamps flashed on the tail, brightly lighting the luminous red cross on the side of the fuselage. The helicopter turned in the wind to fly fast towards the base. It landed just outside the building and paramedics carried a stretcher off the helicopter. A blast of freezing air filled the room as Yumatov opened outside doors, and paramedics wheeled in the Eskimo girl.

A doctor uncovered her face. Her skin was paper-white and her eyes listless. She breathed lightly through an oxygen mask. A drip hung from a matchstick-thin arm. Two Eskimos, a thin woman and a short stocky man, were with her.

'How bad is she?' Vitruk asked.

'Sir, I was not aware you would be here.' The doctor glanced at Yumatov then back to Vitruk who asked, 'Will she live?'

'Impossible to say.'

'She needs to live. Take her to the field theater.' He turned to the two adults. 'We will do our best to save your daughter's life.'

'We are family,' said the woman. 'She is not our daughter.'

'Go with the medical staff. We will see you have everything you need.'

Paramedics pushed the gurney through double doors leading to the field hospital, then through heavy drapes which hung in front to help stave off the icy draught. Once the medics were gone, Vitruk said, 'Send them in, Colonel. It's a go.'

Within minutes, buffeted by blistering snow, a second M-8 helicopter landed on the American island. Spetsnaz special-forces troops spread out and took positions in the south of the village. Vitruk and Yumatov moved from the entrance hall into the cramped command and control center. Two walls were taken up with screens of visual feeds. Vitruk had set up a secure conferencing room deep underground in the base's old nuclear bunker and shared a narrow workbench with Yumatov. Next to them was a chair for the Spetsnaz commander.

The confined space meant Vitruk was working cheek-by-jowl with his men, unheard of for such a senior military commander. But this was not a task that could be done from his Khabarovsk headquarters two thousand miles away. When it was over, the men could tell their children and grandchildren that they had served with Admiral Alexander Vitruk during those days when, together, after centuries and injustice and humiliation, they had restored pride and strength to the Motherland.

Yumatov pulled up a map of the island on his computer and pointed out where they would set up the gun and surveillance posts. Vitruk looked back at the wall screen where soldiers were jumping down from the third helicopter. They rigged up more video feeds from the village. There was a camera on the helipad, three along the shoreline, several going up the hill, and even one in the water-treatment plant and another on the generator.

'We need a position at the top of the island,' said Vitruk. 'Can we get a helicopter up there?'

'Negative, sir. The wind,' said Yumatov. 'Perhaps in a couple of hours.'

'Send a foot platoon up. We need to get a visual on their mainland.' The closest American long-range radar station was at Tin City twenty miles away with an airstrip next door at the settlement of Wales. Vitruk watched soldiers moving along the narrow ice-covered walkways layered up the hillside, going from house to house and taking people down to the school. Villagers were ushered in, stragglers rounded up. He couldn't detect any resistance.

'You need to see the first landing, sir,' said Yumatov. He played back the footage. Vitruk studied the images, the splaying of lights, clumps of mist, snow, and litter skidding with the down-draught. Then a man appeared, confident, excited, welcoming, using his flashlight intricately to direct the pilot's descent. Yumatov froze the image as the helicopter's flood lamp lit the man's face, alert, young, concentrating, his movements profes-sional, trained, familiar with the environment, with a military aircraft, as if he did this every day.

'Do we know who he is?' asked Vitruk.

'We're checking, sir. But he doesn't look like a civilian.'

'Bring that old Eskimo couple back in here,' Vitruk ordered.

Yumatov radioed the instructions. The plastic drapes rose, fell, rattling like a drum roll, and the couple came back in. Vitruk examined them more closely. The man was broad and clear-eyed, his hands calloused from work. The woman carried herself with confidence. She had fashion sense, too, with hair cropped short and a pendant around her neck that looked like a piece of carved ivory from a walrus tusk. They weren't afraid.

'How is she?' he asked, his tone soft and reassuring.

'The doctor is still working,' said the woman.

Vitruk stood up. 'I am Admiral Alexander Vitruk.' He offered his hand.

'Henry Ahkvaluk. She is my wife, Joan.' His handshake was quick and weak. But Eskimos did not measure a man by the strength of his handshake. Not a flicker of expression crossed either of their faces. Vitruk knew the type. They were the ones his alcoholic father had admired. In his sober moments, he had explained to Vitruk how Eskimos lived as one with the environment, how they read the flights of birds, the currents and marine life, and shared their wives to ensure safety for women and children. Vitruk would have preferred that Henry and Joan had been doped out of their heads, not knowing or caring where they were.

'Who was the man on the helipad with the flashlight?' Vitruk asked.

Henry shrugged. Joan stayed quiet. They knew.

'Help me,' he asked again. 'You were with him and the patient.

This man guided in the helicopter. We saw him with you when you carried Akna down the hill to the school.'

They stood together, gutsy and silent. Henry Ahkvaluk's eyes squinted from a life dealing with light reflected on snow. 'I'm sorry,' he said, shaking his head. 'One of the villagers. I don't know who.'

Vitruk let the lie hang, then spoke to the soldiers escorting them. 'Take them back. Don't harm them,' he said, loud enough for everyone to know that physical harm could be an option. When they were gone, Yumatov said, 'A few minutes, sir. We should get something from facial recognition.'

'I want to know everything about that man.' Vitruk flipped the still image onto his laptop screen – a determined figure, wind-whipped but defying the gales, flashing an emergency SOS message. It was a defining image, a lone man in cruel surroundings appealing for help.

EIGHT

Little Diomede, Alaska, USA

Rake sat on the floor of the school gymnasium, legs crossed and hands linked on his head, as they had been ordered. Carrie was next to him, in the same position.

Household by household, soldiers rounded up more villagers, the kids with their tablets, headphones, music, and games; the older ones, defiant, edgy, some in awe, some doped out and barely able to stand. Knives, sharpened metal, anything that could be a weapon was confiscated. They were told to sit by the wall in the order in which they arrived.

So far, Rake had counted five M-8 helicopter landings. To save little Akna, Russia had sent in more than a hundred troops. Ten feet away, by the gymnasium wall bars, a soldier wearing a medical armband kept watch.

'Do exactly as they say,' Rake advised Carrie in a low voice. 'And we'll pull through.'

She shot him a tense look.

'This isn't the Middle East,' he continued. 'These are trained, disciplined men working under orders from their government.'

The gymnasium covered the school's upper floor. A classroom, washrooms, a repair shop, and an office ran off its east side. Each room had a window looking out towards Russia, but none opened wide enough for a person to get through. The repair room door led outside and there was another at the northern end near a stairwell to the top floor. The skylight in the sloping roof was large enough for him to climb through. It was a thought. But then what? How to deal with the soldiers posted on the terrace below? And how could he leave Carrie?

Four soldiers walked in, followed by an exceptionally tall officer in full uniform. His epaulets carried two thin red stripes and three gold stars.

'A moment, please.' He raised his hands like an orchestral conductor. The hum of conversation stopped. 'My name is Colonel Ruslan Yumatov. I understand this is very unusual for you, but I assure you there is nothing to worry about.' He spoke in English with an American East Coast accent. Yumatov walked to the center of the gymnasium, flanked by two men wearing headgear with cameras on top which would be streaming live video back to the base.

'We came here to save the life of Akna,' he said. 'She is now in surgery undergoing an emergency Caesarean section. The doctors tell me the chances for her and the baby are good.'

The colonel paused, as if waiting for a reaction. There was none. Experience passed down generations had taught villagers that the safest path was to stay quiet. Teenagers and difficult childbirth were no novelty to the village, nor were the white faces of an outside power.

Yumatov held up a folder. 'To avoid another emergency, I'm

asking you each to fill in one of these forms that contain basic health questions. My medical staff will take your blood pressure and, in another test, we will check for illnesses such as anemia with just a tiny pinprick of blood from your finger. You don't have to do this, but it could save lives in the future.'

'It's work the US government should have been doing,' muttered Carrie.

'But Russia can't just—'

'They can if they're saving lives.' She was wound up. But they were a team. They would handle this together. Her face became harder. 'You need to escape.'

'What are you talking about?'

'You need to get out of here and get help.'

'Not without you.

'I mean it.'

'We'll be fine. They're not planning to hurt us.'

'Not them. Us. If we're still here when that creep of a new President takes over, he'll come in guns blazing, and won't care about eighty Eskimos locked in a school.'

Rake wanted to say she was overreacting. But she could be right. Could any US President allow the unauthorized presence of foreign troops on American soil? 'You need to get yourself away from here, get word out and keep Bob Holland well away,' she said.

'The Russians are all over the island.'

'If you want to protect us, just do it.' Carrie took a phone out of her jacket pocket. 'There are three contacts in here. Try SL first. She's now the British Ambassador in Washington. I hit the town with her a couple of times in Moscow and Kabul. She'll remember me.' She slipped the phone into his pants pocket and, before he could stop her, pushed herself to her feet and walked towards Yumatov.

The Russian examined Carrie as she approached. 'You are the doctor,' he said.

'Yes, sir. Dr Carrie Walker. I was with the patient. I can help.' Yumatov's face creased with suspicion. His men, professional killers, were being asked to do the work of nurses. Yumatov would be reporting directly to the commander of Russia's Far East Military District. The Kremlin would be listening in and watching. This was one day any military officer would have to get right.

'Who was the man guiding in the helicopter?' he asked her.

'I don't know.' Carrie held his gaze. 'I've come to help your medics.'

'You were with him when our teams arrived.'

'I was with the patient.'

Yumatov gave his response an uncompromising edge. 'What is his name, Dr Walker?'

'I don't know.'

Rake stood up. 'That was me – Captain Raymond Ozenna. I'm a native of Little Diomede. Dr Walker wouldn't know. She only got here today.'

Yumatov spoke in Russian and two soldiers moved either side and loosely held Rake's arms.

'What are you doing?' exclaimed Carrie.

'Captain Ozenna is going to our base to help with the patient.'

'Then I'll come too,' said Carrie.

'Your skills are needed here.'

Rake's mind raced with bad choices. This was his chance. There would be a dozen opportunities to escape between here and the helicopter. Maybe Carrie even planned it this way. 'If I am under arrest, Colonel, handcuff me,' he said. 'If not, let me walk as a free man.' The grip on Rake's arms tightened. He raised his voice. 'If you want this to go well, you should remember there is one thing the people of the Diomede no longer tolerate and that is captivity by the white man.'

It worked. Rake had sowed the first seed of dissent and he felt resentful menace ripple through the gym. Yumatov was smart enough to sense it too. He issued orders for the soldiers to let go of Rake's arms. They did. One held him from behind. The other patted him down and found a knife blade strapped around his left ankle.

'Go, Captain,' Yumatov said softly. 'And, as you say, walk as a free man.'

The guards stayed with him, but kept their hands away. One was tall, head shaved, a powerful man, but with a face of youth and hope that could have made him a military poster model. The other was smaller, wiry, narrow eyes, ferret-like, tougher and probably more dangerous. His face carried a knife scar.

They assessed him like military escorts do. He wouldn't give them time to draw an accurate conclusion. Two against one were probably the best odds he was going to get and those wouldn't last long. He had a home-ground advantage. This was his island and his old school. He would move on his own schedule. He had a couple of minutes at best. The next soldiers would be around the corner.

Outside the gymnasium, Rake slowed at the top of the stairs

where the wall was decorated with photographs of walrus and seal hunts and instructions on how to make kayak canoes and boats from animal skin. He started talking in his bad Russian about how skin boats were used to hunt marine life, even whales at times. Further along there were display photographs of bridges in American cities. God knew who put them there and why, but they bought him more time. 'Brooklyn Bridge.' He indicated an arty black-and-white portrait of the ageing bridge running out of Manhattan. The younger soldier paused to look.

'And the Golden Gate,' said Rake. 'San Francisco.'

'Move,' said the older one.

Rake would have to take him first, and doubted he could do it without killing him. With two trained men, you often had to kill one to show the other that things were serious. 'Maybe one day they'll have a bridge like that between our two countries,' said Rake. 'I've relatives over there, you know. In Uelen. You been to Uelen?'

At the bottom, stairs led straight into a corridor with rooms running off each side that turned at right angles into another corridor. More soldiers would be by the main entrance. He pointed to the boys' restroom. 'Give me a moment.' The older one nodded. Rake left the door ajar. The young soldier kept watch. Rake kept up the chatter, explaining every detail. It was a big restroom so it could take a wheelchair. It had a high ceiling that gave a sense of space and there was a single shining white commode with a stainless-steel rail for the disabled.

He zipped up, flushed the bowl, and moved to the sink, taking time with the soap. In the mirror, he saw that neither man had moved. But their alertness levels had dropped. Naturally. This wasn't Ukraine. They were watching a guy take a piss in a village school. He shook water from his hands, but kept the tap running as he reached for a paper towel. Rake caught the eye of the younger soldier in the mirror. 'They have this idea for a tunnel. Chukotka to Alaska. Sixty miles,' he said. 'You heard of that? Sixty miles under the sea.'

The military equipment was standard – helmet with goggles hitched up on the rim, pouches on the Kevlar vest, a routine issue Vityaz automatic rifle, Makarov 9mm pistol, and a sheathed knife about five inches long, probably with a double-edged blade. The challenge was the radio that was in a pouch at the bottom of the Kevlar. Its wire trailed up to the mouth and earpieces. On an operation like this, it would be button and not voice activated to avoid clustering the radio channels.

He took half a step to his right, shifting his weight as he turned, towel screwed up in his hand, arm raised to drop it in the bin. The tap still ran. The toilet cistern was filling up; plenty of background noise. From the outside, Rake looked nice and relaxed.

Inside he was taut like a spring, and he needed to wind tighter. In a hairsbreadth of a second, he hurled himself forward, the heel of his hand smashing the younger soldier's nose so that shards of cartilage protruded into the brain. He wrapped his arms around the helmet and wrenched back the neck, snapping it and severing the spinal cord. The man crumpled, but Rake held him up as a battering ram, crashing into the older soldier's chest, a solid strike of Kevlar against Kevlar, helmet against helmet.

Rake let go of the dead soldier and kicked the older guard

hard in the groin. As his legs buckled, Rake ripped out the radio wire. He fisted his bloodied fingers, pushing out the forefinger, and struck towards the windpipe.

The soldier was too fast for him, bringing up his arm, intercepting and gripping. He held it with enormous strength, his eyes narrowed into a pinpoint of focus. The two men's faces were an inch apart.

'Stop,' said the soldier in Russian. 'I will help you.'

NINE

The White House, Washington, DC

Stephanie stood to the left of the Oval Office desk listening to the conversation between the Russian and American leaders on speakerphone. President Christopher Swain stood, hand on hip, his eyes moving around the information on screens on his desk. He was an athletic figure with short curly gray hair and the face of a ponderous academic with eyes that emanated authority. A dozen or so officials from Defense, State, and the intelligence agencies clustered around two pastel-yellow sofas that faced each other midway in the room. Holland stood next to Slater by a window in the oval curve.

'I'm sorry to interrupt your evening, Viktor,' Swain said with a tone far more relaxed than the atmosphere of the room.

'Not at all, Chris,' said Lagutov. 'I would have called you, but I only learned this myself from news broadcasts. We have a new regional commander in the east. He told me that an emergency radio call was intercepted at our base on Ratmonova, the island that you call Big Diomede. A pregnant girl's life was in critical danger, and he ordered a helicopter across to help her. In the heat of the moment, no one remembered to let you guys know.

I'm sorry for the panic. But the good news is that I've just heard the baby has been delivered by emergency Caesarean section, a little girl, and both she and the mother are stable.'

'Thank you, Viktor.' Swain kept glancing at his own tablet and a wall screen constantly updated with satellite and radar images. 'And are they still with you?'

'They are,' continued Lagutov in his casual tone. 'The baby has been named Iyaroak, which means apple of the eye in Inupiat, their native language.'

A ticker tape processed from the Situation Room below ran on the screen. *All cellphones jammed. No contact Little Diomede.*

'And are her parents with her?' The ticker read: *Russian attack 4 KA-52s 3 troop carrier M-8s.*' The screen showed radar images of Russian helicopters crossing the border.

'Two relatives are there.'

'That's good. She needs family with her.' The ticker read: *Heavy cloud. No satellite.* Holland paced, a measured contrast against Swain's calmness. Swain's tablet relayed a feed from the Tin City radar station, the closest site to the Diomede islands. Four Black Hawk helicopters were an hour away. Six F-22 fighters had been scrambled from the Elmendorf-Richardson airbase in Anchorage.

'We'll send a helicopter across to pick up the mother and baby and fly them to Nome,' said Swain.

Lagutov allowed a moment of hesitation which Swain filled. 'Jim Hoskins, Governor of Alaska, can fly to Nome with your consul-general. They'll do a photo op. You and I can talk about our friendship and Russia helping an American in crisis.'

'I'm told you don't have helicopters available,' Lagutov said abruptly.

The Oval Office atmosphere tensed. The Russian radar stations on the eastern coastline would detect that Black Hawks and F-22s were close. Either Lagutov was lying or he wasn't being briefed, which could be worse because it meant he wasn't in charge. Or he did know and he was winging it because he did not have a Plan B, unimaginable as it might seem.

'Apparently, that's fixed.' Swain's tone hardened slightly. Prusak motioned that he should keep talking. 'It seems with helicopters we've gone from famine to feast, a Black Hawk at Teller and one at Kotzebue, both mainland settlements. So, we'll send one straight to your base on Big Diomede to pick them up—'

'Hold, Chris,' interjected Lagutov. 'Someone here's updating me.'

The ticker tape read: *Submarines Seawolf-class Connecticut and Virginia-class Washington in Arctic region. 190 minutes out.*

Prusak switched the line so the Russian side could hear nothing.

'If those subs are under the ice, they're not much good against these.' Holland's finger jabbed towards the images of the four Russian attack helicopters.

Defense Secretary Mike Pacolli contradicted him: 'The *Connecticut* carries IDAS missiles that can bring down a helicopter from a submerged position, and if you'd ever seen one of those beasts break up through ice, you would not treat their presence lightly.'

Holland glared. 'This is a ground war, Mr Secretary. It needs boots on ice, not computers under the sea.'

'What else do you have, Mike?' asked Swain.

'Refueling tankers for the F22s are airborne, sir. Drones, two AWACs, and satellites deployed. A marine battalion is on its way to Wales. That is twenty-five miles from Little Diomede. They'll go in by helicopter or across the ice to the island.'

Holland brushed his hand down his cheek, unable to hide his surprise at the speed with which the whole range of American military options had swung into action. His campaign had been against a coward who had failed to protect America. He was seeing for the first time how the authority of one man can deploy such immense military power.

'This is the easy part,' said Swain. 'The tough bit is making sure we don't use them.'

Lagutov was back, his tone formal. 'President Swain, I'm patching you through to Admiral Alexander Vitruk, the commander of our Far East Military Region. He took the initiative to go straight to Krusenstern when he heard of the medical emergency. Admiral Vitruk can enlighten us all.'

'Krusenstern is Little Diomede,' Stephanie mouthed to Swain.

A photograph of Vitruk, tanned, lean, purposeful, appeared on one of the Oval Office screens. As soon as he spoke, voice authentication confirmed that this was indeed the dominant figure who ran the Russian Far East. His bio-data unfolded next to the photograph. A veteran of Russia's campaigns in Afghanistan, Chechnya, Georgia, and Syria, he had forged friendships with the Chinese, North Koreans, and Mongolians. He had been a defense attaché in Washington, DC, had visited Nome and Anchorage, and had even initiated joint US–Russian training exercises out of Elmendorf-Richardson.

'This is a humanitarian mission, Mr President,' said Vitruk.

'They pleaded with us to save these lives and that is what we are doing.'

Without identifying himself, Matt Prusak cut in. He could not allow the President to speak directly to the regional commander of a foreign adversary. The Russian would put it all over their media as President Swain pleading for help. 'We have a Black Hawk en route to bring back the patient, Admiral,' Prusak said. 'You are being patched through to General Davies of our Northern Command with whom you can discuss details.'

'That will not be necessary,' Vitruk replied. 'Your aircraft cannot enter Russian sovereign airspace. If it does, I cannot guarantee its safety.'

TEN

Little Diomede, Alaska, USA

Rake wore the uniform of the dead Russian.

The surviving soldier was Sergeant Matvey Golov of the 83rd Airborne Brigade based in Ussuriysk, north of Vladivostok. Disarmed and with his helmet removed, Golov came across as a squat imposing figure, the surface of his shaved skull rutted like a bad road, his eyebrows thick and his eyes drawn in.

Golov said his unit had left for this mission two days ago. He had family in New York, and didn't plan to become an enemy of the United States. Rake interrogated him quickly and neither believed nor trusted him. However, Golov could have killed him and hadn't, and he would now be Rake's ticket out.

'If you cross me I will cripple you and leave you for your colleagues to finish you off as a traitor to Russia,' Rake told him. Golov didn't respond.

To get across the ice to the mainland, Rake would need more weapons. Russian small arms were not enough. The closest would be in the sealed and abandoned Alaska Army National Guard observation post that stood among civilian homes in the middle of the village. That's if they hadn't been cleared out. No military had been posted to Little Diomede since the 1990s when the post was closed. Weapons and communication equipment were inside, logged, stored, and long forgotten within the army bureaucracy. But Rake had no idea what condition they would be in. More weapons might be further along in a wooden cache underneath the church where they kept seal, walrus, and other meat over the winter months. Don Ondola had hidden them there, and Rake doubted they had been touched since Alaska State Troopers took Ondola away for murdering Akna's mother. Ondola was a rough man, selfish, drug-crazed, and violent. But he knew how to keep a weapon functioning against the wet and the cold.

Rake flipped the magazine out of Golov's Vityaz automatic, ejected the 9mm rounds, and handed the weapon to Golov. Other Russian troops must not see him unarmed. Rake did the same with the Makarov pistol. He took Golov's phone and asked how it worked. The Russian explained that men on each post would be setting up their own Wi-Fi hotspot that only they could use.

They carried the body into the school kitchen and slid it down the rubbish chute where it landed with a thud on the trash of the past days.

Helmets on and faces covered, Golov led the way out of the school. Two soldiers guarded the entrance. There was a short conversation, which Rake had anticipated. Where was the American Eskimo? Golov pointed back inside. Change of plan. The American was staying in the school. They were off to search his house.

They walked on. Troops were positioned between the school

and the helipad. They were on the roof of the old wooden building containing the clinic and launderette and along tiers of walkways that linked the small homes. On the top of the circular concrete water-treatment plant, they were positioning a heavy machine gun. Another machine gun had been set up by the cemetery that overlooked the village. More dangerously, troops were walking up the hillside toward the snow-covered plateau. From there they would have a view to the mainland to see anyone crossing in either direction.

That high watchpoint might make it impossible for Rake to escape the island. It rarely got completely light, rarely dark either because of moonlight. In this second half of the month, the moon hung in the sky, blending with the ice and sun that hovered around the horizon. Rake also had no idea of the thickness of the ice. Someone had gone through it near Wales, which was the closest landfall and where he might go. When he was a child, they used to clear a runway on the ice for a plane to land. Now winter was too warm and the ice too thin.

Rake led Golov up wooden steps to a landing with a bench and space for people to hang out. Two Russian sentries leant on railings, their gaze fixed to where Russian helicopters, red and blue lights blinking, hovered in the sky just behind the border. On the island's helipad, the blades of an M-8 transport helicopter rotated slowly while soldiers unloaded equipment. Rake saw a Kord 12.7mm heavy machine gun, powerful enough to send a wall of lead against an approaching helicopter. He counted three Igna hand-held surface-to-air missile launchers.

By now the long-range radar at Tin City would have picked up what was going on, but not the detail. He needed to get word out that Russia was seriously reinforcing its hold on the island with hostages in the school.

The walkway sloped up. They passed Henry and Joan's house. On the ledge outside sat the skull of the polar bear that Henry had shot with Rake all those years ago. On the rocks in front, the skin of a gray seal stretched between wooden poles. Nearby, its meat hung drying on a line of red nylon rope.

Midway up, they came to the dark-green hut that used to be the army post. The Russians were already there. Tape was spread across its small windows. The door had been broken down and they had put a searchlight in the small watchtower and a machine gun on the roof. Whatever weapons were in there were now off limits. A soldier stood outside. The pinpoint glow of a cigarette shone through his mist of breath.

The soldier spoke to Golov, who replied, not just an acknowledgment, but a longer sentence that Rake couldn't hear because of the wind. The Russian pointed inside the guardhouse, then across the water to the waiting helicopters. Rake shifted his fingers around his weapon. Above them the search lamp went on and off. They were testing it.

Rake turned away, and brought out from his pocket the phone Carrie had given him. There was no signal. But the screen showed a link to the personal hotspot from inside the guardhouse. He drew off his glove to work the keypad and find the three numbers Carrie had given him. The first was her sister Angela with a Brooklyn 718 prefix. Next came a +41 22 code, which was Geneva, someone called Jenny who worked at one of the international aid agencies. Then there was a listing for SL, +1 202 – Washington, the ambassador, Carrie's first choice.

Russian and American signals intelligence would pick up any phone message that went out. It was late evening in Washington and the middle of the night in Europe. The chances were that SL was asleep. Rake wrote the message clear and short. His finger was sliding down to send when two F-22 fighters screamed overhead from south to north along the border. Seconds later two more flew fast and low from north to south. They looped back towards the mainland. The noise faded, and he heard a child's voice. 'Bang, Bang. I'm a Russian and you're dead, Uncle Rake.'

Timo, Akna's seven-year-old brother, appeared from nowhere and wrapped his arms around Rake's legs. He must have slipped away as the soldiers were searching homes. Timo wore a green down jacket, but wasn't dressed to be in the cold for any length of time. His teeth chattered.

The Russian soldier shifted from watching the aircraft to the little boy.

'Why are you dressed like a Russian?' Timo asked loudly. The soldier glanced at Golov, then back to Rake.

The sky erupted with engine noise again. American helicopters from the Alaskan mainland – four Black Hawks and four Apaches – came around from both the north and south edges of the island. Their searchlights swept the village and the hillside. They spread out in a two-tiered line, Black Hawks below, Apaches above, right on the border, flood lamps facing down the Russian aircrews on the other side. The F-22s returned in a deafening roar. Then the American helicopters shut off all their lights and hung ghost-like in the sky. No shots were fired, no missiles unleashed. It was a 'don't mess with us' test of

Russian resolve. Did Moscow want it the easy way or the hard way?

The Russian guard raised his weapon. Rake pressed the Washington number, sending the message just as Golov ripped the phone from his hand.

ELEVEN

The White House, Washington, DC

A message alert flashed on Stephanie's phone. It appeared in a small strip across the top of the screen then faded. She saw it but wasn't focusing. Vitruk's refusal to allow an American helicopter to the Russian base to pick up the Eskimo girl and her baby had drawn everyone's concentration into the narrowest channel.

Holland paced the room. 'Mr President, you must now accept that my first analysis of this crisis was correct. You need to take out their command and control center on Big Diomede island.'

'Then the United States risks losing its ally in Britain,' said Kevin Slater. 'Nor will Europe support—'

'Bull, Prime Minister, and you and Ambassador Lucas know it,' countered Holland. 'Estonia, Latvia, Lithuania, Poland, Bulgaria, Romania will back a strong response. They've been taking Kremlin crap for years.'

'Not if Moscow retaliates against them,' argued Slater. 'You have never witnessed a war on your soil, in your neighborhood, engulfing your family.'

'We should call the German chancellor,' said Stephanie.

'Not from here,' said Slater. 'We need to go back to the embassy.'

From the embassy, they would have secure communications. But for Stephanie there were others who could talk to the Germans and the French. Slater would be better off in the White House because he would know what was going on and it would show Britain at the heart of the crisis.

'You need to make a decision, Mr President,' said Holland.

Prusak flipped to a visual feed from a Black Hawk helicopter hovering between the Russian and American islands. The image was blurred by fog and snow. But there was enough to show two lines of aircraft narrowly separated by the invisible border. Streaks of red swept across the screen.

'They're the F-22s,' said Defense Secretary Pacolli. 'They will keep doing that and the helicopter cordon will stay in place. Meanwhile, we're testing the ice for moving troops on a sea crossing from Wales.'

'Time weakens us,' said Holland aggressively. 'They need to be taught a lesson.'

'Who are they, Bob?' Swain deliberately traced his words with irritation. 'Are they school kids whom we slap on the wrists until they do what we say? At this level, it doesn't work like that.'

'Then how does it work in your White House?'

'We think beyond guns. We don't start wars. We balance the books. We keep our citizens richer and safer.'

'And weaken American power on every continent.'

Swain sucked in his cheek, a habit Stephanie knew from long ago; it meant the President was controlling his anger. 'The Iranians thought they taught us a lesson in 1979 by taking our embassy. That took forty years to sort out. We thought we taught Saddam Hussein a lesson in 2003. We're still mopping that shit pit up today. How do you plan to teach Russia a lesson, Bob? If we take out their base on Big Diomede, what are they going to do? Strike Tin City? Nome? Elmendorf-Richardson, right next to the civilian Lowes Mall parking lot in Anchorage? Then what do we do?'

'Or Ukraine,' said Slater. 'Or the Baltic states. Or break the Syrian alliance.'

Stephanie hoped that would quieten Holland. She was wrong.

'Two days from now, I'll be making the decisions. And there'll be no Russian guns on American soil. You have my word on that.'

'Something's going on in the State Duma,' said Prusak, turning to a screen showing dark-suited men in Moscow's parliament. A Russian commentary explained that the Duma was in emergency session. The camera moved across the hall to the figure of the suave and impeccably dressed Duma chairman, Sergey Grizlov, speaking from the center of the long bench desk at the front of the chamber, flanked by fellow parliamentarians.

Stephanie kept her expression neutral. In a way, she was proud of her former lover and still thought of him as a friend. They were no longer close, but whenever she flipped him an email, Grizlov responded. He was funny, entertaining, cynical, and the smartest political operator in Moscow.

The Oval Office fell quiet. The feed came from Russian television, and Swain moved close to Stephanie, who interpreted. 'They're debating the 1990 Maritime Boundary Agreement.' She glanced at Slater to make sure he understood. 'That's the border between Russia and America.'

'They don't debate. This is a rubber stamp,' said Holland.

No one responded.

'Sergey Grizlov, that's the speaker, is saying the Duma has never ratified the border agreement,' said Stephanie. 'It was pushed through in 1990 when the Russian people were weak. This has impacted badly on the people in the Far East and the country's economy. The United States took fifteen thousand square kilometers of sea that belongs to Russia. With the melting of ice in the Arctic region, many governments are interested in the new energy supplies and shipping routes which have cut the passage from Asia to Europe by four thousand miles or more. Therefore, the correct border now needs to be ratified by the Duma.'

Grizlov moved to the left of the chamber, stopping underneath a large wall screen in the corner. A map showed the mainland of Alaska and Russia's Far East with oil and gas reserves shaded in and colored lines tracking new shipping routes created by the melting ice. A simultaneous English translation now came with the video feed.

'The Arctic region has become the focus of attention for many friendly governments,' said Grizlov. 'By refusing to sign the United Nations' Convention on the Law of the Sea, the United States has broken from the international community, making multilateral negotiations impossible. Russian patience has finally run out.'

A video appeared, grainy, jumpy. The hazy green of a night-vision lens showed paramedics running with a stretcher toward a helicopter on Little Diomede. 'In the past few hours, Russian soldiers have saved the life of an Eskimo woman on this island of Little Diomede, or Krusenstern Island as we call it here.'

The thin beam of Grizlov's pencil torch settled on Little Diomede. A video came up of a man, arms outstretched with a flashlight, on the island's shoreline as if beckoning down an approaching helicopter. Grizlov said, 'These islanders have been abandoned by their own government. They are desperate and pleading with us for help. We have now saved the life of the woman, or should I say girl – she is only fifteen years old – and her baby daughter. Both are well and resting.'

The picture changed to the inside of a clinic with a roof of military green. The young mother lay in a hospital bed next to an incubator. The Duma broke out into applause.

'The conditions we are finding among the community of Krusenstern are truly dreadful,' said Grizlov. The image moved to a large hall with bright lighting and dozens of people separated into groups. There were basketball hoops at both ends, the markings of a court and wall bars on one side.

'In the school gymnasium, we have carried out basic medical tests and found that most villagers are anemic and their immune systems are vulnerable. The children are malnourished. This is a live feed. What you see is happening now. The abuse and neglect of the people of Krusenstern by the United States government is unacceptable under international law.'

Most villagers wore T-shirts or light clothing with thick outdoor clothes piled beside them. The younger ones wore headphones. Some played games on tablets. Military medics moved between them, crouching down, talking. They took temperatures and checked throats and eyes. A blonde woman worked with the medics, but she was not in military green. She wore jeans and a red denim shirt. There was something familiar about her that Stephanie couldn't place.

'How many times did I say that we needed to match Russia gun for gun in the Arctic?' Holland challenged Swain. 'And what did you do? You reduced troops and cut resources.'

Swain's face turned to stone. 'If you speak again, Mr President-elect, I will have you removed.'

'Like Hell you will.'

A faded document, creased and brown with age, appeared on the Moscow screen. The writing was in Russian Cyrillic and at the center was a map.

'This is the original 1867 treaty, when the United States bought Alaska from Russia for $7.2 million,' said Grizlov. 'It was a time when the Motherland was weak. But look at this—' He zoomed in on the map. 'The 1867 border follows a line that goes to the east of Krusenstern Island. It was agreed to keep these two islands as one community, part of Russia, because those living on them were from one family. Our two governments had no right to divide them. You cannot buy people and make them your citizens, forcing them away from their relatives. The concept is barbaric. There was no objection from the Americans. Indeed, many thought the purchase of Alaska was such a waste of money that they called it Seward's Folly after Secretary of State William Seward, who signed the agreement.'

'There is no original treaty,' said Stephanie. 'It's been lost. This has to be a fake.'

The Oval Office was filling up, more uniforms, big figures from the military and intelligence services.

Grizlov split the screen to show the present border running between the two islands. 'The false border was imposed by the United States in 1926 and agreed by the Central Executive Committee of the Soviet Union at a time when the USSR was focusing on internal matters. Even then it was agreed that trade and people would be permitted so that the native people of the Bering Strait would not be divided.' He turned to face the chamber, his expression hard and angry. 'But let me repeat, this exploitative border has never been ratified by either a Soviet or a Russian parliament. Today, in this parliamentary chamber, we are going to correct the historical wrongs. We will reunite the people of Krusenstern and Ratmonova islands. We will ratify the rightful border between the United States and Russia.'

A single screen showed the two islands belonging to Moscow, with a dark patch stretching twelve miles eastward indicating sovereign territory that placed Russia just thirteen miles from the American mainland. The Duma deputies rose to their feet, applauding, shaking hands, embracing. Grizlov repeatedly ran his red pencil beam up and down the new boundary line.

'Mr President, Lagutov is on the line from the Kremlin,' said Prusak.

'Don't take it,' said Holland.

As the Duma's applause subsided, the screen returned to the school gymnasium on Little Diomede.

A message reminder lit Stephanie's phone. She opened it, read it once, then again. She rested for balance against the edge of Swain's desk. She looked back at the screen. Of course! How dumb of her not to connect! The blonde woman, now talking to a tall Russian colonel, was Carrie Walker whom she had met in Kabul, seven, maybe eight years, ago.

They spent an evening hunkered down in the British Embassy with more than one bottle of red wine, while Carrie berated the world for the bloodbaths in the Muslim world. Stephanie liked her. You couldn't be human and work in such conditions without a strong reaction. As they said goodbye, Carrie apologized for making Stephanie her punchbag. 'Next time you need to lash out at someone, it'll be my turn.' Next time, Carrie had looked Stephanie up when she was at a conference in Moscow. Stephanie was British Ambassador, combating an angry husband, and she needed a drinking buddy to talk to. Much to the alarm of her bodyguards, the two of them hit the town, cocktails, dinner, nightcap, and then another. But why was Carrie on Little Diomede? A rebel heart, yes, but with the Russians? Surely not.

Swain was poised to take the call from Lagutov. Stephanie showed him and Prusak the message, *Carrie + 80 held school L. Dio*, explaining that Carrie was the blonde doctor in the video.

'We have a phone track on it.' Prusak read raw data streamed in from the National Security Agency. 'A T-Mobile SIM card registered to Dr Carrie Walker, contract taken out at the Court Street store in Brooklyn. That phone is running through a Wi-Fi hotspot set up by—' He went quiet, digesting the information. 'A private cellphone registered to a unit with the Russian 83rd Airborne Brigade. No individual name.'

'So, did Carrie send it?' asked Stephanie, amazed yet again at the speed with which American intelligence technology worked.

'Unlikely,' said Prusak. 'These are live pictures of her in the school gymnasium. The hotspot is two hundred yards south and at a higher elevation. So, we may have someone out free on the island.'

'Find them,' instructed Swain.

Prusak tilted his head towards the President. 'Lagutov's calling.'

'I warn you,' said Holland. 'You will not negotiate.' His eyes swept around others in the room, many of whose careers would depend on how the new President viewed their loyalty.

Swain picked up. Prusak switched it to speaker. Swain said nothing. He let the silence grow. Then the Russian President said, 'I'm sorry it's come to this, Mr President, but it's out of my hands. The Duma has ratified the new border. We have no problem with the civilian population. But we cannot tolerate a military presence. If you do not begin withdrawing your aircraft, I will instruct my forces to defend Russian sovereign territory.'

TWELVE

Little Diomede, Alaska, USA

The roar of the F-22s faded to a distant growl. They would be back. Two lines of helicopters faced each other like airborne gladiators marking ground to see which would move first. The Russian ones glowed like Christmas trees. The Americans remained darkened, no lights at all.

Rake had to get Timo to safety. Surrender might save Timo's life, but not Carrie's and those of the hostages in the school. He drew Timo firmly towards him, shielding him from the Russians with his body. Timo clung to his jacket as Rake made two simultaneous judgments. Timo's outburst would have exposed his identity to the Russians. Golov would cut his losses and turn Rake in before his own cover was blown. The Russians would be under orders to avoid casualties, which gave Rake an advantage. But trained soldiers do not allow themselves to be shot. Either Rake faced them down or he surrendered and, if he did that, there were plenty of reasons why he would not survive. Golov would need Rake dead to protect himself. He and the others would not forgive Rake's killing their comrade. Surrender would make him a dead man walking.

Golov looked at Rake, eyes squinted against the weather. For a few minutes, Rake had been his ticket to New York, but no more. They both knew it. Once again, they were kill-or-be-killed enemies. Golov was quick, fast, and good, except Rake had emptied his weapon of ammunition, which gave him an advantage, probably for five seconds. Maybe seven. The soldier behind Golov was just a kid, red-faced and feeling the cold.

Rake shot the young soldier in the neck, a single round, just above the flak jacket. The bullet caught the carotid artery and a jet of blood sprayed onto the snow as the man crumpled.

Golov, in a sideways leap, went for the soldier's automatic rifle as it fell. He skillfully picked it up, familiar with the mechanism and moving fast, but as he lifted the rifle the heel of his boot slid under the snow.

Rake hurled himself forward and drew his knife. As they hit the iron-hard surface, he drove it into the side of Golov's neck, withdrew it, and plunged it back into his right eye, twisting the blade. A moment of quiet was broken by a soft cry from Timo and a crackle on the radio, a Russian voice asking about the gunshot. Rake grabbed the radio. 'Turned out to be a kid,' he said in Russian. 'Sending him down now.'

Rake pushed himself to his feet. Soaking blood from the two bodies created a blanket of speckled maroon and red in the snow. He dragged them into the old army post. He went through their pockets. Neither carried ID. He took the radio, ammunition, and the phone. Timo squatted, staring at the snow, shaking. Rake knelt with him and held his face between his hands. 'Look at me, Timo.' The boy raised his head.

'It's OK,' said Rake. 'You're safe.'

'I'm not scared. I'll soon be old enough to kill men too.' Timo looked down again, his hands tightly clasped.

Rake pressed a flashlight in his hand. 'I want you to walk down towards the school. Put your hands high above your head and shine the flashlight into your face.'

Timo nodded.

'Soldiers will meet you. They'll take you to the school and they'll ask you what happened. Tell them you saw nothing. You heard a gunshot. That you're frightened.'

Timo nodded again.

'Good man.' Rake lifted him to his feet.

'Uncle Rake, look.' Timo twisted around to face the Russian island where a firefight between Russian and American helicopters had broken out. A Black Hawk dissolved into an airborne furnace. The fuselage lit up, lurched clumsily, and dropped fast towards the ice. Its rotor blades trailed red and yellow flames. An F-22 roared overhead, a missile speeding out from its starboard wing pod. A Russian helicopter evaporated into a white inferno.

'Go.' Rake pushed Timo gently out onto the path. The boy turned on the flashlight, raised his arms above his head, and walked surefootedly down towards two Russian soldiers who stepped into his path.

Carrie's phone vibrated and lit up with an incoming call from the number that Rake had messaged.

THIRTEEN

The White House, Washington, DC

Like a museum exhibit, Stephanie's phone lay on the Oval Office desk, its signal wirelessly fed into her earpiece and through speakers so everyone could hear. She was making a call to the phone that sent her the message.

'This is Stephanie Lucas. I am a friend of Dr Carrie Walker,' she said.

· Swain sat behind the desk, with Prusak at one end. Holland leant against the wall by the window. Stephanie was at the front of the desk, her gaze switching between three contrasting screens of the burning helicopter wreckage, the Russian parliament, and a calm scene in the school on Little Diomede where Carrie worked with Russian paramedics. Slater stood silent next to Stephanie, arms folded.

Key principals spread around the room. By now the Secretaries of State and Treasury were there together with the Chairman of the Joint Chiefs of Staff, the Directors of Homeland Security and the CIA, and specialists on Russia.

'I am . . .' The voice from the island was drowned out by a

howl of weather. When the wind subsided, Stephanie asked, 'Who are you and where are you?'

'Captain Rake Ozenna, 207th Infantry Group of the Alaska Army National Guard. I am on the island of Little Diomede, which has been occupied by Russian forces. Dr Walker suggested I call. I need to ask now who you are and how secure is this line.'

She glanced at Prusak who said, 'Both ends.'

'It's secure, Captain. I am the British Ambassador to Washington. I am in the White House. You can speak freely. What is happening there?'

'We just arrived—' The rest of the words were lost in the wind. When the line cleared, Prusak signaled for Mike Pacolli, as Defense Secretary, to take over. 'Captain Ozenna, are you in a position to see if there are any survivors from the Black Hawk?'

'I can see the aircraft, but no sign of life, sir.'

'What is the situation on the island?'

'Counting the flights in, I estimate a hundred Russian troops. They have positions on rooftops and up the hill. The villagers are in the school. Any military action targeting the school would result in high casualties of American civilians. I escaped just before the two helicopters went down.'

'Could ground troops make it across the ice from Wales?'

'They would need Eskimo guides. The ice is patchy. A man went through today. The Russians have set up a watch post on the top of the island.'

'Hold, Captain.'

'We take out their observation post,' suggested Pacolli to Swain.

'That would escalate,' said Swain.

'They wouldn't retaliate against the hostages. This isn't the Middle East.'

'Are you a hundred percent certain?'

Pacolli paused, then said, 'No, sir. I am not.'

'Ozenna needs to keep low. We'll get back to him,' said Swain.

'Stay within signal, Captain,' said Pacolli. 'You will have your orders in a few minutes.'

'Do I have to spell this out?' said Holland as the call ended. 'We get enemy forces off American territory. Now!'

'Mr President-elect, I need you to go back to Blair House, consult with your team, and get back to me within the hour,' said Swain sternly. 'I will work with whatever plan you come up with as much as I can. You have my word on that.' He turned to Slater. 'Mr Prime Minister, we'll give you an escort to the embassy. Since you are with me in DC, we will ask European leaders to work through you. Perhaps Britain, France, and Germany could come up with a unified response and bring as many of the European states with you as possible.'

'My hand will be stronger if there is no more military action,' said Slater.

Swain's voice hardened in a way that brooked no opposition. 'I'd like Ambassador Lucas to stay here because of her direct link to Dr Walker and Captain Ozenna. The rest of us will re-group in the Situation Room.'

Prusak looked up from his tablet. 'CNN are publishing their interactive poll,' he said.

'So quickly?' said Slater with surprise.

'It's very basic,' Prusak explained. 'They ask the audience to press a button on a For or Against question. So far sixty-nine percent believe we should just walk away from this.'

'What was the question?' asked Swain.

'"Do you believe the United States should take immediate military action against Russia's occupation of Little Diomede?" And that sixty-nine percent has just gone up to seventy.'

'Bullshit,' said Holland. 'Let's wait for the Fox poll.'

'We'll speak in an hour, Bob,' said Swain. Amid low murmurs of conversation, Swain stepped across into the en-suite restroom. The Oval Office emptied, leaving Prusak and Stephanie alone.

'Does this stink, or what, Matt?'

'Which part? Bob Holland? Your Prime Minister? Viktor Lagutov?' Prusak asked.

'Can you do as these polls suggest? Let Russia take this god-forsaken island?'

'No way. It would mean we surrender the border change, the energy reserves, the gateway to the new Arctic shipping routes, the prestige of America. If we go with it now, Holland will reverse it. So, keep talking, Steph, because I need to know your thoughts.'

'Lagutov's bright, but an academic rather than a leader. Sergey Grizlov's a street-smart wheeler-dealer.'

'Didn't you . . .?'

Stephanie blushed. 'Years ago, when we were young and believed that inside every Russian was a little democrat waiting to burst out.'

'Useful, though.'

'I can call him when the time's right, if that's what you mean. But the one we need to track is Alexander Vitruk. He is ruthless and must have wider military support. If Sergey Grizlov is behind Vitruk, we have a very dangerous situation, because however wretched and remote Little Diomede is, it's not Crimea. It's Russia taking America. Whatever the polls say, you're not going to let them raise the tricolor and declare it Russian soil, whether Holland or anybody else is in this office.'

'Agreed.'

Stephanie swiped her hand impatiently through the air. 'So, what then is their plan – the humanitarian rescue, the Duma session, the new border? It can't stop here.'

'Like I said – a play for the Arctic, control of shipping routes, fossil-fuel resources?'

'Too opaque. Why risk so much now against everything else they have going with the United States – trade, the Middle East deals, terror, penthouse properties, oligarch bank accounts, and Fifth Avenue shopping sprees?'

'They're doing it now because they think they can,' suggested Prusak. 'They took Crimea and eastern Ukraine, and Europe did nothing. They're outpacing us many times over with bases and ports in the Arctic.'

'All of that, yes. But I have a feeling this is about Lagutov's succession. He's playing Grizlov and Vitruk against each other.'

'You think this is all orchestrated by Lagutov?'

'Lagutov is a big theorist with a deep sense of history. Grizlov is his political muscle and is pro-West. Vitruk is his military muscle and leans towards China, the authoritarians, and Asia. Lagutov might be testing which of the two is stronger.'

The side door swung open, and Swain stepped back in. 'I agree with you, Stephanie. But first, call Ozenna. You do the talking, Stephanie. He's the one on the island. Ask him what his plan would be.'

They waited for the line to be set up, encryption secured. A technician's voice came through her earpiece: 'Go ahead, Ambassador.'

'Captain Ozenna?' she said.

'Yes, ma'am.'

'Captain, how best can we use you?'

'I need to cross to Big Diomede. Cut off the snake's head.'

The snake goes all the way to the Kremlin, thought Stephanie. 'What can you achieve there?'

'I can tell you who is where and how to hit them.'

'Would it be better to stay and guide in the Marine units?'

'There are other Eskimos who can do that.'

Prusak shook his head. The civilian Eskimos in Wales had declared the ice unsafe. The Eskimo Scouts were way up north near Barrow on exercises.

'They're saying they can't,' said Stephanie.

'Can't or won't?'

'Explain, Captain.'

'Many will think this is a con, that you're going across to raid homes for narcotics, skins, and guns.'

'We can talk to them.'

'If you're willing to break rules, I know the best man to do this.'

'Go on.'

'He's in the Goose Creek Correctional Center. His name is Don Ondola. He's the father of Akna, the pregnant girl. Get him to Wales, and if there's a way across the ice he'll find it, better than me. Don's the best there is. The ice is thin in many places. He may miss some. Heavy with equipment, men will fall through. You may take casualties. But Don will get most across.'

'Ondola is serving life for murder and rape,' said Prusak quietly, reading from his tablet.

Swain made his decision in a second. 'Get Ondola down there,' he said. 'Send Ozenna across to the Russian base.'

'How long will it take you to get across to Big Diomede, Captain?' asked Stephanie.

'Six hours, depending how the ice is packed. With the Russians watching, could be longer.'

'And you will make it?'

'Yes, ma'am. I know this place. It's my sea. Once we neutralize the base, you can chopper in the men from Wales. If I don't make it, Don brings them across. This way gives you two options.'

Swain gave her a nod. 'OK, Captain. It's a go for Big Diomede.'

'If you use Don, tell him I told you to.'

'We will.'

'They'll be tracking the location of this phone,' said Ozenna. 'Once I'm across, I will use the Russian military radio. You'll need to get Tin City onto that.'

Swain stepped closer. 'This is President Swain, Captain. Good luck and take an American flag with you.'

'Copy that, sir. And thank you, sir. Please, keep that school out of it. My fiancée and eighty American citizens are there.'

The line cut.

'How long to get Ondola to Wales?' asked Swain.

'Two hours, sir,' said Prusak. 'But he's—'

'Do it, Matt, and the three of us will remember this as the moment we staked the future of the free world on a rapist and an off-duty soldier.'

FOURTEEN

Big Diomede, Chukotka, the Russian Far East

'Intercept on call to Krusenstern,' a technician told Vitruk. 'From Washington, DC to an American number, routed through a hotspot of one of ours in the 83rd Airborne. Signal encrypted both ways.'

Vitruk watched images of the two helicopters, one Russian, one American, now charred wreckage embedded on the sea ice, flames leaping, then dampened by the black oil seeping onto the white. His hope had been that he could take the American island without a shot being fired. He had also planned for the high chance of that not happening. He would now step up his reach to make sure America understood it should not mess with him. And he would deceive, too, by offering to cede his advantage here on the border. There didn't have to be blood. At least, not here. 'Break that encryption. Tell the Americans we'll allow them to pick up their injured. We need our own rescue teams out there now.'

On the visual feed from Little Diomede, troops were moving off the helipad, isolating the single Russian helicopter, which, with the outbreak of violence, would be a missile strike target. Soldiers melted into cover around the buildings.

'SU-35s ready to scramble, sir,' reported a technician. The SU-35 strike aircraft would match the American F-22s. They would also escalate.

'Not yet,' said Vitruk. 'Stand them by.'

He spoke to Yumatov in the school on Little Diomede. 'Hold the Eskimos at the school until we have a peace deal. There must be no loss of life.'

'One is missing, sir; Captain Raymond Ozenna of the Alaska Army National Guard.' Yumatov spoke slowly, but he was not hesitant. 'We are certain that he's the one who guided in the helicopter. He has killed two, possibly three, of my men.'

'Where is he now?'

'In the village. He can't have gone far.'

'Find him.'

RAKE FLIPPED OUT THE phone's battery and SIM card so it could no longer be traced. He moved silently around the back of the hut and up the hillside to the next, higher level of walkways where the old church was. He found cover inside a wooden meat cache built like a huge outdoor cupboard, between the wooden struts of the building. Inside was frozen whale, seal, and walrus meat. If, behind that, there was a cache of Don's weapons, he would have a chance of getting across to the Russian island in once piece.

The crossing would not be straightforward. Most of the ocean was frozen over, but there would be channels of open water, carrying chunks of ice on a fast-running northerly current. This was one of the most dangerous seas in the world. If he had been on the island these past few months he would know how it lay this winter. But he hadn't. And there was no one to ask. It was shallow, making the current faster and more powerful. Out there, wind chill would drop minus 20 Celsius to minus 40 with weather that turned at any moment. He would have to check the weapons carefully. The Russian ones he had were close-quarter weapons and would be serviced with cold-weather lubricants. But Rake needed a rifle, an accurate long-range weapon that could take out a man from a distance. Don Ondola was a Diomede man and he understood that although the target of his dreams would not be Russians but agents from the American government interfering with the way he lived.

Ondola's stolen weapons would have come from Iraq, which meant Rake might need to strip and dry them out to ensure no condensation would freeze and lock the mechanisms. He could do that quickly, but he needed to allow time to throw out any ammunition with casings damaged by the weather.

The Russian military gloves were cleverly designed. An outer cover could be removed leaving the trigger finger protected by a material thin enough to work inside the guard. That would prevent lethal cold-weather skin-on-metal contact. Rake had seen a man rip off half his face after resting against a metal rifle stock.

He was well hidden and had a clear view across to Big Diomede. The Russian base was out of sight on the north side of the island. He could see no way of getting to it unseen without going right around Little Diomede, or at least over the top, which would mean having to avoid the Russian observation position up there.

At the back, where the storeroom met the hillside granite,

Rake found carefully packed weapons. There were two pistols, four M-14 carbines lubricated for Arctic conditions, a dozen grenades, and a Remington 700 rifle with a white Gore-Tex sleeve. He even found a roll of kitchen plastic wrap which would keep the weapon moisture-free until he needed to use it.

A dog barked, but it was not Henry's mutt. Then came a crackle of radio communication and footsteps on the walkway. He heard voices in Russian looking for him. Strong flashlights swept around the small hillside homes, illuminating them as if it were daylight.

VITRUK LOOKED HARD INTO the face of the Eskimo soldier standing in front of him. He was no more than five feet four and thin like a wire doll, but strong. This was Sergeant Nikita Tuuq, aged thirty-four, from the village of Uelen in Chukotka. He stood impassive and unafraid, eyes squinted, nose skewed from being broken, his skin young but rough like leather.

'Do you know Captain Rake Ozenna?' Vitruk showed Tuuq a photograph.

Tuuq replied with a nod. Vitruk was familiar with this type of man and allowed the apparent lack of respect. Tuuq belonged to a special Arctic-warfare unit which had flown in from the Khabarovsk headquarters in case the Americans attacked Big Diomede. But that was not why Vitruk had summoned him. The Eskimo's file stated that he and Ozenna shared a US-Russian Arctic search and rescue training course two years earlier in Alaska. Tuuq appeared to be the only Russian soldier who had managed to match Ozenna and another American there, Sergeant

Don Ondola. In unarmed combat, Ondola was ahead. In long-distance tracking, Tuuq had edged in front. In tactical thinking and leadership, Ozenna had shone.

'How well do you know him?' asked Vitruk.

'He is my cousin. Our relatives are in our home village of Uelen.'

It was a good answer because it was half right. Tuuq was smart enough to guess that Vitruk would know this. Among Eskimos, with the fractured nuclear family, anyone could end up as a cousin, and that made them neither a friend nor an enemy. In Tuuq's case, Ozenna was more than just a cousin. After the cold war, when the border was relaxed, Ozenna's father, a drunk, travelled to Uelen to meet lost relatives. During the visit, he had slept with Tuuq's mother. The file said that Tuuq and Rake were almost certainly half-brothers, and Tuuq loathed Rake because of it.

Ozenna's father never returned to America. He vanished inside Russia. Not even the FSB or SVR knew what had happened to him. Some years later, as a child, Ozenna was taken back to Uelen in the hope that he could find his father. The file said Tuuq beat Ozenna up, but gave no details. The man who took Ozenna to Russia was his surrogate father, Henry Ahkvaluk, the Eskimo who had come across with the pregnant girl.

'If you were on Little Diomede, being hunted by us, what would you do?' said Vitruk.

'I would stay free.' Tuuq remained expressionless.

'How would you do that?'

Tuuq spent some moments studying the map on the wall. 'I would cross to Wales to guide the American troops across the ice. Or I would come over here to be their eyes for an attack on this base.'

'Which?' asked Vitruk impatiently.

Tuuq remained impassive, his eyes on the map. 'Here,' he said finally. 'This base.'

'Can you find Ozenna and stop him?'

'Yes. I can.'

Vitruk closed Tuuq's file and, briefly alone, he called an encrypted number at the Russian Embassy in Washington, DC As he had anticipated, the ripple effect of his tiny military incision in the far-away Bering Strait had prompted an early morning crisis meeting at the American Federal Reserve.

FIFTEEN

Eccles Building, Federal Reserve, Washington, DC

By the time Roy Carrol, Chairman of the Federal Reserve, stepped into the high-ceilinged chandeliered boardroom of his head-office building on Constitution Avenue, the Asian markets had fallen and then picked up, unsure how to react to Russian occupation of American territory. News channels broadcast the Duma's emergency session, defining the story as a global crisis. On-screen experts earned their large retainers by predicting the worst.

As Fed Chairman, Carrol's task was to let politicians do their jobs while ensuring no cracks opened in the financial institutions, and not just in the United States. The dollar remained the go-to global crisis currency. If the Russian stand-off threatened stability, demand would build up. Carrol had to see that it was met smoothly. No one person, even one government, could make, break, repair, or damage the global economy. Even so, a word from the Chairman of the Federal Reserve could shake markets. If he spoke, the words had to be right.

'Is this meeting really necessary, Roy, so damn early?' said his ex-wife, Lucy Faulks, as he walked to his place by the tall mantelpiece end of the large oval table.

'And a very good morning to you too, Lucy,' said Carrol, leaning over to adjust the small American flag that hung from a gold-plated stand on the table. Just over twelve hours earlier, he had been examining it with his Russian counterpart, Karl Opokin, while showing him and his entourage around the building.

Faulks was there because she chaired the Federal Reserve Bank in New York, one of twelve such banks in the country and by far the most powerful. Their marriage, of two fiery ambitious economists, had never been smooth. Carrol's appointment over her to the top job broke it. Or at least it did for her. Carrol had never worked that one out.

'It looks to me like some Lagutov grandstanding,' she said. 'If someone leaks that you called a crisis meeting it will only make things worse.'

'We'll have a quorum, so by all means leave, if you need to go shopping.' Carrol pulled out his chair, unsure why he couldn't stop himself using words that were guaranteed to rile the mother of his children. He brushed the black leather seat with the back of his hand. 'But if you'd listened to Bob Holland last night you would be forgiven for thinking we were all standing on the edge of history.'

'Hence we meet?' She eyed him curiously. He was sure he detected the twitch of a smile. She wore a dark pinstripe trouser suit, and had her blonde hair up as if to remind him that added to her formidable will and intelligence she was still stunningly attractive, but, as he had discovered too late in life, impossible to live with. Same old story.

'You happened to be in town. You didn't get my job, but you

got the Fed in New York and you chair the Global Financial System Committee. I could use your input.' He smiled affectionately. 'And besides, I wanted to see you.'

Before Faulks could answer, four other board members came in, led by the stooped, bespectacled Lewis Ash, whose brief was to keep a watch on financial stability. 'Before you ask, Roy, we've reached out to the big six. HSBC, Citi, and J. P. Morgan have already got back to us and insist they would be solid through a world war. We're talking now to Europe, Canada, Moscow, and Beijing.'

'What's Moscow saying?' asked Faulks.

'Karl's in Washington,' said Carrol, mentioning the British Embassy dinner. 'I dropped him at the embassy last night. He didn't seem to have a clue what Lagutov's up to.'

'Based on Ukraine 2014, if it's not resolved in twenty-four hours, we can anticipate five hundred billion dollars in capital flight,' said Ash.

Carrol sat down, thinking about how any military operation with this level of international impact would need parallel financial planning, which pointed to an outside financial guarantor. 'Lagutov would have factored in capital flight and debt servicing,' he said. 'So who's underwriting this?'

A momentary silence fell among them. Lucy Faulks immediately tapped a message into her phone while she took a chair next to Carrol. Most of the huge table was left empty. Carrol's personal assistant came in to take notes. She sat on one of the upright chairs at the far end of the room. The meeting was being recorded.

'This may end up being nothing,' began Carrol. 'When Russia

went into Georgia back in 2008, the economic reaction was muted. That was pretty much repeated in Ukraine in 2014. On the other hand, this time, because America is directly involved, today may turn out to be the longest day of our careers.'

'God forbid,' said Ash a veteran of thirty-six-hour days during the 2007 financial crisis.

'We have two known unknowns,' continued Carrol. 'What is Russia doing and what does it want to achieve? There is nothing new about securing power at home by testing limits abroad. What is new is the decision to pick a fight directly with us.' He stopped on a signal from Faulks.

'Sorry, Roy,' she said. 'There have been large movements of money through Shanghai, Hong Kong, Istanbul, and London, all with a connection to Russia.'

Carrol looked pensive. If true, it meant Moscow was shoring up its capital. And if Karl Opokin was really being kept out of the loop, it pointed to a sophisticated plan. 'We must be certain we can withstand anything that this day throws at us,' he said. 'The second unknown is the inauguration. The President has very few hours left in office. He will try to defuse the situation, but as soon as President-elect Holland steps in it will become more fluid and possibly more confrontational. In the White House last night, Holland wanted us to storm the island of Little Diomede, even if it involved direct combat with Russian troops. That would put pressure on the dollar and the markets. The President has asked Holland to come up with—'

Those were Carrol's last words. A bomb exploded under the table. It splintered the thick wood as if it were paper. It blew out all three of the huge windows, tearing down and setting fire to the draped curtains. It shattered the mantelpiece, ripping a hole in the wall, hurling out plaster and propelling marble fragments around the room like shrapnel. The two chandeliers were torn from the ceiling and with dust and debris fell ablaze into the rising inferno.

No one in the room survived.

SIXTEEN

The White House, Washington, DC

Eyes welling, President Christopher Swain held Stephanie in an embrace. She allowed it for a second – she needed human warmth too – but couldn't stop her concentration returning to the news screens. The cameras focused on the charred rims of three board-room windows, gaping holes, burnt shreds of curtain, and blackened patches along the white walls.

Inside the building two friends had been murdered, just like that. 'Vaporized' was the word the newscasters were using. She had known Roy Carrol and Lucy Faulks for a long, long time. Lucy had been funny and supportive during Stephanie's divorce. She and Carrol were separated by then, but Stephanie could tell she respected him, probably still loved him.

'What's going on, Steph?' Swain whispered.

'I don't know.'

'Russia walks into our territory, and half the board of the Federal Reserve is wiped out in a terrorist attack.' Swain stared stone-faced out of the Oval Office window. 'I'm heading down to the Situation Room. Are you going to your embassy?'

'I'll be wherever you want me, Mr President.' Stephanie hoped formality would prevail over emotion.

'Go to your embassy. Counsel your Prime Minister. I need a strong and unified Europe in the coming hours, its support, its will, its military.'

Prusak stepped into the room. 'They're ready for you downstairs, sir. The President-elect says he needs to be with you. Karl Opokin called from the Russian Embassy with condolences and outright condemnation.'

'The Russian Ambassador?'

'Not yet, sir.'

'Then tell Opokin and all of them to go fuck themselves.'

Prusak flinched. Swain rarely used bad language or a raised voice. 'I have the contacts here of the families, sir,' he said.

'I need the families of the helicopter crew, too,' said Swain.

'They are included.'

'Put Holland off for half an hour, but we must keep him onside. I'm announcing Tom as the temporary chair of the Fed,' said Swain referring to the Treasury Secretary, Thomas Grant. 'What are the markets doing?'

'FTSE and DAX down more than four percent,' said Prusak. 'We're ninety minutes from opening.'

'I suspect there'll be a brief violent dip, then recovery,' said Stephanie.

'Exactly. So how does killing the board of the Fed achieve anything?'

'The best way to undermine capitalist democracy is to strike at the heart of its financial system,' said Stephanie.

'But, a brief dip. Tom moves seamlessly in. No institution crumbles. People keep going to work. Six dead—'

'Eight, sir,' said Prusak. 'Roy's PA was in the room and a staff member was outside the door.'

'Eight is not three thousand and the Twin Towers. I can't believe Lagutov would have authorized this.'

'Agreed,' said Prusak.

'Me, too,' said Stephanie. 'I get the Diomede operation. Lagutov calculates we're not going to go to war over a place that no one's heard of. It is so peripheral, so remote, so unimportant, that it's barely a scratch on the complicated relationship between two nuclear powers.'

'Which reflects those preliminary opinion polls,' said Swain.

'So, what happens?' continued Stephanie. 'A few hours of macho insults, and an announcement to discuss the border dispute. That, Mr President, you could have wrapped up before leaving office. You set up a committee that sits for twenty years and decides nothing. Lagutov's victory is that Russian military muscle achieved what diplomacy didn't and that opens the door for negotiations on a swathe of other things. That would have been possible even with helicopters shot down on both sides. But now, with this attack on the Fed, you can't give them anything. Whoever did this wants a big, big fight.'

Prusak looked up from his tablet. 'The New York Fed says Lucy Faulks was in touch seconds before she died. She wanted to know specifically any movements of money between Russia and China.'

'Were there?' asked Swain.

'Yes. Large renminbi-denominated transfers through Hong

Kong and Shanghai. And the FBI's confirmed that Roy Carrol gave Opokin a tour of the Eccles Building before coming to the White House. Opokin brought six bodyguards from the Russian Federal Security Service with him. They spent ten minutes in the boardroom. Four are clean. Two may not have been fully vetted.'

'In any international incident of the caliber of the Diomede occupation, the Fed chair will call a crisis meeting,' said Swain. 'The Diomede incursion was just after seven last night. Roy called the meeting for seven this morning in time for the nine-thirty opening of the markets here.'

'More in from the FBI,' said Prusak, reading from his tablet. 'Initial forensic investigation points to a Russian military issue plastic explosive known as PVV-5A.'

'That doesn't mean Russia's responsible,' said Stephanie.

'Correct. It's like the AK-47, everyone uses it.'

'Was it on a timer?' said Stephanie.

'They don't think so. They're investigating triggers by cell-phone within a mile radius.'

'We work on the presumption that the Diomedes and the Fed are linked.' Swain lifted his jacket off the back of his chair.

'We'll get you a car,' Prusak said to Stephanie.

'No,' said Stephanie. 'I think it's better if I can get the Prime Minister back here to the White House.'

Swain began leading them towards the door, but stopped mid-stride. 'Are we all thinking the same thing?'

The three close friends looked at each other, working out why Russia was carrying out a coordinated assault against America. Or were their imaginations running away with them?

SEVENTEEN

Little Diomede, Alaska, USA

Carrie judged the gaunt, skeletal man vomiting bile on the floor of the gymnasium to be about forty. He had the sunken eyes of an addict. His name was Tommy Tulamuk, and she suspected a mix of alcohol and a synthetic marijuana drug, maybe even heroin. He was just back from Teller, a settlement on the Alaskan mainland. He shivered as palpitations passed through him. He had a fever and stared at Carrie confused. Cold turkey was a horrible state for any human being. She would ask the Russians for methadone, or if not that, morphine.

She turned him over, bending his legs, and laid a plastic sheet under his mouth. 'Stay here. You're with friends,' she said, looking around for the English-speaking Colonel Yumatov. 'Call me Ruslan,' he had said after Rake left, oozing charm, but with one of those expressions that could switch between kindness and anger in moments.

Soon, the medical checks would be finished and then this would be exposed as the hostage situation that it really was. The cover of health care would become thinner and thinner minute by minute. The gymnasium was a cocoon. The only windows were too high to see out of. Twice she had heard jet fighters. There hadn't been a helicopter for almost an hour. Restlessness was creeping through. But, more than that, over the past few minutes a fresh tension had taken hold among the soldiers and medics.

In the sand wars, as her colleagues called the Middle East conflicts, she had learned how to read soldiers' faces. Something bad had happened. A soldier opened the double doors at the end of the gymnasium. Yumatov walked in, talking on the phone. He ended the call and beckoned Carrie to come over.

'We need morphine over there,' she said, pointing to the man curled up on the floor. 'He's on narcotic withdrawal.'

Yumatov told a paramedic to handle it and looked at Carrie, his expression angry at first, then it became quizzical and confused. 'What is it, Colonel?' she asked amicably, smoothing down her smock, pushing hard on the material as she realized it must be something to do with Rake. Had he tried to escape as she had asked? Was he captured or dead?

'Is it Rake?' she stammered as the thoughts crowded in on her, realizing, too late, that she was using his nickname.

She could tell because of the softening of Yumatov's expression. 'How well do you know him?' he asked.

'He's a colleague.'

'Are you lovers?'

'Just tell me if he's OK.'

A coldness entered his gaze. 'Yes and no.' He turned curtly and walked down the two flights of steps towards the main entrance. Two soldiers took her arms and steered her to follow. She began shaking them off, but their hold was locked. At the school entrance, a dozen troops checked weapons and spoke on radios, tough men about to go out. Off the entrance was the small dining room with three gray steel trestle tables and benches where they had waited with Akna. Sitting on a bench at the middle table was a seven- or eight-year-old boy in a green jacket smeared with dirt from the ice. His eyes were fixed on a school poster about walruses and marine life. He kept still, arms folded, as if in a trance. He had a bruise on his right cheek and a fresh cut on the knuckles of his left hand.

'Do you know him?' asked Yumatov.

'I don't. No.' Carrie started to move forward to treat him. Soldiers pulled her back. The boy's eyes were like misted glass, hiding God knows what behind.

'He's traumatized because of what he saw,' said Yumatov. 'His name is Timothy. Everyone calls him Timo. We think he's the brother of the pregnant girl, Akna.'

Carrie impatiently ripped her arms out of the soldiers' grip. On a signal from Yumatov, they allowed her. 'Why don't you tell me what's happened, Colonel?' she demanded.

'Why don't you tell me about Captain Ozenna?'

Carrie bristled. 'When foreign soldiers mix with civilians you get trouble. You're smart enough to know that.'

'There's something you need to see.' Yumatov turned away towards a stainless-steel counter that separated the dining room from the kitchen, where there was a gas stove and in a corridor beyond that freezers and cupboards. A green canvas tarpaulin was spread over the large workbench. Yumatov peeled it back to show the face of a dead soldier. He looked so young. There was blood in his white blond hair and bruising around his eyes.

The nose had been badly fractured and the head, although adjusted, was slightly skewed to one side. It looked like a broken neck.

'His name was Private Boris Syanko, aged eighteen, from a small place called Kiya up on the White Sea. We'll make him look better before we send the body back to the family.' A soldier handed Yumatov a small red leather pouch. He pulled out photographs of children, snow, dogs, and finally a portrait of the whole big family, Syanko in the middle. He looked like the youngest. 'He was a kid,' Yumatov went on. 'A conscript. Never wanted to be a soldier. But he turned into one of our most promising. That's how it often works. I blame myself. I should never have put him with a monster like Ozenna.'

Carrie took the photograph, looked at it quickly. How could Rake have been responsible for such a brutal murder? A wave of emptiness washed through her. She knew his background as a soldier, knew he could kill. But it was hard to accept that he was behind the death of this boy. She handed the picture back.

Yumatov's voice became steel. 'Your fiancé murdered this young man in cold blood. See the nose. He used a technique of pushing the heel of the hand up against the nose so that splinters from the cartilage embed in the brain. It is cruel and unnecessary. He did that, broke his neck, and threw him down the trash chute.'

'There was another soldier. There were two of them.' Carrie knew she sounded desperate, the innocent clinging on to a belief that the bad cannot be true.

'Yes. Ozenna stabbed him to death. He shot dead another of my men on guard duty outside.' He put his hand on Timo's shoulder. 'We think he did that in front of this little boy, which is why he is so quiet.'

Timo didn't move. He didn't utter a word. He kept his gaze fixed, a feral look, like a waiting wolf.

'The boy's distressed,' said Yumatov. 'No child should witness what he did. Come. I'll show you myself.' He led her through the entrance hall to a small office room at the foot of a flight of stairs. A soldier stepped next to her, carrying her cold-weather gear.

'And take a look at this, Dr Walker,' said Yumatov. On a wall television, an American news channel showed a blackened building, its windows blown out, police and flashing ambulance lights outside. 'The chairman of your Central Bank has been assassinated in a terrorist bombing in Washington, DC. Seven others are dead. They're blaming Russia, saying the chairman of our own Central Bank was visiting the building just hours before.'

Carrie had seen many bomb-blasted buildings and it took a moment to grasp that she was looking at the center of Washington, DC. She took it in, but managed to show no reaction of horror to Yumatov. 'Looks like this is getting bigger than both of us, Colonel,' she said, pulling out the office chair. She sat down to lace up her boots.

Yumatov took a stool next to her. 'I don't know what this killer Rake told you about who he is. But now you've seen his work.'

Carrie finished lacing her boots and put on her jacket. Yumatov muted the television sound, zipped up his jacket, and fastened its belt. He tried again to break Carrie's resolve. 'You are right. You and I are very small in all this. Something big is happening and we are part of it and we can't run away. We must help each other.'

Carrie didn't waver. First, she'd faced horror, now his smarmy manner was beginning to piss her off. 'If you want us to help, Colonel, why don't you and your soldiers leave this island?'

'You're smarter than that. Another colonel would take my place and I would be put out to beg on the streets, or shot.' He pulled his hood over his head and the protective mask over his face. She did the same. 'Be careful out there. The weather has turned for the worse.' He glanced back at his men. 'Bring the boy.'

The pressure and energy of the wind hit as soon as she stepped outside. Each gust threatened her balance. Yumatov moved to take her arm to steady her. She shook him off. He led them up the walkway. The mist was erratic. One moment the village was moonlit. The next, she could barely see in front of her.

A soldier's flashlight lit up a green hut with a sign on the wall that read Alaska Army National Guard. They went inside. Immediately, there was quiet from the weather. Timo came in with a short wiry man in a different type of uniform. The Russian soldiers were in military green. This man was in white and when he took off his mask she saw he was an Eskimo. He spoke gently to Timo. Yumatov snapped on a flashlight which showed two bodies lying uncovered, as if they had just been dragged in.

'The one on the left is Sergeant Matvey Golov,' he said. 'Your fiancé murdered him by stabbing him in the neck. Then he stabbed him again through the eye.' He turned the corpse's head to show congealed blood around the right eye. 'The other one is Corporal Adam Razin, shot in the neck.'

He shone the beam straight at Carrie, making her squint. 'Ozenna used your phone, Carrie. We traced it to you.' Yumatov recited the Brooklyn number with the 718 prefix. 'He sent a message to a number that we have traced to a Mrs Stephanie Lucas, British Ambassador to the United States. Before that, she was ambassador to Moscow.'

The oppression of a surveillance state closed in on Carrie. Russian security would have tracked her visits to Moscow. She had talked on medical panels there. They might even have her night on the town with Stephanie. There was no point in not telling Yumatov. 'I gave the phone to Captain Ozenna.'

Yumatov dropped the flashlight beam, then brought it straight back again into her eyes. 'You need to help me bring your lover in, to stop things getting worse.'

'Then you go find him,' Carrie said calmly, keeping her rage in check.

Yumatov's tone steeled with anger. 'He committed murder in front of a seven-year-old boy. You cannot love this man. For God's sake, Dr Walker, help me before he kills more people.'

'Don't sound so lame, Colonel. Rake's a soldier and that's what soldiers do: kill people.'

Real fury flickered across Yumatov's face. Carrie's refusal would be putting his job and the comfortable lives of his wife and young children at risk. Soldiers tried to take her arms, but Carrie ripped herself free and quickly put on her mask and hood before she was led outside into a curtain of cold. It was now so clear she could see the hillside and flashing red lamps on top. A soldier handed Yumatov a microphone. He tapped it. A clicking sound came from public address speakers placed around the village.

'Captain Raymond Ozenna, Rake, this is Colonel Ruslan Yumatov.' His voice was crisp and firm. 'You need to give yourself in. You will be treated fairly, according to law.'

The wind had gone. They could hear the hum of the generator and a Russian helicopter in the distance. Yumatov let the microphone dangle, then lifted it again and said, 'I understand you won't listen to me, Rake. But Carrie is here, and she will speak to you.'

He held out the microphone to her. Carrie didn't move.

EIGHTEEN

Little Diomede, Alaska, USA

Through the green night vision of a telescopic sight, Rake watched Carrie face Yumatov down. Clouds of breath seeped through her mask. She was alive and acting her familiar stubborn self. Even though that made her less safe, a sense of relief flooded through Rake. Yumatov was learning fast. Rake heard Yumatov making his appeal and Carrie refusing to take the microphone. He feared for what Yumatov might have on her. Did he know that Carrie was half-Russian, that her parents were from the glory days of the Soviet era? How would he use that? Or, better still, how would she?

Rake glimpsed Timo, stepping into the light, then moving back again. The boy was still in his green fur jacket, but what caught Rake's attention was that the Russian soldier with him was wearing not regular uniform, but the white Arctic thermal suit of the American Eskimo scouts with the badges torn off. From the easy manner with which he handled Timo, Rake thought this might be Nikita Tuuq. The last time they met, Tuuq was attached to Russian special forces of the Arctic Joint Strategic Command. The first time they met was when Rake was a child.

He zoomed in on the figure, who kept moving between light and shadow as if he knew how not to be identified. Which convinced Rake that it was Tuuq. If so, was it coincidence? Did Tuuq happen to be the guy on shift, or did the Russians know all about Tuuq and Rake? Either way, Tuuq was being deployed to bring Rake in, which gave Tuuq a just cause to complete unfinished business. There was no way he would let Rake get away this time. If they met, only one of them would walk off alive. Rake lowered the night-vision sight to watch with the naked eyes and assess. Would Carrie and the others be safer if he surrendered now or if he kept going? The same question echoed back to him, but this time with Tuuq center frame. As soon as he surrendered, he would be living a death sentence and Carrie and the hostages would be no safer. If he kept going, the one thing Rake knew was that in head-to-head combat Tuuq would beat him.

As a child Tuuq was sullen, small for his age and wafer-thin. But on the ice, he had the strength of a giant, and the way he handled a sled and dogs had left Rake in awe. Henry had brought Rake and Ondola to the Russian settlement of Uelen for a reunion with the families from the Russian side of the Diomedes, where the Soviets had forcibly resettled them during the cold war. It was the harshest winter, and they had travelled by jeep, dog sled, even on horseback to get there. Henry had hoped to find Rake's father, reunite him with his ten-year-old son, and persuade him to come back.

Tuuq, two years older, had challenged Rake to a race, each with a sled and one dog. The Uelen settlement stood on a long and narrow strip of land with the sea on one side and a lagoon on the other. Tuuq said they would race from two miles out with Ondola staying back on the finishing line as judge. He led Rake through rugged and cracked ice, a more weather-worn landscape than anything he had seen around the Diomedes. There were streaks of blackness like curving rivers and ridges that blocked the path and stood like dominoes. Thick fog patches moved faster than dogs and suddenly blurred everything then vanished, leaving light and clarity. Wind screamed all the time.

Rake's dog was a lean restless black and white husky. His name was Buka, meaning bad temper. Rake was good at calming dogs and on the way out to the start line he had soothed Buka, gently familiarizing him with his command. Before they started, Tuuq walked over, knelt on the snow next to Rake's sled, tilted back his head and cried out with a long undulating howl that sounded exactly like a dog in pain. It chilled Rake and made the huskies skittish.

Back on his own sled, Tuuq let off a whistle to which Buka reacted by sprinting forward. Rake could not control him. The husky veered through broken ice, taking the sled within inches of jagged ice pillars. Terrified, Rake pulled back on the straps, but Buka ran faster and more erratically until without warning his forelegs buckled under him. The dog fell in a violent somersault. The sled smashed into his back. As Rake was hurled forward he heard the crunch of Buka's breaking bones. He lay, listening to the barking howl of Buka's pain.

Tuuq arrived laughing. He drew a knife, cut Buka's throat, and held the bloodied blade inches from Rake's face. 'Go home, you yellow Yankee coward,' he sneered. 'Or I'll make you howl to the moon like a dog.'

Tuuq sledded off towards the settlement. Hours later, Ondola found Rake, who was close to hypothermia with a broken leg. Much longer, and Rake would have died. Tuuq had refused to show Ondola where he was. The next day, Henry took them away. He had failed to find Rake's father. No one had seen him for months. A week later, safely back on Little Diomede and with Rake's leg healing, Henry apologized for taking him there and told him the whole story about his father sleeping with Tuuq's mother, which probably made them half-brothers. If Tuuq had the chance, Henry warned, he would try to kill him again.

A couple of years back, Rake and Ondola had met Tuuq again on a joint US-Russian military exercise. Tuuq was uncommunicative, but he stayed professional and he competed hard. At the end of the week, like a footballer, Tuuq gave Rake his army hat. Rake gave him his white snow gear, which Tuuq was now wearing.

Rake watched as Timo slipped out of sight. Tuuq kept moving, feather-like, gliding, at home with the ice as if he knew Rake was there. Yes, Tuuq had been sent here to get him, brother against brother, Eskimo against Eskimo. For the kill. Because this was Tuuq.

He studied Carrie again and guessed she had made up her mind and wouldn't do what Yumatov asked. An air of foreboding hung between them. There was something fearless about Carrie when she was in a corner. It was up to the Russians to decide how to handle her.

Yumatov handed the microphone back to a soldier. Tuuq stepped into view, stationary and exposed. Timo stood behind him. Yumatov, much taller, leant down to hear what Tuuq was saying. Then he issued an order. Two soldiers took Carrie's arms and led her back towards the school.

NINETEEN

The White House, Washington, DC

Stephanie met Kevin Slater's car as he arrived back at the White House and took him straight to the East Garden. They walked side by side, trailed by the Secret Service agents and officers from Britain's Specialist Protection Command. Light snow fell.

'I've got you a chair in the Situation Room,' she said. 'There'll be a camera there.'

Slater made clear his irritation. 'You brought me back here for a photo-op?'

'A defining image, sir. Britain at the heart—'

'If I'm seen in that room, it means I sign off on whatever Swain or Holland decide.'

'It means you'll be better informed on what to decide.'

'Don't blinker me, Stephanie,' said Slater. 'I will not be conned into siding with the Americans.'

Stephanie stopped under the trees on the frost-covered lawn. She had anticipated a showdown, which was why she had brought them out here. 'When history's written, your party, your beliefs, your manifesto will be forgotten. You will be remembered for what you do right now as events unfold today. You are now a world leader, not an activist running the parliamentary opposition.'

Slater sounded not just unconvinced, but also insulted. 'If I involve myself at all it will be to call Lagutov and not to sit like a puppet with the President of the United States. People remember Blair.'

Stephanie ratcheted up her tone. 'And what exactly will you say to Lagutov? Please get off that island?'

Slater was not retreating. 'I'll explore a settlement. It's what I do well.'

'This isn't a car factory in the Midlands. It's not a pay negotiation. Nor is it about a single island. It's about Russia challenging America. If you explore a settlement you risk putting your name to a stumbling, failing peace initiative.'

Visibly taken aback by Stephanie's bluntness, Slater said, 'I will not blindly follow America into another of its pointless wars.'

'Then show leadership in Europe.'

'Coming from you, that's rich, as you were so keen for us to leave.'

'I'm talking about Europe, sir, not the European Union.'

Slater looked at her sharply. He had been an energetic advocate for Britain's role in Europe. Before he could respond, Stephanie continued, 'Lagutov is relying on two elements, the vulnerability of the presidential transition and a divided Europe. You have the capacity to prove them wrong on Europe.'

'How, when they barely listen to a word we have to say any more?' He stared at her angrily, brushing melting snow off his face.

Stephanie deliberately switched to his first name. 'Make them listen, Kevin. You are the best orator I have ever heard, and you're new. You might not like America, but it represents who we are. Russia does not. America's values, based on our values, have allowed you, a watchmaker's son from Yorkshire, to become the Prime Minister of Great Britain. If we don't help them at a time like this, why should they continue to defend us? Don't mess with this moment, sir. Do you really want to cede all we have fought for over the centuries to Russia's Eurasian Economic Union and, for that matter, China's Greater East Asia Prosperity Sphere?'

'What's China got to do with it?' His voice level dropped with genuine curiosity.

'Apparently, Chinese money is being used to fund the Russian operation.'

'Do we know that?'

Stephanie shared his alarm. Britain was thick with Chinese deals, power stations, technology, infrastructure. 'It's the only country rich enough. At present, we don't know if it's state-sponsored. But that's for later. Right now, I am advising that you have your picture taken in the Situation Room with President Swain. That's it, sir. Show that you're a leader and whose side you're on. Then we hit the phones on Europe.'

'You're persuasive, Stephanie. I concede that.'

'Is that a "yes"?'

'It's an "I'll think about it".'

Matt Prusak stepped onto the White House terrace at the other end of the garden, and signaled to Stephanie.

'It has to be now.' She touched Slater's elbow to start them heading back.

Slater walked with her. 'What are the numbers? Germany and France aside, we would have Poland, Estonia, Lithuania, Latvia, Bulgaria, Romania, Croatia, Slovenia, Czech Republic, Slovakia, Kosovo, Serbia—'

'Maybe not Serbia,' said Stephanie. 'And we might have a problem with Hungary and Poland.'

'Italy, Portugal, Spain, Greece . . .'

'Greece will need a bribe.'

'When hasn't it?'

As they approached, Holland joined Prusak on the terrace, checking his watch.

'What's he doing here?' asked Slater.

Stephanie didn't know, but it would make sense to have Holland in the photo-op with the President of the United States and the leader of its closest ally. She tried to catch Prusak's eye, but Holland, his forefinger raised, was reprimanding the White House Chief of Staff. Prusak listened calmly. Slater and Stephanie climbed the short flight of steps to the terrace. Holland fell silent.

'Prime Minister, thank you for your time,' said Prusak.

'Is there a problem?' asked Slater.

'No, sir. Could you and the President-elect follow the Secret Service agents to the Situation Room, where the President will brief you?'

Slater glanced at Stephanie who shrugged, trying to convince him that she hadn't known and wasn't out to deceive her Prime Minister. Shit happens. Ride with it. Holland and Slater left.

'Holland blew a fuse because Slater's in on the briefing,' said Prusak when they had gone. 'But we have another problem. The

NSA is picking up all traffic coming out of Moscow. Holland made a call to the Kremlin from Blair House.'

Stephanie raised her eyebrows in surprise. 'Holland called Lagutov? To say what?'

'To warn him, just like he said. We don't know Lagutov's response because we haven't broken their code, but judging from the rise in Holland's tone, it wasn't a friendly exchange. He said Russia needed to realize that the United States would be the predominant global power for decades to come. If Lagutov didn't understand that now, he would two days from now, and if Lagutov wanted a fight he'd picked the wrong enemy.'

Trump had broken many of the protocols of transition.

'Can you rein him in, confront him?'

'He doesn't know we know.'

'What's the President doing?'

'He's with Holland in the Situation Room right now, and if you want me to say more I will have to hold you to the letter of your security clearance. You don't even tell Slater.'

Stephanie had a duty to tell her Prime Minister but a wider duty to know as much as possible about what was going on. 'Fine,' she said without hesitation.

'The President has done what any of us would have done. Holland's call might prompt Lagutov to pre-empt, so he's—'

'Gone to a higher level of readiness?'

His voice dropped to almost a whisper. 'An hour ago we were at DEFCON 4. Not any more.'

DEFCON categorized levels of military readiness against attack and could vary from unit to unit. In this case, if she were Swain, she would raise the DEFCON level on the United States

Strategic Command (USSTRATCOM) and the units dealing with the Arctic and Europe. The difference between the two highest levels was timing. At DEFCON 2 nuclear weapons would be ready to engage within six hours. DEFCON 1 was the equivalent of putting a round in the chamber and cocking the hammer.

'Two?' she asked.

'One,' said Prusak. 'He had no choice.'

If two countries have nuclear weapons, the weaker one will fire first. If it doesn't, it will lose. And Russia was weaker than America. Stephanie said, 'We always have choices, Matt. The President made the right one.'

TWENTY

The White House, Washington, DC

Prusak led Stephanie through the main busy area of the Situation Room to a compact conference suite on the left. Swain, Slater, and Holland sat around a small table, their body language stiff. Holland played with his cufflinks. Swain made notes on a pad. Slater looked at Stephanie, his eyes accusing.

'There's no protocol here,' said Prusak to Stephanie. 'Take any seat.' Swain was at the head of a table with only three chairs on each side. Stephanie sat with Slater, Prusak beside Holland.

'The attack on the Fed, the murder of Roy, Lucy, and the others, is brutal,' said Swain. 'But in strategic terms, the impact is minimal. The occupation of Little Diomede is symbolic—'

'Symbolic? With eighty hostages?' interrupted Holland. 'And a terror strike in the heart of the American capital?'

'If you want European support, I suggest you get your ducks in a row,' intervened Slater. 'You cannot take for granted that European leaders who are America's allies now will transfer their allegiance to your presidency.'

'Hold a moment.' Prusak turned up one of the television screens showing Russia Today. The scene was the school gymnasium, laughter between villagers and soldiers, displays of medical equipment, school books and games for the children. The newscast moved to split-screen with the anchor on one side and, on the other, a still photograph of an old document in Cyrillic script described as the original treaty of the 1867 Alaska Purchase.

'The nerve of it!' she exclaimed, then she stood up to point to a line of words on the document. 'They've changed this sentence and are claiming that the original agreement states that the border runs twelve miles east of Little Diomede, putting it right up against the US coastline.' She paused, glancing through the document. 'The rest of the treaty, all seven articles, seems exactly the same as what we have on record.'

The screen returned to the newscaster. Stephanie listened, then said, 'She's saying the seven point two million America paid for Alaska is the equivalent of one hundred and fourteen million today. That would barely buy an apartment block in New York. It was two cents an acre, which would make the land worth thirty cents an acre today. So, it was theft.'

'We paid three cents an acre to buy Louisiana off the French in 1803 and they're not complaining,' said Swain. 'Have we located the treaty yet?'

'They're saying this is it,' said Stephanie. 'The issue of the lost treaty arose when I was in Moscow. Neither you nor they could find the original document.'

'We need to move on,' said Swain. Prusak muted the TV screens. Stephanie sat down.

'Prime Minister, how far will Britain and the rest of Europe support us?' asked Swain. 'If we can come up with a united policy, we can see this problem off. If Europe divides, we're in trouble.'

'It depends what you plan,' said Slater.

'If you're not with us, we'll do whatever it is without you,' said Holland.

'Hold off on the swagger,' said Swain.

'Europe is geographically closer to Russia, so it's more complicated,' said Stephanie. 'We burn Russian gas to keep warm, more than thirty percent in Europe and seven percent in the UK.'

'Mr President,' said Prusak. 'The Defense Secretary asks if he can update us for a couple of minutes.'

'Can it wait?' said Swain.

'He says not.'

A Secret Service agent opened the door and Michael Pacolli walked in. Prusak opened a darkened screen to a map of Europe.

'The Russian navy has been put on a high state of readiness, sir,' Pacolli said, as two circles appeared on the screen. 'It's the equivalent of our DEFCON 2. There is increased activity in Kaliningrad, the Russian military enclave between Poland and Lithuania, and down here in Crimea.' He pointed to the areas on the map. 'Two Novorossiysk submarines left Kaliningrad on January 10th and two more went out from the Black Sea Fleet in Sevastopol the next day. Within the past hour, they have brought three stealth T-50 fighter aircraft into Kaliningrad and four to the Baherove airbase in Crimea.'

'Where are the submarines now?' asked Holland.

'These are diesel-electric vessels. With engines off, running on batteries they are near impossible to track. The Novorossiysk is the quietest.'

'Answer my question, Mr Secretary. Where are they now?'

'We don't know, sir.'

'You didn't track them?'

'We don't have those resources.'

'And damn you, Christopher Swain, for denying us the money to protect America.' Holland pressed the palm of his right hand hard into the table.

Part of Holland reminded Stephanie of Harry, her ex-husband, the use of anger to get what he wanted. Harry imagined himself enveloped in hostility from everyone around him, including his wife, and dealt with it by lashing out. She worked out, far too late, that his temper was a cover for fear. Outside of his general unhappiness, Harry posed no threat. As President-elect, Holland did. His aggression might be pre-inauguration nerves, which were fixable. Or, like Harry, it might be embedded within his mental template, in which case America was in trouble.

Holland drummed his fingers loudly as if waiting for an order to be obeyed. Pacolli stood by the door, ramrod-straight. Prusak's eyes shifted from his tablet to the screen. Slater drew columns on the notepad in front of him. Then, after three minutes of silence, the President sat back, arms folded and said, 'Mike, give me strike options on both Kaliningrad and Crimea.' Pacolli looked relieved to have clear instructions.

Swain continued, 'We screw down Russian companies operating here. Use IRS, RICO, FBI, with the whole toolkit – bank accounts, parking tickets, visas.'

He turned to Holland. 'Bob, Prime Minister Slater advised you to get your ducks in a row. So, I'll tell you how they line up. In Latin America, we will have allies in ten of the twenty governments. Africa, I wouldn't count on more than five and none of the big hitters – South Africa, Nigeria, Kenya. India will stay neutral or side with Russia. Pakistan is with China and China is likely to side with Russia. Southeast Asia will be split. South Korea and Japan are with us. In the Middle East, we may have Saudi Arabia, Bahrain, Qatar, and the Sunni states. But those are fragile monarchies that could flip the other way at any time. Syria and Iraq will be with Iran and Russia. We have Israel, of course.'

'And if things go from diplomatic to hot?' asked Stephanie.

'Fewer allies, far fewer, and a lot will depend on China. Many are in Beijing's pocket, which is why I would strongly advise against the President-elect thinking along the lines of a "for or against us" choice.'

'I'll make that decision with my team,' said Holland.

Swain ignored him. 'Phones, corridors, embassies, trade, education, aid, threats, muscle – use them all.' He turned to Slater. 'Prime Minister, can you deliver Europe?'

'If there's no more combat, I will give it my best shot.'

'Then we hold everything until Prime Minister Slater and I address our people.'

'We don't address "our people" in the UK,' said Slater. 'The monarch does that.'

'An interview. The BBC at the embassy?' said Stephanie.

'No,' said Slater.

'Where then? It can't be at the White House.'

Slater brushed the inside of his wrist with his finger, a habit Stephanie saw several times when he was thinking hard. 'I'll ask Jeff Walsh to set up a session with union workers. Against a

Manhattan backdrop. The Nine Eleven memorial. That'll be recognizable to a British audience and the dockers will be a familiar audience for me. I'll do it better.'

'That would be the Port of New Jersey,' said Prusak as Stephanie's forehead creased with doubt. It wouldn't work, she thought. How could it? An unknown, left-wing British Prime Minister suddenly talking to dock workers in New Jersey. She understood Slater's thinking. His stirring off-the-cuff oratory among blue-collar, working-class backdrops, factories, housing estates, closed coal mines had won him the popular support that propelled him into the top job. Speaking live on television would put him at the heart of the crisis, a British and European leader convincing Americans to do what was right, no stuffy formal interview, the night shift at a container terminal. In one way it was brilliant. But it was too subtle for today's media and therefore very high-risk, the location so surprising that no one would remember a word of what Slater said.

'We need to see your speech,' said Holland.

'I don't know yet.'

'Then let me guess,' said Holland. 'You'll talk about negotiations that will invite Lagutov's Red Army into Europe.'

'We need to trust Kevin on this,' said Swain.

Holland disagreed. 'Europe will cave in, then they'll be on the phone asking Americans to risk their lives to get the Russians out.'

Slater pushed back his chair and stood up. 'I'm a plain-speaking man, Mr President-elect, as are you,' he said. 'I hope, one day, we might respect each other for that. But right now, I'll remind you not to fuck with me, because if you do it will damage America and your legacy will go to shit.'

Holland's face reddened. 'I'll remind you that you are a guest in this room!'

'Matt, fix a plane for the Prime Minister,' said Swain.

'From New York, I will go straight back to London and report to the House of Commons.'

Stephanie got up to leave with him, but Slater said, 'Stay here, Ambassador, where you're needed. My staff can handle this, and I will have Jeff Walsh with me in New York.'

'A message from the Alaska Army National Guard,' said Pacolli, scrolling down his phone. Swain shook Slater's hand and walked him to the door. As he turned back, Pacolli said, 'Don Ondola has arrived in Wales from Goose Creek Correctional Center.'

'The scout?' said Swain. 'The prisoner?'

'Yes, sir. He's inspected the ice. He says there is a risk of casualties, but he can get our troops across.'

The room fell quiet. In their long history of hostilities, there had never been overt, direct, intentional combat between Russian and American ground troops. As soon as they set out from Wales to Little Diomede, that was likely to change.

TWENTY-ONE

Little Diomede, Alaska, USA

Savage winds buffeted Rake as he edged along the ridge on the southern lip of Little Diomede. In the summer, this was a dirt track used for gathering sea birds' eggs and wild vegetables. In the winter, it hardened with frost, then iced over, and now was covered in snow. More came at him in blinding sheets, so thick that he couldn't see his hands.

The bad weather was as perfect as he could have wished for. Swirling snow and fog would keep him invisible. In the lulls, when the wind dropped and the fog vanished, he could see above him a glow of lights: the Russian soldiers were setting up an observation post on the roof of the island. So far, he'd counted three of them. He expected five or six.

He could bypass them and head across to the base on Big Diomede. Those were his orders. He knew the terrain and footholds that would get him around the island. But the weather could clear at any time, making him and the American troops coming across from Wales vulnerable. The Russians would pick them off like ducks at a funfair.

If he were to take the Russians, it would have to be at close quarters. If there were steady wind speed and direction, he could try with the rifle. But in weather like this, wind speed could change from zero to forty miles an hour in a few moments, swinging from northerly to easterly and back again without pattern. The only way to get a clean shot was in the seconds when the wind dropped completely. Even then he doubted he could make six kills, silently, without raising a radio alert.

The track followed a zigzag route towards the top to ease the gradient for climbers. Rake ignored it and went straight up. Even though the rock face was hidden by snow, he knew how to spot hand and footholds. He grasped the rounded edge of a rock and hauled himself up. He leant in, catching his breath. The straps of his pack bit into his shoulders.

He tried to find his footing to the next level, but clumps of snow stuck to his boots making any grip impossible. Holding tight with his hands, he kicked it off just as the wind changed direction threatening to pull him away completely. He held himself still, waiting for the wind to drop, seeing nothing except a swirling whiteness. To go back down now would be as dangerous as to keep going. The wind softened. Its howling energy lessened to buffeting gusts that he could handle. His stolen Russian military gear was good. The gloves didn't tear. The goggles stayed tight. He could feel sweat running down his back. It trickled into his eyes too, underneath his goggles.

His muscles tore with pain as he pulled himself higher, feeling his way with his boots for the next ledges. He reached a familiar point where the hillside rose vertically above him. Twenty more feet and he would be over the edge and on a level with the soldiers. He faced a deep crevice. Above it, within hand's reach, was a rock that jutted out like a pole. He clasped it with both hands and hauled himself higher, fighting the weight of the pack that was tilting him backwards and pulling him down. Fresh feathery snow covered his goggles. He could only see a spinning vortex of white driving into the dark hollow of the crevice. He felt forward with his left hand searching for another hold and found one over the lip. Using both arms, he heaved himself over the top.

He lay in drifted snow, catching his breath. Up there he was exposed, and the wind hit him viciously across the face like a fist. In front was a line of rocks against which the snow had drifted enough for him to hide and watch.

Now he counted six Russians. They were unfamiliar with the island, but were well trained in cold-weather warfare; the way they held their weapons, their respect for exposed metal and how it could stick to human skin and tear it in the cold, how they looked out for each other.

Eskimos had their own way of dealing with the cold, and during the early days of his military training Rake had learned more about Arctic survival, how clothing can slip and how quickly body heat is sapped from exposed parts. Blood freezes so its warmth can't compensate. Circulation stops and frostbite moves in. The victim will not feel a thing until he gets warm. The pain then can be so great that men have told how they prayed to die.

The primary task of the Eskimo Scouts was not fighting, but surveillance. Rake was to be the eyes and ears of America on its sub-zero icy border. Combat was for other units. He had applied and won a transfer to the 19th Special Forces group in

Washington State. They taught him how to shoot and kill men in the cold. In return, he had showed them how to read the Arctic wind and ice. It was this unit that had taken him to Afghanistan, where he met Carrie and where he learned the skills he was about to use now.

Rake laid down the pack, pressed himself against the boulder, and used the night-vision scope. The soldiers had brought up two general-purpose machine guns, powerful night-vision scopes, a satellite dish, and what looked like rocket-propelled grenades. To operate in both directions, east towards Wales and west across to Big Diomede, they had separated into groups of three.

Rake watched for many minutes. From what he could see from the way they acted, how they moved slowly, planning, watching, the Russians were not expecting an attack. He took two M14 carbines from his pack with thirty rounds in each magazine, giving him ten rounds for each target. He shouldn't need that many. It would be fast and at close range. Ondola had lubricated them well. The mechanisms were doing their job. He arranged one weapon on each shoulder.

At some stage, the Russians would gather to eat, to plan, to receive orders. He needed all six in a single cluster.

Minutes passed. The wind dropped. The fog and driving snow cleared. He could see the looming dark ridge of Big Diomede and the moon's glow against a cold black sky. The surface at the top was flat, rocky, snow-covered, and treacherous. The soldiers trod cautiously as they arranged equipment, a machine gun on each side, ammunition boxes hauled up on a sled, a satellite dish, protectively encased, erected on the westerly edge.

Nearby, a soldier was being treated for an injury. The way

the medic was checking him, taking off the flak jacket, it looked like frostbite. Rake counted five gathered around this westerly machine-gun post, leaving one out of sight, presumably manning the easterly machine gun which he could no longer see.

It wasn't perfect, but it was as good as it would get.

He slid out from behind the rocks and eased himself towards the group. Hunting on the ice was all about the kill. You didn't wound. Silently, invisibly, he moved through the snow until he was close enough. In position, he chose his order of targets, judged flak jackets, anticipated moves. The wind remained cruel, the snowfall a blizzard. It would muffle the noise of gunfire.

He squeezed the trigger. A soldier's head disintegrated, spraying bone and brain around him. Another fell, splitting his head on an exposed rock, blood spilling out on both sides like cut fruit. The frost-bitten soldier with no body armor took a straight torso shot. The spill of crimson told Rake he had hit the heart. The medic treating him turned as three rounds cut through his skull. His legs buckled and he folded onto himself, shoulders slumped, feet skewed and barely a face to speak of. A fifth man managed to fire back, but wildly because he had no target. He died a second later.

Rake kept his finger on the trigger until they were all down and the magazine empty. He switched weapons and trod across the rocks to where they lay sprawled, skewed and awkward in snow that was turning dark red and melting with the warmth of their blood. This was an NCO unit, led by a sergeant. He took the radio and reloaded the first M14.

The fog was thick, and to find the sixth soldier he would have to go towards the easterly edge and hope for luck. He crawled on his elbows, fifteen feet at a time, checked, saw nothing, and crawled again. The radio stayed silent.

A lull in the weather brought his target into vision. The moon appeared like a searchlight illuminating the flat barren whiteness around them. The soldier was barely fifty feet away and coming towards him. The man walked carefully, knowing something wasn't right. He held his weapon in his right hand and reached with his left towards the top of his uniform, which Rake guessed would be the radio button.

Rake fired, but it wasn't a clean shot. The soldier stumbled, tried to get his balance, missed his footing on a rock, and fell. Rake pressed the trigger again. The weapon jammed. He fumbled for the second M14, but the soldier, from the ground, already had his weapon raised. Rake twisted away just as bullets hissed by his ears.

Sudden, new fog cut his vision. The soldier was close, but he no longer saw him. Rake drew his double-bladed knife. The fog would lift just as suddenly, without warning, at any second. When it did, one of them would have the advantage. Or the soldier would fire blindly and give away his position. Rake stayed still, barely breathing. Through the fog, he could just make out the darker shape of the soldier edging towards him.

Rake uncoiled himself and rammed the butt of his jammed weapon into the soldier's mouth. His head jerked back, but his right arm clawed, ripping away Rake's face mask. Rake hit him in the neck, then in the temple, and fell to the ground with him. He pulled away his weapon and broke the radio cable. Even hurt and down, the soldier still had enormous strength. The knife was in Rake's right hand. He needed to get it up to the neck, vulnerable above the body armor where death would be near instantaneous. But Rake couldn't. The soldier held Rake's arm in an unbreakable grip. His mask was torn and Rake could see his enemy's face and eyes clearly.

'We don't have to,' whispered the Russian.

But they did have to. There was no other way. Rake's expression softened and he loosened his left arm enough to let the Russian believe he was listening. He stopped trying to bring the knife up which the soldier was resisting, instead shifting his strength to lower it as if relaxing the attack. He saw a flash in the soldier's eyes. Yes, they did have to. With a clockwise turn, Rake plunged the knife downwards, sliding it under the soldier's flak jacket and up through the ribcage. The body arched and the grip fell away. His face contorted in pain as Rake pushed harder and the blade cut through his lungs and other vital organs towards his heart. Blood bubbled from the man's nostrils and mouth and froze. The body went limp.

Rake sealed his own mask, but found himself tearing off the soldier's goggles. He wanted to see the whole face, to show respect. The soldier was brave and rough, but he was a child, like the first one he killed in the school with the poster-boy face. They sent them out so young, and Rake hated them for it.

He put the boy's radio and phone into his bag. He went back to the other corpses and took all their phones. They would be useful because it was safer to use a message from a civilian phone than open the channel on a military radio. They were in protective cases to preserve battery life.

Rake loaded up the sled. He divided weapons, food, and equipment into six separate packs. Even if he lost five in the descent, he would have one pack with which to keep going. He lashed them down. He kept out the night-vision binoculars to look over toward Big Diomede. Clear weather and sturdy lenses would allow him to spot dangerous open channels where sea water still ran. He read the dark and light patches where the sea ice would be strong enough to cross.

He was looking for something else too, which he saw as the moon emerged from behind a leaden cloud, its light falling like a lamp flickering on the ice. Midway between the two islands there was a packed and hard track not yet covered by the new fall of snow. It ended against a tall lump of ice. He thought he saw a ruffle of shadow against the whiteness. It could have been his eyes playing tricks, but he imagined Nikita Tuuq down there, watching. A man like Tuuq could wait like an animal, unseen for hours, even days, nursing his hatred of his half-brother and his mission to kill.

If he were Tuuq he would hide out between the two islands where he could see everything. While Tuuq was out there, Rake would not be able to get across.

TWENTY-TWO

Russian Embassy, Washington, DC

At the moment that Rake was killing the Russian soldier, Karl Opokin, Chairman of Russia's Central Bank, pulled back the lace curtain of the huge windows in the Russian Embassy and looked out onto Wisconsin Avenue. He counted four police cars, two unmarked Lincoln Town Cars, and an untold number of television satellite trucks.

Russia was enemy number one and its embassy was as good as under siege.

Opokin was skilled in balancing Russia's finances between the institutions of organized crime, oligarchies, and government. His whole career had been built on juggling the character of the Russian Federation with the practicalities of twenty-first-century economics. But with the Eccles Building a charred shell and his friend Roy Carrol dead, Opokin felt shipwrecked.

'Speaker Grizlov is calling from Moscow, sir,' said his aide.

Sergey Grizlov, the ambitious Chairman of the State Duma, was a master of political manipulation and tipped as a successor to President Lagutov. Opokin accepted that he might have been the architect of drawing the new border and disputing the Alaska

Purchase, but there was no way that Grizlov, a supporter of all the West had to offer, would have been responsible for this bombing. Opokin let go of the curtain and walked across the room to take the call.

'How are you holding up, Karl?' Grizlov sounded worried.

'What the hell is going on?' said Opokin. 'Roy Carrol was one of my closest—'

'I know, Karl. I know. It's dreadful. I'll be quick because everything is so fluid. The Kremlin is about to ask the Central Bank to set aside funds to help companies caught up in all this. It's short-term, until things settle. To tide things over.'

This was old Russia, thought Opokin angrily. Mess things up and have others clean up behind you. 'How much?' he asked with deliberate caution.

'Well into the billions. I heard twenty.'

Opokin's grief and anger over the bombing turned to steely resolve. 'The Central Bank is independent, Sergey, as you know. I will not release one ruble until Viktor Lagutov makes clear exactly what he's doing.'

'I'm trying to find out myself,' said Grizlov smoothly.

'Then I'll look at it when I get back to Moscow.'

'Which is why I'm calling. What have you said to the FBI?'

The sudden switch of subject made Opokin even more uneasy. 'They've asked to see me, and the police are waiting outside.'

'Do not speak to them. Stay inside the embassy where you have diplomatic protection and they can't touch you.' Grizlov spoke as if it were an instruction, but it was one which Opokin had no intention of heeding.

'On the contrary, as soon as I've dealt with the FBI, I will fly home. I'm needed there.'

'No.' Grizlov's charm vanished. 'If you step outside, they'll arrest you.'

'They can't think—'

'Pictures of you in handcuffs will hammer the ruble!'

'Who did this, Sergey? Who on earth is behind—?'

'Just stay there, Karl. I'll get back to you when I can.'

Grizlov cut the call. Opokin looked across to the television screen to see a head and shoulders static picture of himself together with four others, the bodyguards with him during his visit to the Federal Reserve. Three were shown in passport-style photographs. A fourth, the key suspect, appeared in an artist's sketch. A headline ticker tape ran his name across the bottom of the screen. 'Is this man the bank bomber?'

Blair House, Office of the President-elect, Washington, DC

Determination gripped Bob Holland as he listened to his interpreter speaking to the Chinese President's office in Beijing. The first days of any presidency can mark it for history, and Swain was in the perfect position to stain Holland's legacy. He could see Swain now plotting how to wreck Holland. He wouldn't be surprised if Swain and Lagutov had dreamt up the whole thing themselves.

With clarity and the right words, a great leader could end this crisis within hours. He would bring peace through strength, which is how Ronald Reagan beat the Soviets in the cold war.

Holland had done this in the way he warned Lagutov, leaving no room for doubt about the consequences of taking the wrong path. He was not going to allow China to fund Russia's military attack against America. Plain speaking would put a stop to it. No way would China take American jobs then get rich by selling its products back here then finance an attack on the United States. That would be ending right now.

'Mr President-elect, we have no need for interpreters,' said the Chinese President, Lo Longwei, in fluent English. 'The thoughts of the Chinese people are with all Americans on this dreadful day.'

'Thank you, Mr President,' said Holland brusquely, determined not to be trapped by diplomatic niceties. 'I will be quick, sir. You will not make any funds available to Russia until this crisis is over, and you must condemn its invasion of Alaska.'

'I understand your concern. But I believe your call is two days premature. I have already spoken to your incumbent leader.'

No way would Lo get away with that. 'I need to know, sir – is China with us on this?'

'I would like to express to you personally China's unequivocal condemnation of the attack on the Federal Reserve.'

'I'm talking about Alaska. Russian troops need to leave our territory, and I am asking for your support.'

'This has yet to reach my desk, but I understand it was a humanitarian mission and territorial jurisdiction is very complicated. China has many of its own disputes.'

'I am giving you an opportunity to state your position.'

'I am sure all sides are acting with good reason.'

'You're not hearing me, Mr President.'

'My technicians tell me the line is good. I am hearing you well. China will help in any way to resolve the dispute between America and Russia.'

'I need to tell you that if one cent of Chinese money goes to—'

'We deal in the renminbi and the ruble. Excuse me, Mr President-elect, I have another call coming in.'

The line went dead. Holland held the phone limply in his hand. But it didn't matter. He had put down his marker and China was now running scared.

TWENTY-THREE

The White House, Washington, DC

In the Oval Office, Stephanie listened to the playback of Holland's call. He had shown both stupidity and impatience in demanding so quickly that China openly support the United States. He had irreparably weakened himself in the eyes of China. It was interesting that, unlike with Holland's call to the Kremlin, she could hear both sides of the conversation. The Chinese would have known that the National Security Agency would be intercepting, and it meant they had not encrypted at their end because they wanted Swain to hear their response. She was with Prusak and Swain. Others were on their way.

'What do you want to do, sir?' asked Prusak.

'Nothing openly.' Swain sounded bullish and confident. 'We handle it as they did during the Trump transition. We follow every move Holland makes. We intercept every call. Every time he takes a piss, we know it.'

'They'll react,' said Stephanie. 'China always tests a new President. The question is – with what? In 2001 with Bush, it was the collision of the spy plane; in 2009 with Obama, the harassment of the surveillance ship; in 2016 the taking of the submersible drone. Each was a challenge to your presence in Asia. My instinct is they'll now ramp it up – currency, trade, military – and they'll tie it in with the Russia crisis.'

Swain looked up as three key principals came in, Michael Pacolli from Defense, Thomas Grant from Treasury, and Peter Andrews from State. 'Is Opokin still in the embassy?' he asked Prusak.

'Yes,' answered Andrews. 'He's refusing to speak to the FBI. If he steps outside, we will arrest him.'

Swain moved from his desk to the two yellow pastel sofas facing each other in the middle of the room. He indicated that everyone should share the sandwiches, dips, juice, and coffee laid out on the low table in the middle. Stephanie picked up a plate of sandwiches and held it for Swain, then offered it to Prusak and ended up circling the sofas like a waitress as everyone took one. It was just past three in the afternoon; she remembered having black coffee and an energy bar hours ago and, like her, a few in the room might have napped, but none had properly slept.

'I am not going to confront Holland directly,' said Swain. 'But let his people know that if he speaks to another foreign government without my permission I will use the Logan Act.'

Stephanie's face creased with curiosity. 'Is that the ban on private citizens negotiating with a foreign government?' she asked.

'Correct,' said Swain. 'It dates back to 1799, after Senator George Logan thought he could negotiate with France on behalf of the government.'

'But is Holland a private citizen?'

'He is. Only the President or those authorized by him are allowed to negotiate.'

'It's never had a conviction,' said Prusak. 'Remember in 2015, forty-seven Republican Senators told Iran they would scrap the nuclear deal. Obama got a three hundred thousand-signature petition asking him to prosecute them under the Logan Act.'

'But when Reagan was President-elect in 1980 didn't he call the Iranians kidnappers and barbarians over the embassy siege?' said Stephanie.

'He liaised with Jimmy Carter first, playing soft cop hard cop,' said Swain. 'Holland is not liaising with me. He needs to know he risks indictment so check with the Attorney General how we could get a conviction.'

Prusak looked alarmed. 'Sir, to begin indictment proceedings against the President-elect on the eve of transition—'

'The United States cannot afford the presidency to be undermined during a crisis. I want to see a piece of paper that tells me how we would stop him.'

Stephanie's phone vibrated. Messages and calls had been coming so fast that she had been tempted to turn off the alerts. She expected yet another angry message from the Foreign Office in London, which resented that she was working so closely with the White House and out of their control. But it wasn't. It was an unknown number from Russia. The message almost certainly came from Ozenna. She put the phone on the table for everyone to see. Island top clear.

'Can we confirm?' said Swain.

Prusak read from his tablet. 'The NSA has an ID on the phone,' he said. 'It is on a Russian pay-as-you-go system, SIM card registered in Khabarovsk, headquarters of the Far Eastern Military Command. That's also home base for its special forces Arctic units.'

'They could be playing us,' said Swain. 'What eyes do we have over there?'

'A Reaper drone now and a satellite within the next twenty-seven minutes,' said Pacolli. 'With the fog coming and going every few minutes, the satellite may get nothing. The drone is circling. Images are coming through via Creech Air Force Base in Nevada.'

Prusak switched the feed to the main television screen. The room fell quiet. The image juddered, indicating high wind turbulence above Little Diomede.

'My God!' exclaimed Stephanie. She saw five blood-soaked corpses on a barren snow-covered landscape. They had the most horrendous wounds. On two at least the heads were partly blown away. The brutality gripped the room. The camera moved to a sixth body in a similar location, with frozen blood around the mouth and nose, then pulled away into a wider shot showing machine guns and other equipment, but no human life.

Horror surged through Stephanie followed by excitement at what Ozenna had achieved. Then she felt a flash of worry about the type of man Carrie had chosen to be with. She too had married a man like this. They didn't make good husbands.

'Yes,' said Pacolli after moments of silence. 'It looks like Captain Ozenna has given us a window. With the observation post down, the Eskimo from Goose Creek Correctional Center, Don Ondola, can guide the men across the ice.'

'Do it,' said Swain.

Pacolli repeated the orders into his phone. Secretary of State Andrews took a call and immediately held up his hand to indicate its importance. 'Sir, the Kremlin has contacted our embassy in Moscow. They will take Dr Carrie Walker across to Big Diomede to collect the young mother, her baby, and her guardians. They want our guarantee of safe passage.'

'Why does Dr Walker have to go?' asked Swain.

'The Russian doctor doesn't want to go to our island. Dr Walker will take over the patient's care at the base and accompany her back to Little Diomede.'

'This can't mean they're backing down,' said Prusak.

Far from it, thought Stephanie. She half tuned out of the conversation. To think straight, she needed to get away from the claustrophobic chatter of the Oval Office. Clever people worked in the Kremlin, which meant the White House needed to be cleverer. America had trained a generation of analysts who knew every feuding group in the Middle East and North Africa, but little about the mindset of the Kremlin and even less of Beijing. During the Trump transition, the Chinese stole an American underwater surveillance drone. A few days later they returned it, making things look as if Beijing had backed down. But it hadn't. That was merely a marker for what was to come. Stephanie sensed that with Little Diomede, Russia was doing the same. 'With Carrie at the base, they'll have high-category hostages on both islands,' she said. 'So, my guess is that they're only getting started.' She stood up, phone in her palm. 'Matt, you have this in the system?'

'Every sound you make, Steph.'

'If it's OK with you, Mr President, I'll head back to the embassy and coordinate the Prime Minister's speech from there.'

'When is it?' said Swain.

'The next shift change.' Prusak scrolled his tablet. 'I'll get you a car.'

'It's OK, Matt. I'll cab it.'

A Secret Service agent took Stephanie out through the visitors' entrance where she tagged onto the end of the last tour group leaving the building. Fine drizzle laced with cold air fell on her face. Just what she needed. She walked quickly along Pennsylvania Avenue, then turned north up 20th Street. She put her thoughts in order until she was absolutely certain. If the first conversation didn't work, she doubted the viability of her plan. She brought out a phone, her US one this time, checked her watch for the time difference with Almaty, Kazakhstan, and speed-dialed her ex-husband.

'Harry, it's me,' she said. 'I need your help.'

TWENTY-FOUR

Little Diomede, Alaska, USA

A Russian soldier strapped Carrie into the seat of the helicopter and removed her goggles. Frozen air sliced into her eyes, bringing tears. The aircraft vibrated as the pilot powered the engine. Carrie held her medical bag on her lap. The soldier pulled off her hood and put a pair of red headphones on her. Radio static replaced the wind's roar. Then soldiers loaded three body bags – the men Rake had killed. The tops of the bags were open. Each corpse had a number inked on the forehead. Flood lamps came on, throwing out long dark shadows that raced along the rocky coastline. A gray haze hung over the ice, reminding her how Rake described so vividly the winter sun barely rising above the horizon before quickly setting again.

She heard a burst of Russian voices through the headphones, then the pilot speaking in English. 'American Air Force, American Air Force. This is Russian medical helicopter RF-800238. We are taking off from Krusenstern Island, Little Diomede, on a human-itarian mission. Repeat – a humanitarian mission. American medical doctor Carrie Walker is assisting us. We need safe passage. Repeat – we need safe passage.'

'Stay where you are,' came an American military response. 'Repeat. Do not take off. We are waiting instructions. Remain on the ground.'

Her headset went quiet. Carrie felt the energy of the rotor blades speeding up, thrashing around and around. The pilot flipped buttons. His co-pilot scanned the landscape with binoculars. The two side doors stayed open. A soldier on each side brought down heavy machine guns with belts of ammunition. Carrie was alone in a middle seat, her face numb with cold, her mouth dry. Four soldiers sat in front of her.

The helicopter lifted off, shaking the exposed heads in the body bags. One jerked to the left as the aircraft skewed with a gust of wind. Carrie recognized it as the young soldier Rake had killed in the school.

Instead of turning west towards the big island, they climbed straight up with the nose pointing towards the hill. Wind screeched around her. They rose above the village, its housing clinging to the hillside. Within seconds they were over the top.

Sound came again through her headphones. A different American voice: 'Russian military helicopter RF-800238. You are flying illegally over American territory. You must leave immediately or risk being shot down.'

'American Air Force, we are on a humanitarian mission,' said the pilot. 'Safe passage is required under international law.'

'I will not warn you again.'

Yumatov's voice came in, 'Dr Walker, press the talk button on the cable. Tell them who you are and what you have on board.'

With her hands inside her gloves, she fumbled until a soldier did it for her. 'This is Dr Carrie Walker. I'm one of the Americans being held captive. I am on board this helicopter to retrieve the young American woman and her baby and bring them home.'

'Dr Walker, this is Sergeant Jim Gardiner from the Elmendorf-Richardson base in Anchorage. Are you OK?'

'Yes, I'm OK.'

'Is the aircraft armed?'

'Tell him exactly as it is,' said Yumatov.

Two searchlights came on from each of the skids showing a landscape of snow and rocks.

'There is a machine gun on either side of me,' said Carrie.

'International regulations require arming of aircraft for protection against polar bears,' said Yumatov.

Irritation crept into Gardiner's tone. 'OK, Colonel. No one's cracking jokes around here. Get your aircraft back down on the Little Diomede helipad and no one's going to get hurt.'

The top of the island was a white plateau speckled with dark rocks. The pilot bought the aircraft to a hover. He turned west-wards and tilted the beam of his spotlight. Snow blew across the surface from the rotor blades, and when it cleared Carrie saw a scene that took her straight back to the worst human carnage of Iraq. An overhead light shone on her face.

'These images and our conversation are now being broadcast live on Russian television,' said Yumatov. 'The internal camera is showing Dr Carrie Walker. Are you hearing me, Sergeant Gardiner?'

'Copy that.'

'We need Dr Walker to confirm that these men are dead and to treat the wounded if any have survived.'

'Copy that.' Gardiner's voice stayed flat and carried no reaction.

'We came here on a humanitarian mission to save a young woman's life. Your government must answer to the international community as to why nine of our comrades have been murdered in cold blood.'

'Copy that.'

'Do more than that, damn you. Guarantee us safe passage.'

'I am awaiting orders, Colonel.'

Jagged granite rocks, caked in ice, stuck out from the snow. The helicopter was inches from the ground, swaying so erratically that Carrie couldn't see any way to get down to examine the bodies. In any case, none could have survived. She had seen plenty of gunshot deaths. But these were different. This was Rake's work. One by one, bullet by bullet, he had killed each one of them. A couple had died cleanly, but three of them had been torn up and mutilated by lead.

The four soldiers facing her unclipped their belts and jumped out. They loaded the dead into the back of the aircraft and signaled to the pilot. Rake had killed five. Four men were taking their place. Her headphones echoed with the emptiness of radio static.

The pilot took the helicopter up and turned towards Big Diomede. An eerie band of cloud ringed the island. She saw the shapes of observation posts dotted along its looming ridges. At the bottom, ice glowed against dark rocks. She found herself leaning out, looking down, following tracks in the ice, seeing water flows, huge serrated blocks taller than a person and flat white like a skating rink. She hoped she would see Rake. She scanned the landscape for her killing machine of a fiancé while waiting for an American missile to shoot them down.

As they came around the northern edge, she saw the military base, rows of helicopters, their blades drooping, people moving around, and long white concrete buildings with gun emplacements on the roofs. She counted ten helicopters, six white and four green, of varying sizes. The three biggest, with two sets of rotor blades, were for transport. There were more inside the large open hangars. There were no fixed-wing aircraft, and the short airfield didn't look big enough to take one. Men wheeled trolleys towards them. She smelt aviation fuel. The base formed part of the curve of the mountainside, and with the snow it was difficult to tell what was natural, what was concrete, and what had been hewn out of the granite. The wind was weaker around this side of the island.

Two men in dark green overalls helped her down from the helicopter and led her across the tarmac towards the long single-story building. A wooden plaque of the Russian flag was displayed above the entrance. As the door slid open, she was faced with plastic transparent strips hanging down as extra protection against the weather. She walked through them into a small hallway with bright overhead lights. Warmth hit her face, and the sudden change of temperature set her blood tingling. In Russian, she asked to see the patients. The men led her into a room on the right that looked like a reception area with a set of black leather sofas and chairs and a meeting table. There was a line of stainless-steel food containers on warmers. The soldiers left the room, closed the door, and locked it.

Years of emergency medicine had taught Carrie to eat and sleep whenever she had a chance. The meal was a beef stew with cabbage and rice. She ate fast, not realizing how hungry she was. She washed it down with bottled water and felt strength return. She poured a cup of coffee, black, no sugar.

The door opened with a flourish. She had expected a military person to be in charge, but the short stocky man who strode in was dressed in a dark pinstripe suit with a tiny Russian flag pinned to his right lapel. 'How is your meal?' he asked in English.

Carrie stood up, coffee cup in hand. 'I need to see the mother and baby. Then I will determine if they can safely be taken back to the island.'

'I'm Admiral Alexander Vitruk, commander of the Far East Military District.' He spoke fluently, his English, like Yumatov's, laced with an American accent. He poured himself a small cup of coffee and downed it quickly. 'Come, then, if you've finished; I'll take you to them.'

He held the door open. Several men fell in behind as they led her into a control room with rows of computers and television feeds on the wall. On one screen, there was a split image of Carrie in the helicopter and a map of the Diomede islands. Vitruk took her through a tented walkway warmed by large overhead electric heaters into a mobile field hospital. She had worked in many. This had six beds, three on each side. Akna was the only patient, on a drip, propped up in bed holding her baby daughter.

Carrie wasn't a pediatrician but she didn't like what she saw. The head looked enlarged and the baby wore a gray woolen hat often used for premature births. A monitor recorded Akna's heart and breathing, which were within an acceptable range. The incubator was on the left side of the bed. Rake's uncle and aunt, Henry and Joan Ahkvaluk, sat together on two upright wooden chairs to the right. They stood up when they saw Carrie.

'Are you guys OK?' she asked.

'The baby is very sick,' said Joan. 'She has water on the brain, and they don't know what to do.'

Carrie looked for a bedside clipboard. There was none. 'What medication is she on?'

'They won't tell us.'

She took a tube of antiseptic gel from her pocket, sanitized her hands, and put on a pair of blue polymer medical gloves from her medical bag. She sat on the bed. 'Akna, I'm Carrie. Remember? I was with you before you came here.'

Akna stared at her, eyes dulled by drugs. American military painkillers weren't subtle. Russian ones would be even worse.

'You've given her a name, Iyaroak. It's beautiful.' Carrie checked her pulse, which was slow. She pulled down the covers to see the Caesarean wound. It was clean, without infection. But the stitching was rough, and Akna would be scarred there for life. She put the covers back and turned her attention to the baby. Gently, she slid back the woolen hat. Iyaroak didn't react. Her eyes were tilted down, which was a symptom matching what Joan had described, corroborated by the head size. The soft bones of Iyaroak's skull were being pushed out by cranial fluid that was not draining away as it should, instead putting pressure on the tiny unformed brain. If it were not treated immediately, Iyaroak could be left seriously disabled with brain damage. Or she would die.

'A word, Admiral.' Carrie walked away from Akna. Vitruk followed. 'The baby has hydrocephalus. She needs urgent scans and pediatric surgery.'

'Yes. It is why you are here, to treat here.' Vitruk spoke calmly, but with concern in his eyes.

'I can't do that. She needs a specialist and a big hospital. Nome, or better – Anchorage.'

'We can't fly her there.'

'One of our helicopters can pick her up from here or Little Diomede.'

'We can't allow them over. That is the problem. Politics are in the way.'

Carrie controlled her exasperation, a field doctor up against bureaucratic stupidity. 'OK. Let's keep her in Russia. Which is your nearest big hospital?'

'Providenya. But it's best it's done here.'

Part of Carrie felt Vitruk was being helpful. Part of her knew she was missing something. Given all that was going down, why was the survival of this baby such a big deal for the Russians? She understood the propaganda value of keeping Akna and Iyaroak alive. But things had moved on. She looked hard into Vitruk's expression, but couldn't read him. 'I can't treat her here,' she said. 'The valves that drain the fluid into the bloodstream are not working. We must operate by making an incision into the skull through which the fluid can drain. A tiny man-made valve gets inserted there. For that you need a pediatric neurosurgeon, the valve, and a scanner, and you don't have any of that here.'

'When will she need this?'

'Now.'

'It would take hours even to get her to Anchorage or Providenya. How long before the condition is irreversible?'

'Impossible to say. But this baby's life is in danger, period. Let me talk to the doctor who carried out the Caesarean section and I might be able to judge more.'

'He has left for another emergency.'

Like hell he had! But there was no point in challenging. Carrie ran through options. The best was to fly Akna and Iyaroak directly to hospital in Nome and second best to Providenya. It was better to stay here in the field hospital than be stranded on Little Diomede where there was nothing. She often welled up with anger that governments always had enough money to drop bombs and send soldiers to war, but when it came to saving children they would just wring their hands and shake their heads. And that thought, then, gave her an idea.

'Fly in a pediatric neurosurgeon from Providenya or Vladivostok, together with the equipment needed. We can sterilize this area for the operation.'

Vitruk nodded thoughtfully. 'I will relay your very helpful suggestion to Moscow and Washington. Thank you, Dr Walker.' A smile seeped to the edge of his lips. 'You will now come with me to Little Diomede to tell us what is needed there to keep little Iyaroak safe on her return.' Charm bled from his face and Carrie realized she had been tricked. She glanced towards Henry and Joan, whose expressions confirmed it. By suggesting a way forward, Vitruk would portray Carrie as his ally, colluding with him in the occupation of Little Diomede.

'I'll stay with my patients,' she said firmly.

Vitruk's eyes narrowed. 'You need to come with me. It is not only the lives of your patients that are at risk. The situation is already dangerous.'

'You're the one that made it dangerous, Admiral,' Carrie said, her temper rising. 'You don't have to send soldiers with machine guns to fly out a sick mother.'

'And in return your demented boyfriend killed my men.'

'Fuck you.' Carrie stepped to one side to go back to the bedside.

Vitruk blocked her. 'Swear all you like, but our doctors tell me this baby's hydrocephalus is congenital, probably because the father is such an animal that he screwed his own daughter for this baby.'

Vitruk stood directly in front of her with soldiers, weapons in hands, on either side. She pulled herself back from the cusp of breaking a golden rule of medicine – never lose your cool. Politicians shout. Doctors save. Her duty was not to pick a fight, but to save Iyaroak's life. 'OK, Admiral,' she said, switching to her most warming doctor-patient bedside manner. 'I will come with you. What exactly is it you need me to do?'

Her broad smile caught Vitruk off guard. Confusion spread across his face, so Carrie spelt it out. 'You're the guy with the guns so I'll do what you say, but on condition that what I do for you saves Iyaroak's life. And that will help you because you plan to use a sick baby and a blonde doctor as your propaganda poster in the big swinging dick game Russia is playing with my government.'

Vitruk's face drew in on itself, as if he had anticipated a negotiation. 'Anything else?

'Joan and Henry stay with the patients,' Carrie replied in the same blunt manner. 'You fly in a pediatric surgeon for the operation. I join your propaganda machine.'

'You have my word. So, we have a deal.' Vitruk pulled on his gloves. 'Now we go.'

TWENTY-FIVE

Little Diomede, Alaska, USA

The pounding of the Russian helicopter engine woke Rake from a short sleep in the shelter of a hillside crevice. There was thick fog, and tiny hailstones swirled in a wind eddy at the entrance. He reached outside and checked the straps of the sled. They were tight. The sled remained secure, hanging near-vertically from a spiky boulder from which Rake would lower it down the hillside.

His radio crackled and a voice came through in broken English. 'American Air Force, American Air Force. This is Russian medical helicopter RF-800238. We are returning to Russian island of Krusenstern, known to you as Little Diomede. We insist on safe passage.'

Rake looked for the helicopter. Freezing fog hung in clumps like icebergs in the sky. Fifty yards to the west there was a break and he saw it approaching in a wide loop. Its searchlight soaked into the fog. As it got closer, the rotor draught broke ice shards off the hillside.

They must be searching for him.

The engine labored, its pitch higher than it should be. He

checked through binoculars and saw that the helicopter was tilted forward. Its skids were weighed down by ice which would be hardening as it flew through more fog. Freezing fog clung to aircraft metal like a boot gathering mud in a field. The pilot needed to head towards warmer air because soon it would be too heavy to stay up.

An American voice replied on the radio: 'RF-800238. You are flying illegally over American territory. You were warned earlier. Return to your base now or you will be shot down.'

Rake wasn't a pilot, but he had flown in plenty of aircraft through Arctic conditions. As the helicopter came into full view, he saw the skids were coated solidly with ice. He couldn't identify any deflectors around the engine cowlings that would prevent ice or snow being drawn in. No pilot would deliberately take his aircraft through freezing rain unless in an emergency or under orders from a superior officer. Through the cockpit glass, Rake could just make out the face of this pilot, speaking into his headset to the US military with a tone of controlled frustration, a professional, following orders with which he didn't agree.

If the aircraft stayed where it was, more ice droplets would gather on the rotor blades and other sharp edges, putting on hundreds of pounds of weight. Once formed, the ice could break loose from anywhere at any time, changing the airflow dynamic and plunging the aircraft down or throwing it against the hillside.

It was then, as he shifted his gaze to the main cabin, that he spotted Carrie, sitting rigid, staring ahead, a spotlight shining straight onto her face. It was deliberate. They were using her to tease him out. If he stayed silent, there was a real risk of the helicopter being shot down. If he intervened, he would reveal his position. There was also a good chance the Americans wouldn't open fire and an equally good chance that the Russians would find him anyway. Rake pressed the transmit button of his stolen radio. 'This is Captain Ozenna. Do not shoot this aircraft. An American physician is on board. Repeat, do not shoot down this aircraft. Do you copy?'

'Copy that,' came the American voice, subdued.

'The aircraft is in extreme danger. It is iced up from freezing rain.' He repeated it in Russian so the pilot would hear directly. He added, 'You need to land immediately. Nose up, stay at an angle, and power into the crosswind as you come to the helipad.'

Carrie turned her head as if scanning the darkened hillside for him. The pilot glanced across, then back to the fog in front of him. He powered the engine, following Rake's instruction. A layer of ice cracked and fell from the tail, and the helicopter skewed to the right. The light on Carrie snapped off. Rake closed the radio. He had to get away.

The helicopter's noise faded to a whisper, sucked away by the wind. Directly beneath him the hill fell in a near-vertical drop onto a shoreline of rocks. Rake knew of one narrow passage there to get a sled onto the sea. Even then, there might be ice blocking it or it could be covered with a fast-flowing current of water.

He was out of time to think and judge. From the sled, he took one bag with two Kalashnikovs and one rocket-propelled-grenade launcher, a second bag with grenades and magazines of ammunition, and a third with food. The other bags stayed on the sled. He loosened the rope securing it to the rock until it slipped out of the noose. It lurched downward in a rapid succession of jerks before running lightly on smooth fresh snow, gathering speed until it hit a rut and tipped head on, falling onto its side and spilling the bags it was carrying. Sled and bags tumbled down. One smashed against a sharp granite edge, which ripped it open. Others bounced off rocks and skidded down ice. There was a chance that something would survive, cushioned by snow or caught in an eddy of water; an equal chance that none would.

His breath lingered in the frozen air as he studied the ghostly whiteness that spread between him and the Russian base. Some areas were well-packed and hard. Some were covered with fresh snow making it difficult to tell what thin and bad ice was underneath. He strapped the harness that should have lowered the sled around his shoulders and waist, balanced his packs, and loosened the metal brakes on the ropes that would regulate his descent.

The main thing he remembered from his first-ever visit to New York was that Little Diomede stood at about the same height as the Empire State Building. As a kid on a summer's night, he could run up to the top in less than fifteen minutes. Ever since then, whether going up or down, Rake thought of that iconic American building.

Treading delicately, he lowered himself to his first footfall and stopped, checking his balance and direction. Abruptly, a splutter from the radio that, for a moment, Rake thought was the wind. But it was a familiar voice. 'Hello, yellow Yankee coward. I thought I told you to go home.'

Rake scanned the landscape and imagined Tuuq out there

somewhere, waiting. Tuuq spoke again. 'You're a coward who can't protect his woman.'

Rake had to work out where Tuuq might be. But in that forbidding moonlit expanse, he also needed to keep himself invisible. From around the headland to the south, he heard the slowing throb of a helicopter coming in to land. It meant Carrie was back on Little Diomede and safe, at least from being killed in an air crash in freezing fog.

Just before the radio crackle faded into a static-laden calm, he heard Tuuq's taunting voice again. 'I will find you, yellow Yankee coward. And I will kill you.'

INCHES ABOVE THE HELIPAD, a gust tilted the helicopter to the right, tipping the rotor blades towards the ground. The aircraft jerked back upright, and a slab of ice fell off the side, shattering like glass. The skids settled. Two soldiers hacked away the ice that jammed the door shut. Vitruk removed his headset. 'Do exactly as I say,' he shouted to Carrie above the engine noise. She held her medical bag on her lap, looked straight at him, and didn't reply.

Yumatov opened the door and saluted. Spray from the down-draught peppered his face. Vitruk stepped down. Yumatov held Carrie's elbow to help her out. A television crew was on the helipad filming them. Soldiers worked around the aircraft, clearing it of ice. A six-man Spetsnaz unit stood to one side, ready to climb in. 'Their orders are to find your lover and kill him,' said Vitruk.

'You won't get him,' Carrie shouted back.

'He's not as smart as you think.' Vitruk pointed to ice patterns on the helicopter where soldiers on stepladders were chipping it off the rotor blades. 'He was wrong about the danger. Ice doesn't make a helicopter drop out of the sky. The tail rotor clears because of heat from the engine exhaust. We could keep flying with even more ice than we have here.'

As he talked, Carrie looked around for villagers and could see none, only soldiers. There were no lights on in the houses. The television crew was setting up lamps and two cameras on the school veranda, which must be for a set-piece interview.

'So, you still have everyone in the gymnasium?' she said.

'Yes, because your government is being difficult.'

'If you left, they would have nothing to be difficult about.'

Vitruk didn't answer. Soldiers stared at her as Vitruk and Yumatov led her through the village. She detected anger in their gaze. Nine of them were dead and they must by now know of her connection to Rake. On a single order, they would unleash on her their violent frustration for revenge. A soldier opened the door as they approached the school. Inside they were enveloped in warm stale air and cigarette smoke. Men in the small hallway and dining room jumped to attention.

'At ease,' said Vitruk, the voice of a soldier's soldier. He had been where they were. He had lost friends in battle. Men lining the corridor snapped their heels, and their eyes bored expectantly into Vitruk. If anyone could avenge their comrades it was him.

Inside the gymnasium, there was a smell of sweat and disinfectant, part locker room, part hospital. A baby cried, then another. A mother scolded. From a corner, a boy aired Vitruk a high five. Vitruk told Carrie to explain to him the medical problems she had found. She took him straight to Tommy Tulamuk, the skeletal addict she had saved earlier. A television camera followed. He was sleeping, legs up in the same fetal recovery position as when she had left him. She washed her hands with antiseptic gel. She pulled gently at his right ear and placed a thermometer inside. His temperature had stabilized at 37.2.

'This patient has a narcotic overdose,' she told Vitruk in English, aware of the camera filming her. 'With alcohol, organ destruction is slow. With narcotics, vital organs can reach fragility without warning and suddenly fail. This man is now recovering, and he will live.'

'Thank you, Dr Walker,' said Vitruk smoothly. 'Your work is invaluable to us.'

He walked through clusters of people sitting or lying on the floor, greeting the excited children with a pat on the head or a high five. Most adults, skilled at surviving in harsh environments, didn't meet his gaze and watched with barely any expression. Vitruk reached the wooden exercise bars which stretched right along the back wall. As he prepared to speak, Yumatov beckoned Carrie away out of camera shot.

'Villagers of Little Diomede,' Vitruk began in English. 'Thank you for your patience. I am Admiral Alexander Vitruk and I command this military district. Those are my soldiers who've been watching you from Big Diomede all these years—'

The way he spoke reminded Carrie of her father, using six words when one would do, trying to be loved while clinging on to absolute control. She worked out long ago that it wasn't her father's fault that he had been embedded into the Soviet mindset from birth. Vitruk recounted the emergency rescue and that now mother and child were doing well. He didn't mention the hydrocephalus, nor did he mention Rake. He pointed out how surprised he was at the lack of health care on the island and praised 'world-renowned trauma surgeon' Dr Carrie Walker for helping to save lives. 'Dr Walker's team will make sure you have the correct supply of vitamin and diet supplements.'

A voice broke through from the back. 'We don't need no more white people telling us.'

Vitruk opened his hands in a pacifying gesture. 'Only take it if you want it.'

'Get the hell off our island.'

Vitruk's expression remained cordial. 'We will, and we'll get Akna and little Iyaroak back to the community.'

To the left a door opened. One of the television crew tapped his watch. Without another word, Vitruk walked outside onto the veranda. Yumatov switched channels to show Vitruk lit by broadcast lamps standing against the backdrop of Big Diomede and the wreckage of the two helicopters on the sea ice.

TWENTY-SIX

Washington, DC

Stephanie stamped her feet against the cold as she rang the bell to her ex-husband's apartment. The door opened and, unexpectedly, Harry Lucas looked ten years younger and a million times healthier than when she last saw him. He had lost weight, was trim, fit, and stylishly dressed in a sleeveless green down jacket over a blue denim shirt. His dark hair touched his ears and collar, longer than his usual military cut. Marriage had suffocated him. Divorce had freed him. Whatever Harry was doing now, whoever he was with, had restored him to the person she once loved.

'Thanks for seeing me,' she said, walking briskly in. 'I need your mind, Harry.'

'And you used to want me only for my body,' he smiled.

As she pulled off her gloves, she couldn't help looking around, to see how he was living now. It was an old-style first-floor apartment between Dupont Circle and Rhode Island Avenue with shabby high corniced ceilings, worn rugs from exotic places over wooden floorboards, an open-plan living room, and a kitchen chaotically filled with color and mementos. She recognized some – the mask from eastern Congo, swords from Sudan, portraits of Mao, Hitler, and Stalin, and a table of photos from Harry's time in Congress, posing with the Obamas, the Clintons, Nelson Mandela, Mick Jagger, and an assortment of other famous people.

She looked everywhere except at Harry. What should she do – peck him on both cheeks as a friend? Say 'hi' as they did whenever they talked to each other but reined in open affection because it could be read in a thousand different hostile ways? Give him a hug for dropping everything for her, and for being lucid and sober? She had assumed he was in Kazakhstan negotiating a defense contract, but it turned out he was in DC.

When she had told him what she needed, he replied as if she was asking for a loaf of bread from the supermarket, 'Yeah, I should be able to do that.' Harry had retained his high-security clearance from the military to Congress to the private defense sector. His combat and political background made him a high-worth consultant with an income many times more than hers. Stephanie had left Harry and he had left Congress about the same time, and he had concentrated on identifying fault lines in the government's intelligence apparatus. After Nine-Eleven, the government smashed down the protective agency silos that had compartmentalized classified information so much that no one saw Bin Laden coming. War in Iraq, where Harry served, saw the outsourcing of war to defense contractors who could go into areas government was banned from reaching. Then came WikiLeaks and Snowden, and the silos got built all over again, except in different ways, off the books and deep in the Web. By now, war had changed and money, cyber and social media were superseding guns and bombs. The upshot was that Harry had better access than government to a lot of stuff, and he employed people with better skills at processing it.

Harry led her to a side room from which came soft jazz music and the smell of coffee. He poured two cups, black, handed one to her and turned off the music.

'Whatever Russia's planning, it doesn't stop in Little Diomede,' she said. 'I can't nail it. But I sense it.'

'What is the President's view?' Harry took her coat and folded it over an office chair.

'Swain's playing catch-up. Holland's snapping at his heels. Half the intel community still thinks it's fighting in the Middle East.'

Three computers stood on a workstation that ran the length of the wall. 'We could agree to something over Little Diomede,' Harry said. 'We can't allow the bombing of the Fed. Whoever is behind it knew they were crossing a line. But you're not here for my analysis. You have a thousand experts within a square mile of here who will give you their take on it.' He fired up his computers. 'You want my database.'

Stephanie smiled coyly. 'Right.'

'And I can't even remember if we're divorced yet.' Grinning, Harry sat down and opened the software with a fingerprint and iris scan.

'I'm interested in Alexander Vitruk and Sergey Grizlov,' she said.

At the mention of Grizlov, Harry grimaced, as she suspected he would. At the lows of their worst arguments, he used to bring up her fling with Grizlov as if the affair were still alive.

'Do you think Grizlov's involved in the Fed attack?'

'I hope not. But never say never.'

'Clever girl.'

She felt a spinal shiver at the thought of sleeping with a man who could have ordered anything so brutal. Harry looked at her, lips drawn in, brow furrowed in a familiar expression of concentration. His screens flared to life. 'After you called, I did some checking.'

He showed Stephanie files on Sergey Grizlov, much of which she already knew: the story of a clever businessman who had manipulated his way to the top through the minefields of the Yeltsin and Putin years. She was astounded at Harry's ability to dig deep and wide. He accessed an encrypted network of databases shared by defense and security contractors. Its search engine was more powerful than anything Stephanie had seen on clumsy government systems. The quality of its raw intelligence was exceptionally high.

Harry had found that Grizlov did have a private project that involved Little Diomede. One of his companies had a large stake in a scheme to build a tunnel across the Bering Strait linking Russia and Alaska. It involved Chinese, Russian, and Japanese money.

'But that's business,' said Stephanie. 'Not terrorism.'

'Business and politics. Exactly. Military hostility would set the tunnel project back for decades.' Harry brought up the file on Vitruk. 'Compare it to this.'

The screen showed two sets of pictures side by side. On the left were documents of mugshots and dates. On the right a video showed a younger Vitruk standing outside a low-rise building that looked like an apartment block as his men dragged people out. The date was October 15th, 1999, the city of Gudermes in Chechnya.

'The second Chechen war,' said Harry. 'Putin crushed an Islamic insurgency. These are civilians. Now watch.' Vitruk drew a pistol. He shot dead two women who looked like mother and daughter and then two small boys. A middle-aged man was left alive. Vitruk pistol-whipped him, left him lying in the rubble with the corpses of his family, and walked off. Harry slid to another video with an almost identical scene. Vitruk shot two women and three children and let the man live. By executing mothers, wives, and children in front of their men, Vitruk stripped out the spirit of whole communities. The men's guilt at failing to protect their families would have an effect for generations. Simple and effective. He was cutting the balls off the place.

'Incredible.' Stephanie was unable to help herself asking, 'Where did you get this?'

'Please, Steph, don't get cute and manipulative in getting me to tell you.' Harry gave her a sideways smile. 'I have two other things, and then we work out what Russia is up to.'

He showed a photograph of Vitruk in Syria after breaking the 2016 siege of Aleppo. With him was a Spetsnaz explosives specialist for whom Harry had an identity. Facial imaging matched him, under another name, to one of the four Russian bodyguards who had accompanied Karl Opokin to the Federal Reserve's Eccles Building. 'I'm checking how he was recruited and how he got onto that detail.'

'Even then, how did he plant the bomb?'

'We don't know exactly, but he had expertise, and he and Opikin are now hunkered down in the Russian Embassy refusing to talk to the FBI.'

Stephanie took a long drink of her coffee, relieved that Vitruk, not Grizlov, was reflecting Russia's dark side. The feel-good moment didn't last long because she didn't know to what extent Grizlov was working with Lagutov and how far Lagutov was backing Vitruk. Had he ordered or known about the Fed attack? Grizlov too?

'One final thing on Vitruk . . .' Harry pushed his chair back and waved his hand dismissively at the screen. 'I won't show you because it's too bitty. A year ago, Vitruk invited a Chinese general by the name of Bu Zishan to his headquarters in Khabarovsk. Bu had just been appointed commander of Shenyang Military District, which adjoins Vitruk's Military Far East region. Vitruk laid out the red carpet, sent a plane to pick Bu up, hosted a big banquet, caviar, vodka, women, the works.'

'Not that unusual . . .'

'No. But I checked anyway. Breaking through a near-impenetrable web of business activities, I found that after the meeting Bu and Vitruk set up a company in Panama that doesn't do very much at all. Now people only tend to do that when they expect a shed load of money to be coming their way.'

That too wasn't unusual either, thought Stephanie. After the Chinese and Russian state-run command economies unraveled, private-sector business arrangements became the default of government institutions. They needed to make money simply to pay salaries and pensions.

'Bu has a track record of being hawkish,' said Harry. 'Before moving to Shenyang he spent years masterminding the South China Sea dispute.'

Stephanie stood up, sipped more coffee, and paced the length of the room. 'This is great, Harry—'

'But you still think it's something else.'

'Yes.'

Harry, suddenly distracted, looked up at a television running silently on the wall. It showed Vitruk in an Arctic combat uniform, on Little Diomede island, standing by a pole where Russian troops were raising their white, red, and blue national flag on conquered American soil.

TWENTY-SEVEN

Washington, DC

Vitruk came across as the exact older version of the man Stephanie had just been looking at in Chechnya, with a leathered face and a smile for the camera that wasn't enough to cover the hard cruelty in those photographs. The framing went to a wide shot of Vitruk with a Russian reporter. In the hazy distance was Big Diomede island. A logo said the interview was live, but Stephanie couldn't be sure because Fox was taking it straight off the Russian channel. Harry turned up the volume.

'Yes, of course, without doubt, Russia utterly condemns the attack on the Federal Reserve, as do I,' said Vitruk.

'Then why raise your fucking flag now?' muttered Harry.

'That was an act of horror that has nothing to do with my government,' Vitruk went on. 'America has many enemies, including among its own people, as we know. Everything I am doing here is being conducted under international law.'

Vitruk spoke about the medical evacuation and the new border, and Stephanie ran scenarios through her mind. What was his endgame? The presenter even pressed him on the hostages in the school, and Vitruk insisted the villagers were there voluntarily. What exactly was he doing and why? She repeated the question to herself until it echoed like a chant. The screen split, with Vitruk on one side and shots of Carrie on the other working with paramedics in the gymnasium, blunt but effective propaganda. It switched again to the corpses on the plateau at the top of the island with both the presenter and Vitruk expressing shock and outrage. Harry's face creased with curiosity.

'We've got someone out there,' explained Stephanie. As she outlined the barest details, she realized now how crucial Ozenna would be to what unfolded next. She told Harry of the decision for him to cross to the Russian base.

'Tough one,' Harry said after a pause, thinking. 'My guess is that Vitruk will fly back to the base as soon as he's done with the TV and he'll have worked out a way to protect his aircraft from us taking it out.'

'If we could kill him, would that end it?'

'What do you think, Steph? You said you had something else in mind.'

She poured herself more coffee, mixing the hot with the tepid, and kept pacing. 'When did we last have a showdown like this with Moscow?'

'Ukraine 2014.'

'That wasn't a direct confrontation.'

'The cold war—'

'Yes, but I mean a head-to-head challenge.'

Harry took a moment. 'Way back. 1962. The Cuban missile crisis.'

'And what happened then?'

'The communists wanted to put missiles in Cuba, a hundred miles from our coastline. We came to the brink of nuclear war. Then Moscow backed down.'

'That's the point, Harry. It didn't "back down". Moscow withdrew only when we promised to take our missiles out of Italy and Turkey.'

Harry looked at her quizzically. She had piqued his interest. Even if she were going off on a crazy track, he wanted to hear it. That was how it had always worked between them. Stephanie stopped, put down the cup, and folded her arms. 'No one's putting missiles on Little Diomede. There's no need. But Moscow does need to create leverage to get us away from its borders in Europe.'

'Breaking NATO's ring of steel.'

'Correct. It needs a bargaining chip to achieve that. The only other time Moscow directly threatened American territory was Cuba, and it won concessions. Lagutov begins the crisis now because Swain is on his way out and Holland is raw and new. Holland will step straight into this with a team that has no experience of working together. Bush had more than six months in office before Nine-Eleven; Kennedy had more than eighteen months before Cuba.'

'And your point?'

'If this is Russia's game plan, then it's not Vitruk going rogue. It's Lagutov, Grizlov, the whole Russian government.'

There was a quiet knock on the door. Harry's gaze drifted over as it opened enough to reveal a young woman, dark hair loose on her shoulders, wearing a red silk robe. She could have been taken from a magazine cover. Harry held up his hand with

splayed fingers as if to say five more minutes. She flashed
Stephanie a silent smile, and the door closed. Stephanie unfolded
her arms and reached for her coat. Harry shrugged as if to say,
You threw me out when I was a loser; now I'm recovered and
I've gone for someone younger and less complicated.

'I'll get back to the White House, run stuff past them,'
Stephanie said, fighting an urge to ask who the woman was. Was
it serious? For how long had he been seeing her? Was it better?
She pursed her lips to hide conflicting feelings. If she asked, they
would start circling each other and it would get scrappy; it always
had and there was no luxury of time for that now. Harry had
helped her tonight. A lot.

'Hold on. What's this?' Harry's concentration returned to the
TV screen. Fox News was interviewing Carrie directly inside the
school gymnasium. Carrie was angrily gesticulating. Harry
turned up the volume. The anchor had a reputation for aggressive questioning. 'So, you agree then with the Russian assessment
that the people of Little Diomede have been neglected?'

'I'm a doctor. Don't draw me into your politics.' Carrie's face
was etched with irritation. 'Check our findings here against
neighborhoods in any American city and compare how normal
or bad it is.'

'When you say "our," who are you referring to?'

'I am working with Russian military paramedics.'

'Cooperatively?'

'We are medical professionals. That's what we do.'

'Then, I have to ask: Do you feel right about coming on air
like this?'

Carrie tensed. 'I don't know what you mean.'

'You are helping the Russians in this military operation against America. Your parents are Russian—'

'My father's Estonian.'

'They were both citizens of the Soviet Union. Therefore, I have to ask, Dr Walker, because our viewers will want to know, what your loyalties are to Russia?'

Every muscle in Carrie's face seemed to stiffen. Her eyes sharpened. Stephanie remembered one evening when they got drunk together while she was splitting from Harry. Carrie told how she dealt with whatever operating-theater shit was thrown at her. Stay focused. No crying in surgery. Keep punching on. That was what she delivered now, upfront and personal to the anchor: 'How do you feel about promoting an enemy state while drawing your seven-figure salary behind your studio presenter's desk?'

'Excuse me, Dr Walker!' The anchor looked stunned.

'Your network has just given Russia millions of dollars of free publicity.'

'That's not the—'

'Yes, it is!'

'Dr Walker, I have to—'

'Don't you dare cut me off! I'm here because I was ordered at gunpoint to go on air to tell your audience what I've seen and done. And you consorted with Moscow—'

'What I meant was—'

'Your question was phrased to imply that I was being unpatriotic.'

'I appreciate it must be stressful—'

'You asked if I felt right about supporting the enemy.'

'Yes, I did.' The anchor recovered her composure, but only for a second.

'I feel fine about it. And I'll tell you what's happening next. In the next few minutes I'm being ordered into a Russian helicopter with Admiral Vitruk to fly three miles across to Big Diomede to help in an operation to drain fluid from the brain of a one-day-old United States citizen. Why don't you keep your cameras rolling, and ask your audience if they want President Swain to comply with your definition of patriotism and shoot our aircraft down?'

'There's that bit of intel we wanted,' said Harry, as the newscast switched to a commercial break. 'Vitruk protects himself by taking Dr Carrie Walker with him.' Harry held Stephanie's coat to help her into it. She took it from him and did it herself.

'Tell me I'm wrong,' she said. 'By painting Carrie a traitor, they're making her expendable.'

'Yes. They won't touch her on this flight. But if they choose to strike later and the casualty cost is limited to, say, eighty Eskimos and a traitor, then yes, they could get away with it.'

'That would be Holland, not Swain,' said Stephanie.

'Don't underestimate Swain.'

They walked to the entrance. Harry opened the door to a blast of cold night air. To her surprise, he kissed her lightly on the lips, then hugged her. 'It's good working with you again, Madam Ambassador. We'll fix it, you and I.'

STEPHANIE WALKED INTO THE Oval Office where Swain's advisors were watching her Prime Minister address shift-change workers on the New Jersey docks. The television shot was stunning, Slater raising his arms, turning to the Statue of Liberty, the camera moving from the Manhattan skyline to the transfixed expressions of his audience. Slater stood next to Jeff Walsh, the union leader she had met at that dinner that now seemed so long ago. They looked like two ageing revolutionaries, brothers in arms, voices for the forgotten and ignored.

When Slater had suggested that he make this speech, she'd thought it a crazy idea. If his task was to rally support in Europe, why would a British Prime Minister make his case to American dockworkers in the middle of the night? Why not do it with a few discreet phone calls?

But she was wrong. Slater had warmed them up and they looked as if they were hanging on his every word. He spoke about the universal aspiration of mankind, a bond that no one nation could break. 'A bond forged by working men and women, like you, not jumped-up politicians seeking a cause for war.' A single wolf whistle was picked up by others to create cheering applause. 'Way to go, Kev,' came a shout, followed by another. 'Right on, Europe.' Slater wrapped his arm around Walsh. 'Shoulder to shoulder. Shoulder to shoulder,' he shouted, and the chant ran like a Mexican wave with fists pummeling the air, dockers linking arms and the camera director skillfully picking out the faces of firemen, police, paramedics, the civilian heroes who kept people safe.

'And my message to the Russians on Alaska is clear and direct,' Slater continued as the cheering subsided. 'Leave, and leave now. Leave and be free.' Sleet across lamps, breath on faces, the camera moved from him to the crowd, the stamping of feet, the raising of arms. No one else could have pulled it off as Slater had. She disagreed with just about all his policies, but she had never heard a finer orator or seen a more skillful working of a crowd.

'And to my colleagues in Europe . . .' Slater was saying as Stephanie's phone lit up, a message from Harry. She read it and looked up, stunned and afraid. Prusak was on the phone too, his eyes on the television. The Defense Secretary took a call. A moment later, the Secretary of State did the same. The Chairman of the Joint Chiefs of Staff took two fast steps to the Oval Office desk. 'Sir, they're saying we shot down another Russian heli-copter.'

'Who's saying?' said Swain.

'Tin City radar station picking up Russian military traffic. It's the one Dr Carrie Walker was on.'

Stephanie re-read Harry's message – *Vitruk's helicopter down.* A Moscow number on Stephanie's phone lit up. Sergey Grizlov.

TWENTY-EIGHT

Little Diomede, Alaska, USA

Ten minutes earlier, wedged into cover just above the ice-floe edge, Rake had fixed a rocket-propelled grenade on a launcher, hoping to hell he wouldn't have to use it. If he did, he would need to destroy the approaching helicopter with one shot because he doubted he would have time for a second. Smoke from the grenade propulsion would expose his position. The trick with this weapon was to fire and move. But the only place he could go was onto the sea ice, where he would be a perfect target for the helicopter's fire power. He wished the helicopter crew would adhere to basic military rules and stay at least four hundred meters away from the hillside and out of range of an RPG or assault rifle. At that distance, thermal imaging would only create confusion and they would have difficulty spotting him. But those were rules for regular troops, and these were special forces whose mission must be to kill or capture him. The weather was clear too, and there were stars, the moon, and clarity of vision. If he were them, he would take the risk and come closer.

His analysis was right. The Russian helicopter flew around the north edge of the island and followed contours that rose almost straight up. At one point, the aircraft was so near that its rotor-blade draught ripped away the snow that gave him cover. Rake could see outline figures of soldiers inside. He counted four, but there would be others. The helicopter pulled away, climbed like an elevator, then began a slow vertical descent for the real search. Floodlamps lit the landscape that men would be scouring with trained eyes. Thermal imaging would pinpoint him. He could only stay hidden for so long, a minute, probably less. Within a few seconds of them spotting him, he would be dead.

Rake steadied the launcher against his shoulder and adjusted the sight. The crosswinds were well over ten miles an hour, which skewed his chances of a first good hit. He needed to allow for helicopter draught too, and that changed from moment to moment. He made ready the second grenade just in case. He scanned the landscape, checking for cover out on the ice. At about seventy-five meters, he thought he saw an ice wall. This was a glass-half-full view of the world, the part of Rake's character that Carrie said she found attractive, the belief that he might be alive enough to take another shot if he failed with the first, might even make it out to new cover on the ice.

Rake waited, letting the aircraft get closer, gauging the wind, judging distance, what the enemy could see. Then, when the helicopter was less than a hundred meters off the hillside, the arc of the lamps sweeping down towards him, Rake tightened his finger on the trigger. The fuel tank would have the most impact. But he needed the fattest target area and the fuel was in the tail, too slender. He tilted the launcher up, waited a beat longer; it turned out to be a beat too long. Heavy machine-gun fire smashed into the hillside above him. Rounds sparked off rock. Snow sprayed across his goggles. It was random firing, to flush him out, but the next burst could cut him in two.

Rake fired.

A huge cloud of blue and gray smoke enveloped him and trailed out towards the aircraft. His position was exposed. Rake loaded the next grenade while expecting a wall of hot lead to cut into him.

Nothing came.

His shot hit the underbelly, violently tilting the aircraft backward. He fired again. More blue and gray smoke, and the fuselage peeled open like a can. Flames spread back toward the tail. The aircraft rolled away. As the pilot tried to keep control, it lurched the other way, and that was when he saw a flash of blonde hair. Carrie turned towards the window, its glass blackening with fire, her eyes dark with terror.

Rake dropped the grenade launcher into the snow. How he could have done that? Why hadn't he thought? That's how their twisted minds would work; use a civilian as bait. Then why didn't they make her more visible? If he'd seen her, he'd never have . . .

A shrieking whine came from the stricken aircraft. The rear rotor blades stopped dead. Flames encased the tail. The fuselage was torn and the pilot had no rear power. He would only have a few seconds left in the air, to hunt for the safest glide angle, struggling to stop a lethal spin.

Rake scrambled out of the crevice onto the sea. The ice was patchy as if walrus had been there, their body warmth melting it. Thick broken ice sheets floated in channels of dark water. The pilot managed to get the nose up, but there was no way the aircraft could get back to base. A soldier smashed his rifle butt through a cracked window. Rake ran out into full view, jumping over weak ice patches. He moved unpredictably to avoid being a target, but deliberately made himself visible to show the pilot where the thickest ice was, the safest place to crash land. The ice around them was weak. It got stronger bit by bit further north, not far, maybe half a mile. Rake pointed and gave the pilot a thumbs down. *Bad here.* He raised both arms, hands vertical like parallel blades, slicing them down repeatedly towards the north. *Good there. Trust me.*

The pilot powered the blades, pitching the nose up like a rearing stallion, the tail ablaze, wild flames dancing, reflected on the ice. Rake glimpsed Carrie again. She looked at him, rigid, focused, her terror gone. 'So sorry,' he mouthed. 'I love you.' It was ridiculous. She wouldn't hear, couldn't lip-read it from that distance. Could she even see him; would she understand? But he had to do it, because in a few seconds she could be dead. Her expression didn't change.

The pilot gave his wounded aircraft a final burst of speed, then cut the engine, letting the blades rotate freely in the air to give more stability. It kept going forward, foot by foot, but not far enough. Either he could try to reach stronger ice and risk a mid-air explosion. Or he could take a chance and crash-land on weaker ice. Rake watched him conduct a work of art. The pilot brought the helicopter down so that the burning tail brushed the ice to dampen the fire to try to stop it catching the fuel tank. Some flames were extinguished, but not all. Then he could hold it no longer. He levelled out and the skids settled heavily on the ice.

Rake unclipped a radio from his belt and called through, knowing that both sides would pick up: 'Tin City. Tin City. This is Captain Rake Ozenna. Do not intervene in aircraft activity on northern edge of Little Diomede. Repeat – do not intervene. Russian aircraft is down with casualties. This is a humanitarian operation. Let Russia handle it.'

'Copy that,' came the American voice across the crackling channel.

A BLADE OF WIND CUT through a smashed window into Carrie's face. A soldier opposite was slumped, his foot shredded by shrapnel that had torn up from under them. She couldn't tell if he was even alive. Another had his hands clasped over his eyes, and blood streaming out from between his fingers. Chilled air mixed with tail-fire heat sent warmth and cold into the cabin.

'Out! Now!' Vitruk shouted.

She unclipped her seatbelt just as the helicopter jolted, throwing her against Vitruk. It stabilized, then with a scraping of metal the ice gave way, and the side of the aircraft fell through. A spray of frozen water flew up into her face, unforgiving and brutal.

Vitruk slid the door far enough back to climb out. He reached down and pulled Carrie to him, gripping her arm as she started back towards the burning wreckage. 'The wounded!' she shouted.

'Get back. Further!' yelled Vitruk.

The pilot was out, guiding them to a firmer area he had

identified twenty meters away. Soldiers stumbled from the wreckage. They carried two wounded colleagues and brought them to Carrie. The one with the injured foot had bled out. He was dead. The other would live, though probably blinded. Carrie recognized the faraway throbbing of an engine which became louder as three helicopters reached them from the base. Their floodlamps lit up the survivors. She could see Rake still there, a tiny distant solitary figure, so far away that he was long out of small-arms range. Vitruk's gaze was on him too. An incoming helicopter snapped on more lights and broke away towards him.

A jagged piece of shrapnel protruded from the eyes of the wounded soldier. They lowered him onto a thermal blanket. Iced blood was hardening on his face. His teeth chattered violently, pushing the embedded metal towards his brain.

'He needs to get to the base!' Carrie opened her medical bag to give him a shot of morphine. Suddenly, alarm spread across Vitruk's face and without warning he hurled himself against Carrie, bringing her down. Her face was pressed hard into the ice, cold stinging her skin, Vitruk's weight on top of her. She heard a high shrill whine of wind that at first sounded like a gust kicking up surface snow. But it was the fuel tank of their helicopter exploding. A fireball rose into the air, throwing a hot cloud of aviation vapor over them, and a plume of thick black choking smoke, laced with orange flame, that faded and was taken by the wind. When Vitruk finally let her up, she turned to her surviving patient, but didn't have to check his heartbeat to know that he too was dead.

Four soldiers stood up, readied weapons, adjusted snowshoes, and set off to find Rake on the wasteland of cold that stretched out endlessly in front of them.

RAKE CONCENTRATED ON CARRIE. From where he stood, he could see that she was alive and seemed uninjured, scrambling away from the crashed helicopter. Then came the fuel-tank blast which hid her in smoke. Then it cleared and he watched her get up. She put her glove to her face in what looked like a regular frostbite check after skin contact with ice. She examined a patient. Carrie was doing what she did best, being fine, being with the wounded.

Then Rake saw four men moving towards him like sentinels, meaning that he was exposed and they knew where he was. He had to get himself into cover.

All he had was a Makarov 9mm pistol and a Vityaz automatic rifle with no reputation for accuracy. Its two-hundred-meter outer range was about where the enemy was now. The rest of the equipment lay scattered on the hillside behind him.

To surrender would be suicide. Russia needed to display his dead body. To his left stood the ice wall he had identified earlier. Over the winter, ice walls grow like snowballs gathering soft snow. Their origins are iceberg slither that appears above the water. Then in gale after gale, water and debris flung against them make them bigger each time. Rake had seen ice walls in many shapes. This one looked low and long, no more than four feet high, but it could extend fifty feet down towards the seabed. He judged it to be at least six-feet wide which was enough to stop a high-velocity small-arms bullet. If he could get there, he might be able to take all four men before another helicopter came close. As he ran towards it, he saw the flash of a shot. It went very wide, probably out of range. That was good. It meant his enemy was angry and impatient.

More gunfire chipped off the top of the wall, spraying ice pellets towards him. He made it to cover and lying flat, elbows embedded in snow, he tried to line up a shot. The wind was erratic and he hadn't sighted the weapon for the cold. His target was moving too quickly, but if he could not make a kill now, it would mean close-quarter fighting. They weren't far away, but they had separated and were approaching from both sides. Even he wasn't good enough to take them all. He didn't know a man who could.

Rake did not pull the trigger. His finger was not even inside the trigger guard. But bullets tore into one soldier's face, destroying the head and sending out webs of blood as he fell to the ground. A second soldier, although thirty yards away, died in exactly the same way. A sniper's shot. The two surviving soldiers ran towards him, firing at the same time. Their bullets smashed uselessly into the wall. A third soldier was hit in the legs, his screams shrill and haunting like those of any young men suddenly wounded.

Rake heard the low-pitched whine of a snowmobile coming fast from the east. The fourth soldier flattened himself on the ground.

In camouflage, Arctic white, the snowmobile was military issue. From the tone, it would have carried a 1,000-cc engine, and could be moving at sixty, maybe seventy miles an hour, slowing to navigate an ice hazard, then speeding up again. The driver looped around checking each of his targets and signaling Rake to keep the fourth soldier covered. Rake tensed, trigger poised, but the Russian surrendered. The driver took his weapons, stood him up and pointed for him to walk back to his people. The soldier obeyed. Whoever this was, he was alone; he didn't want prisoners, but he didn't kill for the sake of it.

The snowmobile approached and Rake saw the driver was encased in the full skin of a polar bear. It would have weighed more than fifty pounds, but Don Ondola carried it with no more effort than an overcoat. The last time Rake had seen Ondola he was in court and Rake stood as character witness. There wasn't a lot to say when a man got drunk, killed his wife, and raped his daughter, although that last one wasn't even on the charge sheet. Ondola might be the finest outdoorsman in Alaska. He might have saved Rake's life the day Tuuq left him to die in Uelen. But drink is drink, murder is murder, and the law's the law. He had asked Rake only one favor and that was send him the polar-bear hide in prison.

Ondola pulled up next to Rake, got down, and lifted the skin. His face was thin, skin stretched and creased with a grin. 'They said I could find you out here,' he said, as if bumping into Rake in the village. 'How you doing, Rake?' A gloomy mist swept along the ground. Lights from the Russian troops were blurred, and the beams of floodlamps splayed and bounced off the whiteness.

Cluttered with gear, filled with appreciation, Rake embraced him. 'So, you brought the marines across from the mainland?' he asked.

Ondola nodded. 'They're on standby. They've been told to stay put.'

A siren started up from near the crashed Russian wreckage. Both men watched through binoculars. A medical helicopter hovered inches above the ice. Two bodies were lifted on board. Carrie climbed up, followed by the commander and others. The door slid shut and the aircraft turned quickly and flew nose-down, low and fast, towards the Russian base.

Rake and Ondola didn't have long. The Russians would come for them again, with more men and aircraft.

'You heading across there?' asked Ondola.

'Those are my orders unless they sent you here to tell me different.'

'They didn't send me, Rake.' Ondola fidgeted with his weapon. 'I split. I'm not going back to prison.'

'You'll be running all your life.' Many times, Rake had tried reasoning with Ondola, but his brain wasn't wired like that.

This time, Ondola pre-empted him. 'Up here,' he flattened his hand on his head, 'I don't think straight and I do bad things. Only place I'm any good is out here in the wild.' His mind might be tortured, but his face was calm and, given what he had just done, he seemed untroubled. 'I heard Akna's over there, with a baby.'

'She is.' Rake scanned the landscape.

'I'll get you there,' said Ondola.

Rake glanced at the snowmobile. 'No chance with this.'

'No. They'd cut us down. I brought more skins.'

The best camouflage on the ice was animal skin, seal, walrus, polar bear. No synthetic material matched it. Ondola took a collapsible sled from the back of the vehicle.

'Go back,' said Rake. 'It's not worth it.'

'I need to see Akna. Tell her I'm sorry.'

The ice was harsh, shimmering, with shades of contrasting gray, white, and darkness. It reminded him of a burning hot desert in Iraq. 'They sent Nikki to get me,' said Rake.

'Nikki Tuuq? Is he out here?'

'Yes. Somewhere. I saw him with Timo.'

Ondola pulled a magazine from his weapon as if checking it. 'How is Timo?' he asked softly. Timo was Akna's half-brother. Ondola had raised him like his own son until the night he killed Akna's mother.

'Timo's fine. Henry's watching over him now.'

'Henry wants me dead.'

They lifted the skins onto the sled. Rake wanted to say more, to persuade Ondola to serve his time so he could walk free and try to get better. But not here. Not now. And besides, Ondola's mind was set.

'Can I beat Nikki Tuuq?' asked Rake.

'You can't,' said Ondola. 'Not alone. Nikki's too good. You'll need my help.'

TWENTY-NINE

The British Ambassador's residence, Washington, DC

Stephanie stepped across the checkered black and white tiled floor of her residence, suddenly filled with nostalgia. By God, she had held some strained meetings here, lavish parties too, but nothing compared to what was about to unfold. She weaved through ornate gold pillars and headed to the dining room, stopping abruptly at the entrance.

Harry had called her moments after Carrie's helicopter went down. She was replying to Sergey Grizlov's message that asked her to get back to him as soon as possible. It wasn't his usual number. She dialed, but it rang out. No reply. No voicemail.

Then Harry's call interrupted. He had received information connected to Vitruk from the Japanese intelligence community. It was complicated. They must meet, and he needed a secure place to operate, somewhere to coordinate private, government, home, and foreign intelligence, completely off the books if need be. They had swapped suggestions. Harry's apartment was fine for a visit, but it wouldn't work for what was needed now. His was in an unsecured office block in Crystal City, near the Pentagon, where many defense companies were based. The

Pentagon, the White House, and any other government property would be impossible because of government control. Securing and sweeping a hotel suite would take too long. Harry suggested Stephanie's place, the British Ambassador's residence, which she immediately queried: 'You said off the books. This is British government property.'

'British books ain't American books,' Harry said, and Stephanie had agreed.

From his time in the military and on Congressional committees, Harry's contacts in the global defense world were second to none. He was trusted, known to return favors and to keep his word. Stephanie spoke to Slater who, to her surprise, immediately gave her the go-ahead.

Now, standing in the doorway of her elegant dining room, Stephanie was amazed at how quickly Harry had turned this museum piece area into something resembling the planning center of a military boot camp. The long graceful table, usually set for thirty, was covered in maps, diagrams, phones, and laptops. Four men worked around the table, wearing ID passes around their necks. Two marker boards hung on either side of the tall marble mantelpiece, one with calculations, the other with a list of countries with red, green, and white crosses next to them. 'We're trying to build up support,' said Harry as he weaved round the table towards her. 'The more intel we muster, the safer it will be.'

'Explain,' she said impatiently. 'And keep it simple.' Stephanie still had no idea what 'it' was, except it had come via the Japanese.

'You were right, Steph, on the Cuban missile crisis comparison. If this intel is correct, Moscow is making a similar play, except this time using Asia as the theater of confrontation.'

A flush of anxiety hit Stephanie as she thought of Grizlov's message. Was he warning her? Was it the first step in a negotiation? If so, why didn't he pick up? Back in the Sixties, she hadn't even been born. But her father rarely stopped talking about the thirteen days when the world came to the brink of nuclear war. One of her first memories was him carrying her down to the basement of his scrappy used-car showroom to acquaint her with his bomb shelter and shelves of provisions.

Harry flattened his hand on a map on the table which showed East Asia, running from the east coast of India to Hawaii. 'The Japanese have a long-time intelligence asset at the Sinuiju border crossing between North Korea and China,' he said.

'You mean an agent, a spy?'

'Yes, I do. And a couple of hours after the Bering Strait kicked off, three sports utility vehicles, a black BMW, a white Toyota, and a gray Chinese-made Chana, followed by a white Kia truck, passed through that border. The convoy's VIP status meant that no papers were needed. Identities, even the number of passengers, were not logged. The vehicle windows were blackened. But the Japanese asset managed to look through the surveillance video. He found what I regard as intelligence gold dust.'

Questions tumbled through Stephanie's mind, but she held them back. She was crying out for the top line, but this was how Harry operated. He built blocks of evidence so that his conclusion would not be questioned. North Korea was a dynastic dictatorship, a buffer state between authoritarian China and democratic South Korea, that controlled the thoughts and movements of twenty-five million people, ran labor camps for tens of thousands, executed people with abandon, and had dodged just about every international sanction to develop a nuclear weapons system. Whether it would work or not was anybody's guess. But the bombs were there, and the Trump presidency had brought things to crisis point. North Korea was China's ally. But the big question was: why was Harry telling her and not his own people?

Harry continued, 'For a few seconds, as the BMW pulled away onto that bridge into North Korea, the driver's window came down and a cigarette butt was dropped onto the road. The hand that held it was white. The agent enhanced the pixels enough to ascertain that in the front passenger seat was another Caucasian, about fifty, with spectacles, his head slightly turned towards the camera. Defense Intelligence Headquarters in Tokyo identified the passenger as Dmitri Alverov, aged fifty-two, designer of ballistic missile re-entry vehicles. Alverov works at the Moscow Institute of Thermal Technology and has been photographed twice in Votkinsk, the factory eight hundred miles east of Moscow where the Topol-M missile is made. This is Russia's most lethal long-range ballistic missile. It's not Alverov's first visit to North Korea. He was there from October 7th to 18th last year when he visited the Toksong nuclear weapons facility, which is three hundred miles north-east of Pyongyang.'

Harry pointed to it on the map, tracing a route down from the North Korea–China border to the capital Pyongyang and then looping up again to the nuclear site at Toksong, reminding Stephanie how Russia, China, North and South Korea, and Japan all got crushed together in this part of the world. The Sunuiju crossing lay at the south-west end of the border. She shifted her finger to the north-east, inadvertently brushing Harry's hand.

'Why didn't they bring it in here?' she asked. 'The direct crossing between Russia and North Korea. No need to involve China.'

'That's only a rail crossing. Vitruk would need the flexibility of road transport, which is why he sought Chinese help.'

'On Alverov's first crossing, was the vehicle window up or down?'

'We missed him at the border, but why?'

'They could have thrown out the cigarette butt anywhere. They have ashtrays in the vehicle. So why bring the window down here, where they know they're being watched? Were nuclear scientists being absent-minded? God forbid! Or did they want us to know they were going through? And if they did, why?'

'And, of course, you have a theory.'

'Yes, if we run with our Cuban missile analogy. Kennedy knew the Russian naval ships were on their way to Cuba and that was the beginning of the negotiations. If Moscow wants a deal, far better to start talking now than when the missile has been readied for launch. Unless, of course, it's a bluff.'

'No.' Harry shook his head. 'They couldn't bluff on something like this.'

She tapped the China side of the border. 'Isn't this the Shenyang Military District?'

'It is,' said Harry. 'Run by the same General Bu Zishan whom Vitruk lavishly entertained last year.'

'And would he need Beijing's authorization to let the Russian team through?'

'No. He has a lot of independence.'

'Would Vitruk need authorization?'

'Alverov and the Institute of Thermal Technology are in the

Volga Military District. The commander there is a rival to Vitruk and an ally of Sergey Grizlov. So, yes; my guess is that Vitruk would need to reach out, beyond his arc of control.'

Which meant that Vitruk's operation must have been sanctioned by Lagutov; not just Little Diomede, but, if Harry's intel was right, ratcheting it all the way to nuclear confrontation. The timing of Grizlov's message suggested this was the case. Stephanie checked her phone to see if he had messaged again. Nothing. 'Grizlov tried to contact me.'

'I know.'

And how the hell did he know that? He must be plugged directly into the highest classification of signals intelligence. 'Explain, please.' Stephanie shifted her weight and looked him straight in the eye. 'No, forget that. First give me your overall conclusion as to what you think is going on.'

'If we were not dealing with the Bering Strait crisis—'

'But we are—' Stephanie began.

Harry cut her off. 'If we were not, my analysis would be that a rogue Russian team was showing North Korea how to build a long-range missile that can avoid US counter-measures. But since, as you say, we are, I have to assume that an authorized Russian team is assembling a missile in North Korea with the intention of launching it against the United States, or at least threatening to.'

'Hence the Cuban comparison.'

'Install your missiles with a proxy, then negotiate away the American missiles in Europe.'

'The Soviet missiles never got to Cuba. The Topol-M is already in North Korea.'

'That's why I needed to talk to you first. The transition, Steph, in particular the acrimony between Holland and Swain, is leaking like a gas can peppered with gunshot. Holland's people brief against Swain, Swain's against Holland. Ten thousand experienced staffers are clearing their desks at State and Defense alone, all looking for new jobs. We cannot afford to share this through the usual channels.'

She understood where he was coming from, but it wouldn't work. Harry was always the impatient wild card that tore up the rule book. Sensible Stephanie reined him in.

'No,' she said, dialing Prusak. 'You need to brief the President.'

'Didn't you hear me, Steph? I'm not briefing because it will leak. And how to explain the source of my intel? What reputation do I have? A failed congressman from a rival party who quit because he couldn't hold his drink and keep his marriage together?'

Stephanie paused the dialing and put her phone on the table like a peace offering. Harry pointed at the men working in the room. 'These are my guys, but they're here privately, OK? If I bring my business direct to the Oval Office, half my clients will melt away.'

'You brief the President as Harry Lucas, chief executive of—' She stopped as she momentarily forgot the name of his company. Harry let her struggle for a few seconds, half-amused that she had been caught out. Stephanie picked up. 'Your reputation speaks for itself. Just do it, for Christ's sake.'

'You do it.'

'I can't, I'm British.'

'The way this is going down, you might as well be a Mongolian pagan dancer.'

Stephanie didn't mean to, but triggered by the tension and the outlandish image conjured up by Harry, she laughed, a real belly laugh. It had been the pattern of their marriage; where his mood hardened, she would react, and at the height of their anger, he would come up with a ridiculous line that cracked her up.

'Sorry. Yeah. I forgot,' said Harry, chuckling too. 'We're not married anymore so we don't have to yell at each other.'

'You've still got your cute side.' She took his hand and squeezed it. 'If all this fails, Swain, me and Slater are the scapegoats. It's not right, but you know how these things work. No one will know you're involved.'

His face opened, resistance gone. 'OK. You win. I'll do it, and tell Matt to get Frank Ciszewski over from Langley.'

Good. She had won him round. They understood enough of each other's minds to know that this was far bigger than the two of them. But as Harry was unhooking his coat from a stand by the door, he announced a counter-deal. 'I need something from you.' He put on his coat, keeping his eyes on Stephanie. It wasn't a sexual look, as he used to give her. He was studying her, measuring her, playing a thought through his mind, until deciding what to do with it. He handed her a phone. 'Afterward, try Sergey Grizlov on this. It's registered to Narva on the Russia–Estonia border. He won't know it's you, so he'll likely pick up.'

'But—'

'No buts, Steph. Like you say, just do it. I know it wasn't just one night with him, Steph. It was a full-blown affair. He'll tell you more than he'll tell anyone else. When you speak to him, just ask him outright what the fuck is going on.'

His suggestion was simple and brilliant. For some inexplicable reason, as she wondered what she would say and why Grizlov should reveal anything to her, Stephanie felt her heart pound. Harry was reading her mind. 'I've been tracking him. For what it's worth, I know he still holds a candle for you.'

THIRTY

The White House, Washington, DC

A smell of coffee and pizza hung in the Oval Office. Suits were crumpled, faces unshaven, eyes red and focused. By the time Harry and Stephanie arrived everyone, including Holland, was there and Swain was ending a call with the Chinese President. 'He's refusing to condemn the Russian occupation of Little Diomede,' he said to the room. 'He referred to it as a routine border dispute and raised our issue with them over the South China Sea.'

'We could take out their South China Sea positions in half an hour,' said Holland.

'Then what?' said Swain dismissively. 'Fight wars on two fronts?' He addressed Stephanie. 'New Jersey was a work of art, Ambassador. I must ask the Prime Minister to lend me your speech writer.'

'That would be him, sir, and he's on his way to London now.'

'So, is Europe with us?'

'Depends how many more aircraft get shot down. It'll hold for a day or two. After that, as always, Europe will fracture.'

Swain turned his attention to Harry. 'Good to see you, Harry. What've you got for us?'

Harry told it exactly as he had to Stephanie: the convoy, the Japanese agent, the camera catching the white forearm, the missile scientist Dmitri Alverov. He ended with Stephanie's question: whether the team wanted to be spotted and if so, why?

Swain gave nothing away. No anger. No apprehension. No surprise. He drank from a plastic bottle of water, and his gaze shifted to two of his trusted security principals, the lean and alert Mike Pacolli from Defense and the rotund and avuncular CIA director Frank Ciszewski. He asked what either of them had that added to or contradicted Harry's analysis.

Pacolli described a North Korean defector who claimed to have worked as an engineer at the Toksong missile site. 'He says it's been expanded a lot since the Trump presidency crisis. It's a large, deep underground facility with four independent silos and launch pads and, from his description, it could have been redesigned to accommodate the Topol-M.'

'Going back over our IMINT,' said Ciszewski, glancing across to Stephanie. 'That's imagery intelligence, Ambassador Lucas. Examining vehicles from known armament factories and matching them with traffic going into Toksong, it is possible that between September 28th and October 7th dismantled parts of a mobile Topol-M were transported to North Korea. That would coincide with Alverov's first visit. Nothing is concrete, sir. We've been at it for an hour. It's a job that should take weeks.'

'That was before the election,' said Prusak. It was a salient observation. In October, a month before voting, the polls were neck and neck, meaning that Russia would have been making contingencies for this operation now regardless of who was in the White House.

'We need to call Lagutov. Tell him to back off,' said Holland.

Being President isn't that simple, thought Stephanie. She caught Harry's eye and checked her phone. It was filled with messages from everywhere, but nothing more from Sergey Grizlov. Prusak saw her, his eye questioning. She shook her head. 'Where is Captain Ozenna?' Swain asked.

'Still alive, but Russian troops are closing in on him,' said Pacolli. 'Since then two have been killed.'

'That man is lethal,' said Holland.

'It may not have been him. Radio traffic indicates that the shooter was the Eskimo tracker from Goose Creek Correctional, Don Ondola. He stole a snowmobile and escaped after guiding our men to Little Diomede.'

'You mean without orders?' Swain raised his eyebrow with a complex expression of anger and respect.

'Essentially, yes,' said Pacolli. 'He's an escaped civilian prisoner.'

'Where is he now?'

'He may be with Ozenna.'

'A damn stupid idea to use either of them,' said Holland. 'We need to get them back and under control.'

Swain ignored him. 'Could they get to the Russian base, and do we still need them there?'

'The base becomes irrelevant, if the North Korea play is real,' said Pacolli.

'It is real, because it's moved into our frame,' said Swain.

If Carrie was still alive, thought Stephanie, she would be at that base now, as were the mother, her baby, and two of her family. That made five American civilians. But would they be safer if Ozenna made it to the base, or if the base were left alone?

Harry spoke, half-answering her question. 'The operation is being run by Alexander Vitruk and right now he is on that base, sir,' he said. 'We don't know exactly what he's doing, but I can tell you this: we can knock a North Korean missile out mid-flight, no problem. But with a Topol-M, we would be up against world's finest long-range ballistic-weapons science in the world. It has a good chance of getting through. So, if we want to stop this, we need to stop Vitruk.'

Harry nailed it hard. In the jugular. Holland stiffened, his face reddening, mouth open but, like an actor who had suddenly forgotten his lines, unsure of what to say. Pacolli and Ciszewski stood with hands clasped, alert, ready, awaiting instructions. Harry bristled with purpose and confidence.

Instead of showing pressure, Swain's face took on an extra-ordinary aura of calm. 'The marine unit remains on standby on the north of the island,' he instructed. 'It only moves in if there is a real fear for the hostages in the school. Tell Ozenna, if you can reach him, that he has a window to complete his mission. If Ondola is with him, use him too.'

Holland found his voice. 'You cannot do this without consul-tation. I will inherit your mess.'

'You have no standing, Bob,' Swain replied softly. 'By calling Beijing, you undermined our national security in the middle of a crisis. But the presidency is bigger than one man, and to see something like this through, a President needs the full support of the American people. Therefore, you should step back and distance yourself from my decisions.'

'But where are these decisions, Mr President?' Holland's tone was laced with sarcasm.

Swain checked his watch. 'It is now just past two in the morning. I will give Ozenna an eight-hour window to get to that base. In that time, we need to establish the existence of the Topol-M and what's going in Moscow. Ambassador, are you able to follow up on your message from Sergey Grizlov?'

'Yes, sir. I'll try,' said Stephanie.

'If we hear nothing from Ozenna and have made no progress by ten o'clock, two hours before the inauguration, I will assume the worst.'

Swain paused as if making sure the choice he had made was right and fully understood. Those receiving his orders were some of the most powerful men and women in the United States. They hung on his next words.

'After the window closes, we will hit the Big Diomede base and, if necessary, risk and sacrifice the hostages in the school.'

THIRTY-ONE

Big Diomede, Chukotka, the Russian Far East

The first helicopter delivered casualties from the crash scene. Carrie flew in on the second one with Vitruk. Head down against driving snow, she walked quickly across to the base's main building. Inside, icicles on her coat melted quickly against a blast of hot air from a wall heater just inside the door.

'Why don't you thank me for saving your life?' Vitruk said, shaking with cold and anger as he took off his coat. Water dripped from his jacket sleeve and collar.

Carrie said nothing.

'The Americans killed eleven of my men,' said Vitruk. 'Russia saved the lives of two Americans.'

'You've said that before,' said Carrie, pressing the skin of her face to check she had feeling everywhere. The skin exposed to cold was on her upper right jaw where her mask had ripped. Feeling was returning, which meant frostbite had not set in.

'The baby is having the hydrocephalus operation now. Fuck you, Dr Walker. Fuck you and all your people.'

'I need to treat the wounded,' said Carrie dismissively. She was damned if she was going to rise to his rage.

'We have our own doctors.'

A soldier came through the swing doors from the control room and handed Vitruk a piece of paper with a single line written on it. Vitruk pulled off his gloves. Melting snow and water pooled on the concrete floor. He spoke curtly, and the soldier went back inside. A heavy vibrating hum came from the apron outside, another helicopter taking off.

'What do you know of Henry Ahkvaluk?' asked Vitruk.

'Nothing. I met him yesterday morning at the helipad.' She lifted her medical bag onto a table and opened it. Everything was in place despite the crash.

'What's his relationship to the girl?'

'Uncle or something. I don't know.'

'Why did he come over here?'

'I wanted to come. Rake wouldn't let me. Henry and Joan volunteered to accompany Akna.'

Two soldiers opened the control-room door. Vitruk walked in, instructing Carrie to follow. It was more crowded than before. Men were on edge, the light dimmer. Blue and green splayed from screens onto faces. She took in the television feeds – maps, anchors, the Fed building rubble, the Russian parliament, Little Diomede. She stepped through a short passageway of cold, then into the warmth of the field hospital.

Three beds were taken by soldiers. One was dead, his face covered with a sheet that wasn't long enough to go over his boots. On the next, a nurse treated a man for a cut to the head and a gash on his right hand. He must have been the one who hit the ground to avoid the gunman. On the last bed, closest to the door, lay the one whose legs had been shot. He had curly dark hair and bit on a cotton pad against the pain, his young face contorted, eyes squeezed closed. He didn't utter a sound.

On the other side of the hospital tent, a surgeon and nurse worked inside a sanitized area, screened off with translucent heavy-duty plastic. Little Iyaroak's life must be hanging by a thread.

'They're finishing. The surgeon thinks it's a success.' Vitruk pointed to Joan Ahkvaluk, whom Carrie hadn't noticed because she was obscured by the plastic screen on an upright chair against the wall. Vitruk's expression was strained, his eyes immobile, fixed on Carrie. 'Her husband has escaped. You need to speak to her.'

Carrie shivered at the thought of anyone being outside, alone and unprotected. Joan's hands rested on her knees, her wrists handcuffed together, her eyes closed.

'Joan, it's Carrie.'

Joan looked up. Her face carried a confidence that Carrie rarely saw in a woman, total calm even though her husband would be in extreme danger.

'I need to—' Carrie began.

'Don't do their work.' Joan lifted her arms to put a finger to her lips. 'Henry has gone. That is all I know.'

'I know,' said Carrie. 'But all this is out of our control.'

'This is our land. It is in our control.'

Carrie squeezed her hand and walked back to Vitruk. 'How did he get out?'

'Our carelessness.'

'She has no idea where he is.'

'That's not the point.'

'What is the point?'

Two soldiers lifted Joan from her seat and unlocked her cuffs.

'We're going out again,' said Vitruk.

A dread of the dark, cold, and wind enveloped Carrie. Joan, a soldier each side, walked ahead, silent and composed. Water was still running down Carrie's coat as she put it back on.

'We won't be long.' Vitruk's voice was empty, eyes dark with resolve.

A sub-zero wind tore across Carrie's face as she stepped out. Her eyes streamed and she struggled to adjust her goggles. Six soldiers led them down a path beside the main building towards the shoreline. In less than a minute the wind died and there was clarity. A soft moon cast a grayish-white light over a landscape peppered with odd shapes. It was such a different one from the one Carrie had left not long ago. Without the wind, it was as if she could see for miles.

Some of the ice was smooth, polished, and reflecting light like globes. Other parts were jagged and black where dirty sea water had been thrown up by gusts and instantly frozen. The most dominant in front of her was a wall of ice about fifty meters from the shore. It must have been twelve-feet high and thirty-feet long. Rake had once explained how it would have built up over weeks from wind shear created by the island's hills. A concrete pier jutted out towards it from the shore.

'The Eskimo took advantage of our helicopter casualties,' Vitruk shouted close to her right ear. 'He offered help. We brought him out here. Fog hit and he escaped. The Eskimo woman will find him for us.'

A soldier unlocked Joan's cuffs and pinned a GPS tracker to

her coat. Another soldier walked out to the pier, laid down a white mat, then set a rifle on a bipod and adjusted its telescopic sight. Another did the same to the left of where they were. Two more snipers set up on the roof of the building behind them.

'Mrs Ahkvaluk,' said Vitruk. 'You will walk out so your husband sees you. You will beckon him in. If he does not appear, one of my men will wound you, first in the arm, then in the leg. If he doesn't come then, you will know he is not worthy to be your husband. We will collect you, and Dr Walker will treat your wounds. My men are skilled. You have nothing to fear except pain. Do you understand?'

'You cannot do this!' shouted Carrie.

'Let him,' said Joan. 'He will not see me again.'

Vitruk signaled his men. Two took Joan's arm and led her down the pier. She walked smoothly, her steps skillfully working the unevenness of the frozen surface. Seamlessly, the end of the pier became a boulder of ice. The soldiers let go her arms. Without looking back, Joan walked. Once she leant down, using her hands to lower herself from a rock. After that she kept going, looping to the left of the ice wall.

'Henry Ahkvaluk knows the layout of this base,' said Vitruk as they watched Joan's figure get smaller and smaller. 'I can't afford to let him get to the other side.'

'Then why bring him here?' said Carrie. 'Why bring any of us here?'

'Take a look.' Vitruk handed her his binoculars. They powerfully magnified Joan in an aura of black and green, defining her against the landscape.

'Two o'clock to her right. Do you see?'

There was someone moving forward, right arm outstretched, breaking into a run. For sure it wasn't Rake. He was too tall. It had to be Henry. Carrie remembered what Rake had said, that Joan and Henry were one of the few intact married couple on Little Diomede. Now, trying to meet on the ice, they were both running towards their own deaths.

'Bring him in,' she told Vitruk. 'And watch over him properly this time. Do not shoot him.'

'He's too dangerous. He knows too much.'

'Bullshit,' screamed Carrie. A soldier grabbed her wrist and brought her left arm up hard behind her back, causing excruciating pain. The moon, low in the sky, cast a shadow from Joan, long and gray, that moved by her side. Bleak desolation stretched from horizon to horizon. There was none of Rake's romance, only a terrifying deadness that killed those who challenged it.

Carrie wished Joan would vanish into one of the fog patches that floated around her. Instead, she stopped. She held up both hands like a traffic cop telling Henry to go back. Vitruk spoke to the closest sniper, lying a few yards from them. He gave orders in his radio.

'No!' yelled Carrie, her arms pinned to her side by a soldier.

Vitruk barked an order. Orange flames from an exploding cartridge leapt from the breach of the rifle.

THIRTY-TWO

Big Diomede, Chukotka, the Russian Far East

To Vitruk, the way the night-vision lenses conflated the image looked as if his soldier had fired a second shot from the pier.

That wasn't the case.

The soldier was killed by a shot that came from out of the ice.

There was no convulsion, no arterial blood. The bullet came in at the top of the neck and severed the spinal cord. The body slumped instantly and lost life. Only a handful of men in the world could make such a shot. Vitruk had seen it only once before. He moved back just before another bullet struck the ground exactly where he had been standing. The second sniper looked up to sight the target. He was shot in the face.

'Take her in,' ordered Vitruk. Carrie was dragged to cover between the two buildings. Vitruk stayed exposed, moving back and forth so quickly that no marksman would get a shot. He looked for human movement and saw none.

A soldier ran up to him. Coming to a standstill, clicking his heels, he handed him a note. 'Sir, urgent—' He was about to salute when Vitruk hurled his body weight against him, throwing them both to the ground. A shot smashed into the wall behind them and, through a tiny flash, he thought saw the location of the trigger.

'Floodlamps,' he shouted. The wall of ice lit up like castle ramparts. Vitruk signaled toward the roofs of the two buildings. 'Field of fire along the top.'

Each building had a 76mm anti-aircraft unit and two Kord 12.7mm heavy machine guns. There was a deafening roar of large-caliber gunfire. Snow chunks broke away like exploding masonry. Ice spun into the air. Mist mixed with gun smoke as layer after layer was peeled off. No one caught in that onslaught of lead could survive.

'Hold fire.'

Through binoculars he saw the marksman.

'The ridge.'

Two bursts of machine-gun fire slammed into the target. Vitruk swept the wider area through his night vision. There was no Joan Ahkvaluk out there; no husband. They would be next. But he had the sniper. He checked the mutilated top of the ice wall again and didn't expect what he saw. He looked with his naked eye, patch by bullet-torn patch, to make sure he was missing nothing. He checked again through the binoculars. A shape lay flat and skewed from the gunfire. But this wasn't a gunman. It was the skin of a wild animal, blended in with the ice. Staring directly at him like a calling card was the black skull of a dead polar bear. The killer had gone.

A heat of fury ran through him. He knew only one man who could have achieved what this marksman had, and he was Nikita Tuuq. Yet this was someone as good, probably better. Both were out there, which meant that Tuuq was compromised. Vitruk pushed himself to his feet and banged his gloved hands together. Should he summon back Tuuq, who would have gone to ground? His phone and radio would be off. They had a system of emergency flares. Red for recall. Orange for standby. Green for proceed to the kill.

Vitruk shared his soldiers' own anger. So many hours into the operation and he had achieved little except the death of his men. Another two comrades were dead. Just over an hour ago, three more had died, two on the ice and one in hospital. The helicopter shot down, the six men on the top of the American island. It was a stream of catastrophe, the reality of war.

'Sir—' The soldier he had saved clambered up next to him. 'Thank you, sir.'

Vitruk read the note. It was from the Kremlin.

'They want you now, sir. In the communications room.'

Vitruk gave orders to check the ice wall, but to leave the bodies where they were. He would examine the trajectory of the two lethal shots which had avoided the soldiers' Kevlar vests. He walked back inside the main building and, without taking off his coat, headed down steep spiral stairs into the old nuclear bunker sixty meters beneath the ground. It was a high-ceilinged chamber hewn out of the granite, the sides cylindrically curved like the hull of a ship and sealed with reinforced lead and concrete to protect hundreds of troops. Moisture dripped because of the outdated ventilation. The door to the communications room was open. He pulled out a chair and opened a bottle of water. A technician left, closing the door behind him.

'Alexander, are you there?' Lagutov's voice was hesitant and tired.

'Yes, sir.' Vitruk pulled off his coat.

'Holland called President Lo in Beijing and Lo called me. He is worried. I am worried. If we do not resolve all this before the inauguration there may be a war of such strength as the world has never known before.'

'What did Holland want?'

'For China to condemn Russia. Lo cut him off. But he is nervous about his economy.'

'We need to hold firm,' said Vitruk. 'Not even Holland would risk taking on both China and Russia.'

'But will China hold its course?'

'The Chinese do not like direct confrontation. Leave it with me, sir, and I promise we will win.'

'You mean I should trust you as my successor.'

'Yes, sir. And sacrifice me as a renegade, should I fail.'

'Which you will not.'

Vitruk had not told Lagutov about the deal he had made with General Bu Zishan, commander of the neighboring Shenyang Military Region when, a year earlier, he had hosted General Bu and an official from the North Korean People's Workers' Party to an extravagant banquet at his headquarters in Khabarovsk. He had won agreement from both men in exchange for promises to transfer Russian missile technology. Nine months later, he had covertly sent to North Korea two dismantled long-range intercontinental ballistic missiles, the Topol-M – 'topol' meant 'poplar,' the tall evergreen tree. A Russian team assembled them in the massive underground facility at Toksong where North Korean engineers rebuilt the launch pad to fit, then left. The Topol-M was generations ahead of North Korea's own missile design, which was basic and untested. The Topol's speed of 15,000 miles an hour meant it could avoid detection to penetrate America's anti-ballistic-missile shield. To launch, they only needed to arm and fuel it.

Lagutov would have known that Vitruk had plans to ratchet things up. He might even be aware of the North Korea operation. But, so far, he had not asked. Lagutov was half urbane courtier, half brutal apparatchik, but his soul lay in the warmth of an academic library where decisions and their impact were safely embedded in the pages of history books.

'I am tired, Alexander, and you are full of energy,' he said. 'Your television interview was inspiring. Russia needs you in Moscow.'

This was Lagutov, offering Vitruk the mantle on condition that he won. His return to Moscow would need a dramatic entrance, an arrival at the Kremlin from a far-flung part of Russia's newly expanded empire.

Vitruk calculated distances and obstacles. Alverov and his team had successfully crossed the border and were now at the Toksong site. One missile would be fueled and prepared for launch from a silo. The other would be taken in a trailer and hidden above ground. It was on a robust carrier that could handle off-road terrain and, like a nuclear-armed submarine, would be near impossible to find. If they began fueling now, there could be a launch before the inauguration with the hidden missile still at large as President Holland took office.

'Leave China to me, Viktor,' said Vitruk, deliberately using the Russian President's first name.

'Is it dangerous?' asked Lagutov.

'It is necessary.'

Vitruk waited for the secure line to clear, then put a call through to General Bu in China's Shenyang Military Region.

THIRTY-THREE

Big Diomede, Chukotka, the Russian Far East

Carrie shut the door of the small en-suite shower. There was no bolt, but the door to the main room was locked, the same one where she had been taken when she arrived. Food remained on warmers, the coffee stewed and tepid. The shower water ran ice cold, then jumped to steaming hot. Carrie peeled off her damp clothes and felt cold sweat on her back. Sweating under thermal clothing was dangerous. Outside, once human movement stopped, sweat froze on the skin, sealing it. She needed to wash it off before going out again. The shower temperature settled and she stepped under.

Head tilted back, water running down her face and soaking through her hair, she processed what had happened, absorbed images so they didn't lash back at her and skew her judgement. The way a helicopter burnt; how a young man died; how she clung to her medical bag, always hunting out the injured; pushing Rake from her mind, admiring and despising his skill at killing all at the same time. There was madness in the human mind. If she hated this life so much, why did she seek it out? Except, on Little Diomede she hadn't hunted for war. It had found her.

The bathroom door opened to a rush of cooler air.

'Finish up,' said Vitruk from outside. 'I need to talk to you.'

A cloud of steam covered her. 'Give me a moment,' she said, keeping hidden her anger that he was trying to exploit the vulnerability of her nakedness. She was a doctor. She knew the human body better than he. She pulled a towel from the rack, dried quickly, and dressed.

'You OK, Admiral?' she said, stepping out. 'Are you finished with fucking things up? You need to rehydrate, check for frost-bite—'

'I was raised in these parts. You don't need to tell me.'

If he wanted to play the psychological intimidation game, bring it on. 'Sure as hell a lot's going wrong for you. Two heli-copters, thirteen men, and you're holding women and children hostage in a school. I can't see any hero fighting for his country here.'

Vitruk lifted the lid off a stainless-steel food container releasing a sweet, poignant smell of beetroot and beef. 'Just borscht, and in here it looks like potatoes and seal meat,' he said. 'We'll eat.'

He ladled food onto a plate, handed it to Carrie. She took it. No point in not doing so. The human body needs nutrition, water, and sleep. Vitruk helped himself, taking a seat on the other side of the table. Carrie kept her eyes on her meal. The food, bland and over-salted, warmed her. Vitruk pushed a phone toward her. 'You need to call Ambassador Lucas. She is working with President Swain in the White House. Tell her your fiancé must be ordered in. He must stop, or more of us will be killed.'

Carrie didn't touch the phone. She kept eating, taking time to chew and swallow. Vitruk kept his gaze on her, waiting. Carrie said, 'Do I tell her where I am, who I'm with, describe the layout of this base that you said was so dangerous to know?' She wiped her lips clean with a brittle white paper serviette and looked straight back at him. 'Or do I tell her it's all over and you are taking your men off Little Diomede, and everyone can go home?'

'You tell her to stand down Captain Ozenna.'

Carrie forked her food. 'You've got the number; you talk to her.'

Vitruk leaned forward. 'You know Stephanie Lucas.'

'Not that well.'

'Enough to call her and say she needs to order your fiancé to surrender.'

'She can't. She's British.'

'She's in the White House. It can be done.'

Carrie took another mouthful and washed it down with bottled water. Vitruk waited, his stare intrusive, threatening. 'Even if he's ordered to, he won't surrender,' she said.

Vitruk picked up a remote, turned on a television screen on the wall, and flipped it to what looked like a military surveillance feed. 'There are eight hundred American troops on the north side of the island. Work with me, Dr Walker. Please. These men are like sitting ducks and I can call an airstrike on them at any time.'

'Why would you do that? Lose more men and helicopters?' She tried to keep her expression casual. 'I will not be part of bringing Rake in because, like you say, he is my fiancé, and if I were in your shoes, I would kill him for what he's done.'

'When I kill him, I will be doing you a favor. No woman should be with a man like that.'

'Why? Is that what your wife said about you?' It came out fast, straight and blunt, and Carrie wasn't even sure if she gave it a moment's thought that she was comparing Rake to Vitruk. She bit her lower lip as her hard-assed expression weakened for a second, enough for Vitruk to notice. His face went dark as wood. Elbows on the table, he rested his chin on his hands. He smiled, not triumphant, not false either. It smiled of regret, and his voice softened. 'My daughter was like you, sharp, unafraid. Pretty, confident. Larisa would be your age, now, if she had lived.'

He paused, seeking Carrie's curiosity to hear more, a trap she would not fall into. A father grieving the loss of a daughter did not diminish Vitruk as the monster who had ordered his men to shoot Joan. She stayed quiet.

'Larisa died in a snowmobile accident,' he said. 'Slammed into a tree because I was drunk.'

'You don't get daughters back by killing people. Go see a therapist.' Carrie kept her expression closed.

His eyes trembled and he gripped his fingers together. 'I know the mind of a man like Rake Ozenna. It is about war, hunting and killing. He will not be a good father to your children. Whatever dreams you and he have will come to nothing.'

Carrie forked the last food around her plate. Was he playing her or, in this strange place and moment, was he unloading the mess of his own mind? One thing her job had taught her was that some form of humanity lay inside the worst of people. But none of that solved the situation right now, so she said flatly, 'Looks like you and I are negotiating again. I'll treat the wounded, Admiral, but I'm not making that call.'

Like lightning, Vitruk switched to anger. 'Damn you, woman!' He banged the table with his fist. Coffee spilt. 'You have no idea what is at stake.'

Carrie pulled a paper napkin from the holder to soak it up. 'You're right, I don't. But I do know that if you order your troops off Little Diomede and—'

'Grow up!' Vitruk's tone was hard, but measured again. 'I saved your life out there. If you don't make the call, give me one reason to keep needing you.' His eyes were powerfully aggressive as if to expel any doubt about his intentions. Carrie had to stop herself from shaking. She was about to reply, but found her throat constricting. Whatever she said would have come out limp, hesitant, and pleading. There was something else, something more than Rake. Vitruk only wanted to use Carrie now as a direct line to the White House, and she had lost count of the injured and dying she had treated because they had challenged power against which they could never win. Vitruk had the guns. He might be merciless, but he was not stupid, and she had revealed her self-doubt. He checked the phone, punched on the dial, slid it across to her, and said, 'Stop being a stubborn, high-minded, destructively moral bitch and ring your friend.'

As soon as she hesitated, both she and Vitruk knew she would make the call.

THIRTY-FOUR

The White House, Washington, DC

The vibration from the incoming call woke Stephanie from a short deep sleep on the couch in Prusak's office. She fumbled with her phone, working out where she was. Prusak was by her side. He put in an earpiece for the line intercept and checked his tablet. 'From the Russian base,' he said.

Stephanie pressed the answer button.

'Steph. It's Carrie.' The tone was calm and professional.

Stephanie gripped the phone harder than she should. 'Carrie! Good God! Are you OK?'

'I'm at the Russian military base on Big Diomede with Admiral Vitruk who instructed me to make this call,' Carrie said like a doctor delivering a bad diagnosis.

'The helicopter . . . the crash . . .' Stephanie stumbled on her words. 'Are you hurt?' Phone pressed to her ear, she swung her legs off the couch to sit upright.

'Yes, I'm fine.' Carrie's short precise answer shook Stephanie into doing the same. Vitruk was bound to be listening. This was not a time to show emotion. 'Are you captive?' she said.

'Correct.'

'Is Captain Ozenna with you?'

'He is not.'

Stephanie shot a look at Prusak who shrugged as if to say that not even the NSA with all its gadgets had located Ozenna. He patted his hand in the air: Stephanie should hold back and let Carrie talk. An echo peppered with shots of static hung for a few seconds until Carrie said, 'The Admiral has some requests. He needs a guarantee that the marine units on the northern side of Little Diomede will remain on standby. He wants Captain Ozenna and the civilian Eskimos who are at large with weapons between the two islands to give themselves up. Once that is done he is sure that a solution can be found without further confrontation. He warns, however, that any attack on Big Diomede island will be considered as an attack on Moscow and there will be consequences.'

Prusak mouthed that Stephanie should speak to Vitruk directly. 'Thank you, Carrie,' she said. 'That is very clear. I need to speak directly to Admiral Vitruk.'

She heard Carrie talking in a low voice. When the line picked up again, it was Vitruk. 'Hello, Madam Ambassador. I trust my requests are clear to you. They are small and I insist they are carried out.' He spoke with an East Coast drawl, peppered with diplomatic charm, the type Stephanie had handled for years.

'Your first responsibility, Admiral, is the safety of civilians, including Dr Walker.'

'Civilian safety is in your hands, not mine. Since we rescued the pregnant teenager, Russia has saved lives. America has taken them.'

Prusak pointed towards the Oval Office. 'All right, Admiral.

I'll take your wish list to the President. You have my word on that.'

'Dr Walker is sitting with me,' said Vitruk. 'Please be quick. We are at a most critical stage.'

Prusak circled his finger in the air for her to keep the conversation going.

'Critical stage? What do you mean? We are talking about winding things—'

There came static, clicking, then silence. Stephanie turned the phone round and round in her hand. His reference to a critical stage must mean the missile, nothing to do with Ozenna, except Ozenna could be the only obstacle that now lay between Vitruk and success. A few hours back Vitruk would have thought he had a whole army to take Ozenna out. So far, he had failed.

'Steph, we need to brief the President,' said Prusak, opening an adjoining door to the Oval Office. Stephanie desperately wanted to freshen up, splash some water on her face, but that would have to wait. She combed her fingers through her hair and followed Prusak in. Harry was there, unshaven and still wearing the same clothes. She counted twenty-two people, Pacolli, the Chairman of the Joint Chiefs, others she recognized, including Holland, who was by the window looking subdued and thoughtful. The conversation halted and Prusak signaled Stephanie to speak. She ran through the call recounting the demand that Ozenna surrender and the US troops remain on standby. She ended on Vitruk's warning about a critical stage. 'Does anyone know what he means?' said Swain.

'Obviously, it's the transition,' said Holland. 'Six hours from now, they'll be dealing with a new President.'

'He said we are at a critical stage, not about to go into a critical stage,' said Stephanie.

'It has to be the North Korea play. That's why he needed to communicate directly with the White House,' said Harry. 'He was saying that he knows we know about it, the first step of negotiation.'

'We don't negotiate,' said Holland. 'Kennedy didn't with Khrushchev when they tried to put missiles in Cuba. I'm damned if I'll negotiate now.'

Wrong, thought Stephanie. Swain caught her eye and she kept quiet. History lessons must wait. Prusak tapped her elbow, and she guessed from his expectant expression that they were thinking the same thing. She nodded. Prusak reminded the room that Stephanie had received a call from Sergey Grizlov, speaker of the Russian Duma. Would it be worth her trying again to get through to him?

'To ask him what?' said Holland.

'Ask him straight,' said Stephanie. 'Is Russia planning an imminent missile strike against the United States?'

'Would he know?' said Holland.

'We can judge a lot through voice analysis,' said Prusak.

'Do we have his whereabouts?' said Swain.

'He went into the Kremlin an hour ago,' said Prusak. 'He may be with Lagutov.'

'Ask the question and add in nuclear, an imminent nuclear-missile strike,' said Swain.

'Once it's asked, they will know we're on to them,' said Harry.

'Your point?' said Holland.

'The question might be the catalyst to a launch, depending how ready they are.'

'They're not going to launch if they want to negotiate,' said Swain.

'That could hinge on who is actually running the Kremlin,' said Stephanie.

'Is Ozenna still bound by the deadline, sir?' said Pacolli, who was lining up airstrikes less than four hours from now.

'Nothing substantive has changed.'

The finality of Swain's statement abruptly ended the quick-fire conversation. Stephanie understood Swain's thinking. Obliterating the base before Holland took office threw down a marker to stop hostilities before the world was plunged into all-out war. It also gave Holland a choice. He could continue his plans to strike the Russian mainland and North Korea or he could sue for peace. Swain was giving him a clean plate.

'I'll ask about an imminent nuclear strike against the United States and its allies,' said Stephanie. 'That would cover Japan and South Korea.'

Swain nodded. Harry said, 'Use the Narva registered phone.'

Swain looked quizzical and Harry explained about the phone registered to the city in Estonia that was mainly populated by ethnic Russians. But Stephanie disagreed. Why should Grizlov answer a direct call from a stranger in Estonia when he might not from her? 'I'll try mine first, then the Narva phone,' she said.

Harry said nothing. No one spoke. She scrolled to the last call from Grizlov and dialed. It rang three times and went to voicemail, a woman's voice asking callers to leave a message for Chairman Grizlov. She cut the line. 'Should I leave a message? "Call me" – something like that?'

'No,' said Swain. 'But try again.'

Stephanie switched phones, punched in the number, and gave

it a full minute. No one moved. The silence in the Oval Office was oppressive. Prusak put his finger to his earpiece for the intercept. She pressed Call and caught Harry's gaze of approval as the first ring sparked up, then two more and she heard her former lover's voice. 'Speaker Grizlov, can I help you?' His voice was friendly, full of charm and confidence. She detected no background noise, no traffic, no hotel lobby music, no muttering of other voices.

'Sergey, it's Stephanie. I need to know—'

There was a click, the same bouncing electronic silence, the same voicemail. Stephanie cut the line. Was that her one shot? He had declined her call on her known number, picked up the unknown one, heard her voice, and run away? Or was it a bad place to talk? Too risky? In which case, would he call back? An atmosphere of disappointment enveloped the room, then Holland asked, 'How would we take out this Toksong missile base?'

Pacolli answered. 'A GBU-57 bomb dropped from the B-2 stealth will drill down into the bunker before exploding. That's a fifty three hundred-pound warhead which would destroy everything at that launch site.'

'What would be the radiation leak levels?' asked Swain.

'Limited, sir. Secondary aircraft could deliver foam sealant to the strike site that would hold long enough for ground forces to get there—'

'Whose ground forces?' asked Holland.

'They would be North Korean or Chinese,' said Pacolli.

'They would have to be ours,' said Holland.

'That would be impossible in the time frame.'

'How long to do that strike?' said Holland.

'Fourteen hours from the order, sir,' said Pacolli. 'They're at Whiteman's Air Force Base in Missouri. Or we could be there in three hours out of Osan, South Korea with the HVPW and F-35s. That's a smaller, more versatile version of the bomb, but it could work.'

'I don't like the word "could",' said Holland. 'It has to be a single strike. Where is our closest nuclear launch?'

'USS *Florida*,' said Pacolli. 'She's in the Sea of Japan and carries nuclear armed cruise missiles. That would be a strike within a couple of hours.'

'And is that "could" or "would" destroy?'

'Guaranteed, sir. A conventional strike with a GBU-57 out of Missouri or a nuclear strike from the USS *Florida* are certainties. The F-35s from Osan – their payload might not have the explosive power to do the business.'

'I recommend the nuclear,' said Holland. 'North Korea's been a live unexploded mine from another era for too long. To protect America, we need to get rid of it and move on.'

Harry spoke up. 'Sir, if we collapse the North Korean regime, it would take a hundred thousand troops two months to secure all of its nuclear arsenal during which time renegade generals will be hawking nuclear material to terror groups around the world. It will take another two hundred fifty thousand troops to stabilize the country, and the humanitarian crisis would make the Middle East look like a school picnic outing. And to get anything done we would have to work closely with the Chinese and the Russians.'

★

HARRY HAD NAILED IT AGAIN. There was another pause. Stephanie kept coming back to the same question. Is it just Vitruk? Is it Russia? Is it Russia and China?

'The economy, Tom?' Swain asked Treasury Secretary Thomas Grant, who was also the temporary Federal Reserve chair. Grant spoke slowly and with confidence. 'A conventional single strike will wobble the markets, but they will hold, depending on the response. Nuclear would create panic that could rupture the global economy into deep recession.'

'But worse if that Topol-M with a nuclear warhead hits Hawaii or California,' said Holland.

'Strangely, sir, not. It would have less of an economic impact.'

Holland's brow creased with suspicion. 'You've got to be kidding.'

'This is not a time for kidding, sir. The United States is stronger and more versatile than either Russia or China. If we strike first, the markets will see it as the world's biggest economy becoming unpredictable and out of control.'

'There is no love lost between China and Russia,' said Stephanie. 'The deep mistrust is exactly what Nixon exploited in his 1974 visit. If we get China onside—'

'Screw the Chinese. They let that damn missile across into North Korea,' said Holland. 'We used nuclear weapons on Japan in 1945 to save lives and bring peace. That is what we will be doing here.'

Power was shifting away from Swain. In a few hours, Swain, Prusak, Pacolli, and others would be gone. At some stage, Stephanie would have to speak to Slater, mid-Atlantic on his way to London, but not yet. She had another idea. It wasn't that it would work, or even change things. But it bought time and offered an alternative to the world's first nuclear strike since 1945. 'Why don't we comply with Vitruk's wishes?' she said.

'Are you crazy, Ambassador?' said Holland.

'The troops are on standby anyway. We can't contact Ozenna. We can comply and do nothing. We call him. Keep up the conversation.'

The common sense of Stephanie's suggestion rippled through the room. 'Do it,' said Swain. Stephanie flipped her phone over in her hand and dialed Vitruk again.

THIRTY-FIVE

Big Diomede, Chukotka, the Russian Far East

On a small table lay the phone on which Carrie had spoken to Stephanie Lucas. It was ringing, but Carrie couldn't reach it. Her left hand was cuffed to a vertical metal rail, on the chair where Joan had sat. Vitruk was by the doorway, headset on, deep in conversation. When Vitruk had brought her in, she noticed a strained and concentrated atmosphere, and fewer than half a dozen men who had now left. In the hour she had been here, she had counted four helicopters taking off and three coming in. She guessed Vitruk was emptying the base because he expected a strike as soon as Holland was sworn in. Rake was somewhere out there, but she couldn't imagine what he was doing, what he was thinking. She couldn't place her fiancé in her mind because she wasn't sure any more who he really was.

The soldier who had been shot in the legs lay awake, staring, eyes wide open at the ceiling, occasionally mumbling to himself. The other man was silent and still. Akna slept. The corpse was gone from the bed across the ward. The pediatric surgeon had gone, too, and he had done a bad, rushed job. In the incubator, the baby wriggled, awake, mouth open, crying, but no sound came out. Iyaroak was badly positioned with the weight of her head on the wound. Blood clotted the bandage that needed changing. Bacterial meningitis and encephalitis were a real risk, and Carrie had no idea which antibiotics they were using, if any.

Hailstones pounded loudly on the military canvas. She heard the slow throbbing of another helicopter starting up, ferrying men out of the base. It took off. The fifth. The phone ringing stopped, then the keyboard flashed with an incoming message. Vitruk could see it, but kept talking. Carrie stared at him, the cuff cold on her wrist.

VITRUK LISTENED TO THE measured argument of President Lagutov over the phone while watching Carrie, her expression thoughtful and angry. He had ordered an evacuation of the base and had only a skeleton of highly trusted men left.

'The Americans are calling us constantly and we are stalling,' said Lagutov, sounding resigned but determined. 'Sergey Grizlov tells me to negotiate, but my faith remains in you, Alexander, to make this work for the Motherland.' There was barely a cigarette paper between the success and failure of any military operation and Lagutov was giving Vitruk that one last high-risk shot.

'Thank you,' said Vitruk. 'Sergey would make us Western puppets again.'

'I have authorized you for Kavkaz,' said Lagutov, referring to the Russian military communications system used for a nuclear-missile launch. 'You will receive unlocked codes in the next five minutes. You are the only one with these.'

As the line was disconnected, Vitruk looked across to the ring tone coming from the phone just out of Carrie's reach. He would deal with it, but only after he had one more piece of information. An hour ago, General Dmitri Alverov was still thirty minutes out from North Korea's Toksong missile-launch site. He had assured Vitruk that if the North Korean engineers had followed orders, they would be able to launch within an hour of his arrival. Vitruk called through again. Alverov had arrived and the team was at work. 'It needs to be just after the inauguration,' said Vitruk.

'Without a warhead, we can,' said Alverov. 'The missile would be more accurate without it.'

'The first from the silo will be unarmed,' said Vitruk. 'The second mobile launch will be armed.'

'Armed?' It wasn't a question, more an exclamation of excitement, a departure from his usual scientific detachment. 'That will be a great pleasure, sir.'

'Is your team united?'

'We cannot let the past years of humiliation go unpunished.'

Vitruk was convinced that Alverov's mood was being reflected throughout Russia. Once the Americans had hit this base, the Russian people would fall in behind him and Vitruk could push through a decisive victory. He had already decided that Pearl Harbor would be the most symbolic target. America could beat Japan, but never Russia.

On the ice between the Diomede islands

Driving pellets of hail smashed against Rake's goggles as he stood between two men in the last stages of exhaustion. The power of the ice storm cut visibility to just a few feet. He couldn't see Henry because of the swirl in front of him. But he could hear his voice, and Henry's fury carried on the wind. When Rake cupped his hands protectively around his goggles, he could make out Don Ondola, silent, passive, a giant of a man, whom Henry would kill if he had the chance, but whom they all needed to stay alive.

Henry was a level-headed man, except on the issue of Ondola. Henry had raised him like a son and saw his crimes as a personal betrayal. He had given evidence at the murder trial, framed in a way that would cause Ondola to be locked away for life without parole. Ondola had said he was sorry. He broke down in tears, but had meant it only because he was sober. As soon as he touched drink the monster in him would return. Henry had pledged that if his adopted son ever became a free man again, he would kill him.

Rake and Ondola had found Henry in the cover of the ice wall, watching Joan walk out from the coastline. He had escaped the base with the barest of protection and was rigid with cold, scarcely able to move. They gave him a hide and warmed him. Ondola climbed the wall and set up his firing position with the aim of killing Vitruk. Only then did Henry reveal himself by running towards Joan. Rake and Henry brought Joan to safety as Ondola killed two Russian marksmen, but failed to hit Vitruk. He escaped after a field of lethal machine-gun fire cut the ice around him and left his polar-bear skin as a calling card not to mess with the Eskimos. Now, in the shelter of the wall, Joan brewed coffee and prepared military self-heating meals that Rake had taken from the Russians.

Despite where they were, all they were up against, Henry stubbornly stuck to his pledge, even though Ondola had just saved his life, even though he knew he could never beat Ondola in a fight. Ondola had arrived back as the weather turned bad again, and Henry confronted him. Rake stepped in between them. The environment was at least as lethal as a human enemy, he said, and if they fought between themselves, the weather and the ice would take them all.

Ondola beckoned Rake, who took a step towards him just as a whistling gust roared through. He almost slipped, but steadied himself in time. 'You and Henry go to the base,' shouted Ondola. 'I'll watch your back, keep Joan safe. I'll handle Tuuq if he comes.'

Rake pointed to Little Diomede. 'Joan wants to go home. Can she make it alone?'

'To the village, yes. She cannot get around to the Americans on the east side.'

'Eat with us while we have cover,' said Rake.

Ondola shook his head. 'Henry won't—'

'I'll handle Henry.' Rake took his arm. 'You need energy.'

Like pushing into a tidal surge, Rake led them against the weather, noise drowning out everything. He sensed rather than saw Henry until he blocked their path, stopping only inches away. 'Keep him away, Rake. I swear by God—'

'We need him.'

'We don't.'

'He's sick in the head, Henry. He needs help.'

'He murdered—'

'Out here, Eskimo does not harm Eskimo, whatever the past,' shouted Rake. 'We will feed him, and when it's over I will return him to the prison. You have my word.'

'Or I'll kill him.'

'If it comes to that, I'll kill him to save your hide.'

Once behind the ice wall, the clatter of flying hail fell silent. The wind dropped, and they ate fast and hungrily and were done in minutes. Henry drew a plan of the base in the snow, explaining the hangars, the main building with the control room, and the field hospital tagged onto the back. 'If Carrie is still there, she'll be in the field hospital here, or in the room directly on the right inside the main door. This long room that runs into the hospital is the control center.'

'Vitruk's quarters?' asked Rake.

'None. It's too small, too crowded.'

'What about the bunker?' said Ondola. 'Deep, down a long staircase, where they kept Uncle Anik when he was arrested in 1988.'

'I didn't see it,' said Henry.

Anik, an obsessive hunter, had followed a herd of walrus into Russian waters. The cold war was full on, and he spent a month deep in an airless Soviet bunker on Big Diomede. Or so legend had it.

'So how do we get in?' asked Rake.

Henry drew the pier and gun positions along the coastline. Ondola added the ice wall.

'Can we do it from there?' asked Rake. 'We use the ice wall as cover?'

Henry and Ondola shook their heads. 'This whole side is exposed,' said Henry.

'Then we go here.' Rake used a spike of ice to show the spot on Henry's map where a cove would be. It was a third of a mile from the base. When growing up, they had played at trying to cross to Big Diomede undetected. This was the only place where intrusive rock formations blocked the lines of sight from the ridge watch towers. 'Has anyone been caught here?' Rake asked.

Henry forgot his animosity for a moment as he looked at Ondola. Both men shrugged as if to say neither knew, which meant no one had. If they made it onto the tiny rock beach, they would be clear.

'Then the Russians might not have it covered.' Rake pointed to other landing spots to the south. 'Here, here, and here people have been intercepted, and this is where Anik was caught. I reckon if the weather stays bad we have a chance of getting in undetected.'

'I'll be a decoy,' said Joan. 'Go to one of those places with a white flag. They won't shoot.'

Rake didn't like it. After Ondola's killing of the two snipers, the soldiers would be nervous and trigger-happy. 'It's too dangerous. Joan, you come with us as—'

Rake was about to say more when they heard a dog's howl. A quiet wind carried it towards them from the direction of the Russian base. At first it was soft, undulating, almost singing, but it became loud, a throbbing cry, piercing, cutting through the air. It stopped abruptly and Rake's radio sprang to life. 'Watch the sky, yellow Yankee coward. It's my orders to cut my brother until he dies.'

To the west, over the coastline of Big Diomede, a trail of glowing yellow sparks climbed into the sky. For a moment, Rake thought it was machine-gun tracer. But the trajectory was wrong and it kept climbing until, like a firework, it burst into a shower of green stars that lit up a large area beneath, before streaming away, extinguished by the wind.

THIRTY-SIX

On the ice between the Diomede islands

Through the night's blackness Rake found the cove that would lead them onto Big Diomede. He recognized it by rock formations that jutted out like a hanging roof from the cliffside making a canopy over the beach. Underneath, protection from the weather had created a fast running channel of water about four-feet wide between sea ice and the frozen shingle of the beach. They needed to jump the water to get onto the island.

Outside the canopy, wind and cloud cut visibility to inches. There were no stars, no moon, no lights from the Russian base or from the village on Little Diomede. Ice leading to the channel was flat, scoured by months of battering by hailstones that stuck like barnacles to the surface. Spotting weak patches was near impossible.

They had kept watch for Tuuq and got this far. In this weather, they might not see him until they collided. Or he could already be on the island, even on the base. For sure, Tuuq was still out there. Ondola stayed well behind. Henry moved forward, testing with a pole, until he reached the edge. He locked grip with his boot, braced himself, and jumped across. Rake pushed the sled to the channel. He unstrapped the rucksacks and one by one threw them across to Henry. Rake moved back, and Joan stepped past him to the same spot from where Henry had jumped. Henry held out his arms to bring her in.

Suddenly, the sound of fracturing ice cut through the air. The surface cracked into a hairline fissure. Joan stayed stock-still. She knew the dangers. Any sudden thrust to jump would break the ice completely. The fissure widened. She shifted weight. More ice broke. Her foot caught in the crack and she stumbled, struggling to stay up. Rake moved towards her, gliding more than running, keeping his steps light and fast. He lifted Joan in time to keep her feet clear of the water. Her voice rasped on fast shallow breaths, telling him she was all right. He carried her back and lowered her down. She steadied herself, pointing to an area to the right that might be safe. Rake let her make the judgement. They had all been raised around rotten ice, taught how it could kill. Foot by foot, prodding around her, Joan tested the strength until she was confident enough to jump. Henry caught her as she landed. A few yards to the left, Rake identified a fresh safe patch for himself.

As if from nowhere a break appeared in the scudding clouds and moonlight bathed the landscape. The wind dropped. It might only last seconds, but Rake signaled for everyone to stay still. He could see a light from the base. It was close, about three hundred meters. The plan was that Joan would stay outside the fence with a radio and a Russian phone. Rake would secure Carrie, which probably meant killing Vitruk. Only then he would report back and get orders. Henry would deal with Akna and the baby.

Henry edged forward to help Rake cross the open channel. Rake locked his boot; the ice was a clear blue and he was certain it would hold. He was coiling himself for the jump when a formidable hold took him around the neck and threw him down hard. Hands gripped like a steel vice, pressing on his windpipe with enormous power. Green eyes bore down, vicious and cruel, the face that threatened him all those years back ago on the sled in Uelen, not the soldier with whom he had trained, but his half-blood brother with a dark empty hole of hatred inside him.

'Bye bye, Yankee coward,' Tuuq whispered, his breath on Rake's face. Rake was pinned. Tuuq's fingers closed tighter, draining him of strength. Tuuq's expression was primordial, without conscience, a hunter whose quest was not food or skins. He could have shot Rake, but he needed to do it by hand. Nikita Tuuq killed in order to kill. Nothing else.

Rake's sight blurred, his thinking muddled. Tuuq's face became his. He became the Russian soldier who pleaded with him there didn't have to be a kill. Rake gave no mercy. Nor would Tuuq. Across the channel, Henry had his weapon raised, but with no clear shot. Where was Don Ondola? He must be dead, killed by Tuuq on his way in. A few yards away, snow lay in a broken jumbled heap where Tuuq had been hiding, covering himself, and Rake had missed it.

How stupid they had been! They knew Tuuq was out here. He would remember the cove just as they did. He had come, and waited.

Rake lifted his boot and crashed it down on the ice, lifted and crashed it again, and again. Tuuq kept his hold. If Rake succeeded and the ice broke, both he and Tuuq would disappear into freezing water. Their survival wouldn't be more than a few seconds. But it would be a different kind of death and give a clear run for Henry and Joan to get to the base.

The ice shattered, but not under them. Rake's pounding impacted further along where a whole section gave way, splitting like an earthquake, creating a gaping hole, slabs listing into the water which spilled over and ran down towards them.

Drawing on last reserves of energy, Rake pushed his chest high enough to smash his forehead against Tuuq's skull, hitting him on the bridge of his nose, loosening the hold on his neck. Rake turned his body, freeing an arm to drive his fist into Tuuq's crotch. In those hair-trigger seconds, it was the best Rake could do, and it wasn't enough. Tuuq slashed his hand across Rake's face, cutting his cheek. He got his fingers back around Rake's throat, harder this time, more urgent, dispensing with the luxury of the long kill. Tuuq fought as if untouched, blood streaming down his face. Rake was suffocating. Strength failed him. His arm wouldn't move. His leg couldn't lift his boot. His muscles were gone. He felt no pain around his throat. His will was stripped away by the reality that an oxygen-starved brain would not function and soon he would die. Tuuq loomed, his head slanted back, waiting, his gaze intent through the goggles. He was the victor. Rake saw Carrie, face caked with soot from a bomb. Then she went and there was haze. Rake's mind played memories. His brain was without oxygen. There was no road to the greater good. All that killing had been for nothing. Soldiers die; it was his turn now.

A smile lit Tuuq's eyes. He reared back and let out that dog howl, keeping up the cry as he leaned forward, gripping harder, squeezing, his voice surging and rolling louder and shriller next to Rake's ear, that primeval wail of death that had haunted Rake for so long. As he howled, Tuuq twisted Rake's windpipe, kneading his fingers in the last act of killing.

Then, suddenly, his hold broke.

Ondola smashed a metal ice pole across Tuuq's head, gashing his skull. Tuuq toppled. Ondola hit him again, slicing the pole up under his jaw. Rake rolled himself out as Tuuq pulled a knife and scrambled to his feet.

'Go!' shouted Ondola.

Rake drew freezing air into his lungs, and pushed himself up. He stumbled, found his footing. Ondola, his own knife in hand, swung towards Tuuq's face. Tuuq side-stepped and hurled himself forward, hands clasped together, knife held like an executioner, and used his power to bring it down with absolute force towards Ondola's neck. Ondola shifted an inch. The blade sliced his cheek and Ondola crumpled under Tuuq's weight. Rake started towards him.

Henry's voice. 'Rake. Over here!'

Bent double, Ondola staggered, legs buckling. Tuuq drew back the knife to plunge it into the exposed back of his neck. But Ondola was ready for him. In a lightning move he deflected the arm and sank his knife into it.

'I've got him!' Ondola yelled. 'Go!'

Tuuq crashed his elbow into Ondola's head, bringing them both back to the ground.

'Now, Rake.' Henry's voice. Sensible, firm. 'We need you here.'

Rake ignored him. Tuuq's right arm was raised to plunge the

knife into Ondola. Rake propelled himself forward, leaping up to kick Tuuq in the head, or anywhere to deflect the blade. His boot struck Tuuq's shoulder, but it was enough to skew his balance. Tuuq fell back, his hands empty, the knife embedded above Ondola's sternum, deep in his throat.

The ear-splitting fire of an automatic weapon splayed across the ice. Henry emptied a magazine towards Tuuq who jerked as a round thudded into his body, but moved quickly, using the ice as cover. Bullets cut through in a circle around him, but missed. There was silence. Rake needed to help Ondola, but he couldn't until he dealt with Tuuq. Henry fired a burst of three, stopped. He had no target. Then came a tearing roar. Water sprayed up like a geyser and the frozen sea tilted as if in an earthquake. Clawing at the edges of broken ice Tuuq slid down, his blood trailing through the water.

'Brother!' Tuuq cried out in Russian. 'Help me!' Rake ran to him, holding out an arm, an instinctive reaction to anyone caught in bad ice. Tuuq's face caught in reflected moonlight had lost its hardness. For a flash, Rake imagined his father there. He lay flat on strong ice and stretched out to take Tuuq's hand. As Tuuq reached for him, Henry fired twice, one shot in the forehead and one straight through the mouth. Tuuq slid silently into the water.

Ondola lay still, gloves holding the knife blade, keeping it in his throat to stem the bleeding. He managed a smile. 'I told you . . . to go . . .' Rake pulled out a bandage and a pack of blood clotting agent which he tore open.

'Don't,' said Ondola. He didn't move his hands from the knife. His eyes were clear. 'This is . . . a good place to die . . .'

Rake dropped the bandage to put his hand on Ondola. 'You're a good man,' he said.

'You're my brother.'

'Stay with us. We'll get help.'

'Go save my daughter.' Another smile. Frailer. A last spark of life in his eyes. 'Tell her I'm not all bad.'

THIRTY-SEVEN

British Ambassador's residence, Washington, DC

Stephanie paced the dining room in the British Embassy, back and forth between the mantelpiece and the long table that was splashed with mid-morning winter light. Maps and charts lay among laptops, tablets, and part-drunk cups of coffee. Harry leant against the wall in a far corner, working contacts on the phone with a second line open to the Situation Room watch commander.

She had repeatedly rung Carrie's phone and got no reply. She kept asking herself what it might mean and dealt with that by protecting herself in diplomat thought: Don't speculate. Just keep working. She dialed Carrie, then Grizlov, alternately, one after the other, aware that minutes were ticking down to Swain's deadline to take out the Russian base. She understood his reasoning. She hated that she was part of it and that Carrie was there. Stephanie owed her big time for standing in as a bar-room therapist that night they hit the town in Moscow when Harry was being such a shit. She knew that diplomats at the American and British embassies in Moscow were burning contacts to get to Grizlov or anyone who could make sense of what was happening. But they had all gone to ground.

Then Grizlov picked up, his voice filled with tension. 'Hold, Steph. Stay on the line.' A click. Emptiness. She mimed to Harry that she had Grizlov. But he was already looking her way, must have heard from the Situation Room. Grizlov was back, no charm, no introduction, taut to breaking. 'Vitruk's on his own, Steph.'

The finality of his tone brought goose bumps to Stephanie's neck. 'Can you stop him?'

'I need time. If you strike, we have to strike back.'

'We don't have time, Serg. You've got to—'

Grizlov ended the call with a terse 'I'll get back to you.' Prusak was immediately on the line. 'Voice analysis is coming up as genuine.'

Genuine what, she thought angrily. Her palms were sweating. She was shaking all over. All the fucking gadgetry in the world and they still couldn't stop blowing each other up. She kept herself measured and said, 'The President must stand down the strike, Matt. We've talked to one of the good guys.'

'Yes. I'll ask him, Steph. Well done.'

Blair House, Office of the President-elect

Bob Holland checked himself in a long mirror and smoothed down his dark pinstripe suit to rid it of creases caused by his thermal underwear. Outside the temperature was below freezing. Wind-chill on the podium would send it lower. Holland could not be seen wearing an overcoat for his inauguration.

There was knock on the door which opened with his

six-year-old son Casper scuttling around the legs of CIA director Frank Ciszewski. Holland's wife, Nancy, picked Casper up, carried him out, and shut the door.

'Ambassador Lucas made contact with Sergey Grizlov. He described Admiral Vitruk as being on his own. He has asked for time to resolve,' Ciszewski said, handing Holland a thin folder. 'The President has delayed the strike on the Big Diomede base. But we have these. They show a mobile missile launcher moving out of the Toksong site in North Korea, sir.'

Holland examined a collection of grainy photographs. 'When was this taken and where is it now?'

'Just over an hour ago. We know the broad area, but not enough to target it.'

The image showed the snub nose of a huge missile emerging from a cluster of trees. Much of the photograph showed cloud cover, but Holland could make out the edge of the trailer and a set of front wheels.

'When could it launch?'

'Any time.'

'Range?'

'Los Angeles and the West Coast are its outer range, flight time about half an hour. We cannot guarantee a successful intercept. The missile is designed to avoid our infrared detection satellites and tracking systems. It could carry six nuclear warheads, each on an independent re-entry vehicle. The likelihood is just one, but we have to factor for all six.'

Holland's Senate job had not been one of making impossible choices. In less than an hour, he would have to make one. 'What would you do, Frank?' he asked the CIA director.

Ciszewski's avuncular face stiffened. 'I can give you our intelligence, but I cannot make your decision.' He was not unfriendly, but he was adamant.

'What's Swain doing?' said Holland.

'Like you, sir, he's getting dressed while trying to end this thing. His view is that any pre-emptive action without knowing the exact location could blow back badly on us.'

Holland checked his watch. 'I need you in on a conversation with the Joint Chiefs.'

'We can schedule for 13.15.'

'No, now, before the ceremony. I don't intend there to be a mushroom cloud over Los Angeles because I was too busy fixing my tie pin.' Holland dropped the satellite pictures onto a small table by the mirror.

'I'll fix the meeting, sir,' said Ciszewski.

'At 12.01 all of our assets must be ready. We go before I finish my speech.'

Big Diomede, Chukotka, the Russian Far East

Henry's firm grip took Rake's arm as he jumped the narrow channel onto the island. He looked back and saw Tuuq's wrist caught on the edge of ice, his body visible in the water. Ondola lay on his back, staring upwards. Rake couldn't tell if he was waiting to die or already dead. The gunfire might have alerted those left at the base. But the wind was blowing off the island and they may have heard nothing. Rake hoisted a pack onto his shoulders and set off up the hill with Henry and Joan following.

The hillside was steep, the ground firm with a track between the rocks. Soon they sighted the base, protected by high granite cliffs with a narrow opening that gave access to the sea. There were no walls, no razor-wire fence, no watchtowers even. The geology of the island and the environment gave defense enough. Soldiers in watchtowers along the top usually kept vigil, but now the watchtowers were empty, the guards gone.

Rake crawled forward to the edge of the rock and used his night-vision binoculars to examine the base. It appeared through light fog as an example of the faded Soviet dream at the edge of the empire, a series of drab low-rise buildings with no style, no grandeur.

The buildings formed a ring around a central helipad with a second landing spot about a hundred yards to the east right on the shoreline. A helicopter was parked in the open near a hangar. An engineer worked, alone up a ladder near the tail where a panel hung open.

Three jeeps were visible, one by the hangar, another to the left of the main building. Two overhead lamps protruded from either side of the door, but they were unlit. A light shone inside. He counted three snowmobiles by a ramp to the sea. He saw no dogs. That didn't mean they weren't there. They would be trained for air-scent because of the way water neutralized a dog's smell. With the wind blowing due south hard against them, it was unlikely a dog, however well trained, would pick up anything.

There were no signs that Vitruk or Carrie were even still on base, nor that they had left. Once Carrie was safe, he didn't mind what happened. They could never pick up as before, a couple filled with dreams and infallibility. Carrie would return to her hospital or head out to some difficult place. He would go back to his unit to be posted to the latest shit-hole foreign politicians had created for native people. His worst prospect was ending up wounded and captured, paraded in front of the television cameras, then sent to the cold danger of a Russian prison cell.

Fog slid across the landscape. By keeping close to the black granite of the hillside, Rake was confident that they could get down to the base unseen in a few minutes. A wall of snow had built up at the bottom right on the edge of the helipad's concrete. Once there, fog and darkness would give them cover. To get further, they would probably have to shoot the helicopter engineer which meant more killing. Walking in with a white flag wouldn't do the business. He put Stephanie's number into two of the Russian phones and handed them to Joan and Henry.

They followed a narrow track with Rake using night vision to detect sensors and trip wires. There were none. When the slope levelled, they took cover behind the pile of snow. Henry drew a rifle from a rucksack. With the storm gone, the wind was quiet which would help the shot. The engineer climbed down the ladder and vanished inside the hangar. Henry set up his weapon with a field of fire that would cover Rake and Joan as they went in. Rake wanted Joan to stay back, but she refused point blank. She was responsible for Akna and Iyaroak just as Rake was for Carrie.

The way the moonlight reflected off the snow gave no cover across the helipad. The distance to the main door was less than a hundred feet, an eight-second run. They would go one at a time, Rake first, then Joan as soon as he was outside the door and gave the all-clear. Twenty seconds at most, then inside to the unknown, the best they could plan for. If the engineer reappeared, Henry would kill him.

Rake left cover and ran.

THIRTY-EIGHT

Presidential limousine to Capitol Hill, Washington, DC

A toxic silence hung between Swain and Holland as their heavily cocooned vehicle made its way along Pennsylvania Avenue in a convoy of flashing lights.

As had been the practice since 1837, the President and President-elect travelled together to the inauguration from the White House towards Capitol Hill. Their Vice-Presidential and First Lady counterparts rode in limousines behind them. The tradition started when Martin Van Buren succeeded Andrew Jackson who was his ally and mentor, a transition far removed from the distrust between Swain and Holland.

Through the limousine's darkened windows, Holland watched crowds lining the sidewalks. His banners were predominant. He was no longer a campaigner. He was stepping into the highest office in the land. Swain was yesterday's man. Holland held the cards. Eventually he broke the silence by saying, 'I've ordered strikes for 12.01.' He reeled off the targets in North Korea and Russia.

Swain didn't answer. Holland settled back in his seat and drummed his fingers on the arm rest.

Big Diomede, Chukotka, the Russian Far East

His pistol in his right hand, Rake pushed the door. It gave way. He eased it open, signaled Joan to run across, and ushered her in. They both flattened themselves against the wall. Straight ahead was a dirty cream-colored wall with two windows that looked out to the sea. He heard the hum of a generator, but the only light came from the moon outside. To the left strips of heavy transparent plastic hung down across the entrance that Henry said led to the control center. Rake couldn't see inside. He sensed no movement there. To the right, a door was ajar to another room. Joan waited for Henry. Rake stepped across and pushed open the door. It was a formal reception room, with a set of sofa and chairs and a conference table. Against the far wall steel containers stood on cold hotplates. Next to them were urns for coffee and hot water. Rake ran some over his finger. It was tepid. Light came from a connecting shower room. Inside, damp towels hung on rails, and warm water dripped from the shower head.

Rake came out, leaving the door open. Now Henry was with Joan. Rake pointed to the control room, and Henry pushed through the plastic strips. The clattering noise they made against each other broke the quiet. There were four rows of computer terminals, six to each row. The screens were dark, as were larger ones on the walls, and the overhead fluorescent lights were off. There was a smell of smoke and sweat. The room was cold, with no heating.

Henry moved further towards the door that led to the field hospital. Beyond it a single lamp shone through more plastic strips. Rake signaled for him to stop. They were too exposed. No gambler would have taken odds on them making it this far.

Henry and Joan stood silent and still, each with their own thoughts. Who knew they were here, even where exactly they were? This was not a base with just one lone helicopter engineer. So, who was left?

Henry led them to the hospital. Light came from a single fluorescent strip over a bed in the far corner with an incubator next to it. Joan walked fast towards it. Henry stayed back, watching. Unlike the other room, the heating was on. Rake spotted a body on a bed opposite. The way the legs were splinted and bandaged, he guessed this was the soldier Ondola had shot from the snowmobile. But he had died here in the field hospital from a single gunshot to his temple. The round had gone through the brain and was embedded in a splintered wooden strut in the next bed. Vitruk's work.

Akna lay on her back, her eyes open and expressionless; the bag for the drip in her arm was streaked with saline stains and empty. The baby, her tiny head wrapped in a blood-stained bandage, twitched her arm in an uncovered incubator. Joan reached inside and rested her hand on Iyaroak's forehead. On the floor, lay Carrie's medical bag, bandages, syringes, and medicines scattered, as if it had been ripped from her hands and flung down. Outside, a helicopter engine started.

British Ambassador's residence, Washington, DC

Stephanie listened to Prusak, phone in hand, through an earpiece. He told her about the CIA satellite imagery of a Topol-M leaving the Toksong launch site on a truck. 'At the end of his inaugural speech, Holland will announce that he has launched military action against North Korea and Russia.'

'Unless we neutralize Vitruk,' said Stephanie.

'That's the thing,' replied Prusak. 'Holland wants to mark his presidency by teaching Russia a lesson it will never forget. The moment he has sworn the oath of office, the strikes will begin. The first missiles will hit targets around 12.12. Holland's inaugural speech lasts fourteen minutes and twenty seconds, allowing him to end it with the announcement.'

'We can't let him, Matt.' Stephanie's tone was determined and angry. On the television, she saw Swain just feet from Holland, who was the only prominent figure at the inauguration without an overcoat or a scarf. The President-elect stood upright, head high, no spectacles, no evidence of human vulnerability, ready to take the oath of office. Dignitaries quietly shuffled. Wind blew hair over everyone's eyes. A microphone stand needed to be steadied. Coughing reflected the cold. Overall, there was silence and expectation. Shadows and light speckled in different ways as clouds passed overhead. The white dome of the Capitol towered above them all.

They had time, but not much. In a few minutes, the Vice-President would be sworn in, after which there would be prayers, the marine band, readings, songs, and poetry that would last until noon. During that thirty minutes, Swain remained President of the United States. The second Holland was sworn in, Swain would be powerless. The new President would be the commander-in-chief. War was his to wage.

The Vice-President stood opposite the Chief Justice and placed his left hand on a tattered brown leather-bound Bible. The television anchor told viewers how this Bible had been passed down from the Vice-President's great-grandmother who had carried it with her on the sea journey from Ireland to the United States. President-elect Holland would be taking his oath on the gilt-edged velvet burgundy Bible owned by Abraham Lincoln.

Harry, hunched in the corner, kept talking, phone to his ear, hand gesticulating with frustration. Stephanie ran through her few options. Once Vitruk was neutralized, Britain and other European governments could force Holland to pull back. Until then, he would have legitimate grounds. She began another text message to Grizlov: 'You have to—'

He called before she had finished.

'We're holding back, Sergey. You have to—'

'Steph, you're not hearing me,' replied Grizlov, his voice raised and angry. 'Vitruk thinks he can win. I cannot stop him. Understand. Only you guys can.'

We can't, thought Stephanie. Not without going to war. 'Where is he?'

'On the base. But it has a bunker. If you strike, he can still operate and we will have to strike back.'

'He's your monster. Sergey. You need to deal with him.'

That she couldn't tell him more. She had given warning enough. Stephanie found herself trembling again. How could this be? Russia wasn't a horror extremist group. It had institutions, lines of command. 'Give me something, Sergey,' she urged. 'Help us. Don't just tell us what you can't do.'

'He's been authorized.' Grizlov's tone was low, controlled, bursting with fury. 'We have a system called Kavkaz. Your guys will know how it works.'

'What do you mean, he's been authorized?'

Grizlov said nothing.

'Sergey, for God's sake—'

'Enough, Steph. Enough.' Grizlov was gone.

She felt dismal and afraid. 'Kavkaz,' she told Harry. 'Vitruk has been authorized for Kavkaz. What the hell is that?'

'It's their nuclear code suitcase,' said Harry. 'Except it's now all electronic. He can work from a phone.'

Prusak's voice came down the line. 'We've tried the North Koreans. They deny anything at Toksong. The Chinese are silent.'

'Dmitri Alverov? The launch team in Toksong?'

'NSA has his number. Not getting through. Hold a moment . . . There's something happening on the base. We have a track on Ozenna.'

The Vice-President stepped back and the US Marine Band struck the first chords of 'America the Beautiful.'

'We have fourteen minutes, Steph,' said Prusak.

THIRTY-NINE

Big Diomede, Chukotka, the Russian Far East

Rake's phone lit with Stephanie Lucas' number. He hesitated. But it was inauguration time, which could bring in a strike on the base in just over twenty minutes. He answered.

'Captain Ozenna. Matt Prusak. Our tracking has you at the Big Diomede base. Can you confirm that, and that you can talk freely?'

'Correct, sir.' Rake spoke in barely a whisper. His cover was a stack of oil drums from which he could see, facing the hangar, the white MI-8 helicopter, red medical crosses emblazoned on its sides.

'Are you with Admiral Vitruk, or do you know where he is?' asked Prusak.

'Negative.'

'Vitruk plans to launch an ICBM. We need you to confirm him neutralized or dead before the end of President Holland's speech. That is before 12.15 Eastern Standard.'

'Copy that, sir.'

'Whatever is necessary, Captain.'

'There are American civilians here, sir.'

'If I can reverse these orders, Captain, I will. Until then, understand that civilian casualties will be far higher if this man wins.' Forfeit lives to save lives, the concept of collateral damage that had been drilled into Rake from his first days in the army.

Rake had less than fifteen minutes. He watched the helicopter in front of him for signs of human movement. The panel just underneath the tail wing hung open and the steel ladder lay fallen on the apron. Five circular windows ran along both sides of the fuselage. A lone pilot sat in the cockpit, his gaze down on the control panel and his right hand dealing with a switch above him. He was wide open to attack, dangerously visible through the transparent panels that made up the front of the aircraft. Rake was unsure if this was the same man he had seen working on the tail.

From where he was, Rake could see only two of the windows. Henry, on the other side of the hangar, was able to check them all. He signaled that he saw no one else in the aircraft. That didn't mean there wasn't. Henry lay still on the ground in black darkness near the hospital entrance, ready to fire into the cockpit. Joan was with Akna and Iyaroak.

The draught from the slowly turning rotor blade snapped a sheet of ice from the roof of the hangar. It smashed onto the apron like breaking crystal, throwing chips against Rake's face.

Then Vitruk appeared, darkening the arc of a helicopter lamp as he stepped into view, half a profile obscured by mist and light but enough for a shot. Vitruk stayed where he was, part visible, part in shadow. He didn't walk briskly to the helicopter as he should have done once on the tarmac. He was directly facing the hangar as if he knew Rake was there, and a lightning glance to Henry who had a better-angled view told Rake why – the tautness in Henry's face, his finger relaxed on the trigger just as Rake's own finger was tightening to fire. Carrie was handcuffed to Vitruk's right wrist. As she became more visible, she looked uninjured, walking upright and decisively next to Vitruk. She had on the same green parka. It was torn on the right shoulder and ripped across the left sleeve. There was a dark smear down the front.

Rake's lethal orders smashed like a meteorite into his concentration. It beat the hell out of him. Carrie was here because of him. She would die because of him. He would have to kill her. He tried to think straight. Instead, a world flashed in front of him without Carrie, bleak, black, apocalyptic. No color. He saw himself going mad like Don Ondola.

Vitruk kept walking towards him. He was wearing full dress uniform. He wore a blue-gray fur hat with a red star at the front, its flaps dropped over his ears, and medals adorned the chest of his greatcoat. He carried a phone in his right hand. As he moved closer, his thumb ran up and down as if he were stroking it, moving slowly from bottom to top.

Vitruk had positioned Carrie so that Rake could not make a clean shot. He could see no way of killing Vitruk without risking Carrie . . . without killing her . . . If he didn't shoot Vitruk and Carrie now, they would all be dead from an air strike on the base in a few minutes. What was the difference? And if he allowed Vitruk to go ahead . . . The White House Chief of Staff's voice bounced violently around his thoughts – *The casualties will be far higher if he succeeds.*

Vitruk stopped, lit by the helicopter lamp, midway between

the hangar and the aircraft. He pulled Carrie to his side. Rake could see her more clearly now. Her face was masked, her eyes goggled, her hands gloved, the hood of her green jacket pulled over her head. Strands of blonde hair blew about on either side. Her head was turned toward Vitruk. She looked nowhere else.

'I know you can see me, Ozenna.' Vitruk's voice was loud and confident. 'I can guess what your orders are. To kill me, whatever the cost. But the missile that your bosses in Washington are so worried about is activated in two ways.' He held up his free hand with the phone. 'One is by pressing a four-digit code on the dial pad of this phone. The other is losing my pulse, which the phone is monitoring through this strap around my wrist. Just to be sure you understand, Ozenna – if my heart stops beating the missile will launch. So, if you kill me to save Carrie, thousands and thousands more innocent people will die. I've arranged it like this to relieve you of the dreadful choice your country has forced upon you.'

Rake stayed quiet. He looked across to Henry, who was locking in a rocket-propelled grenade. Rake signaled for him to hold.

'Are you hearing me, Captain Raymond Ozenna?' said Vitruk.

Rake said nothing.

Vitruk continued. 'The American attack will come in just over ten minutes. Dr Walker and I are flying in this helicopter to our airbase at Egvekinot and then by plane to Moscow. Carrie will be thanked for her work and awarded a medal for her bravery by our State Duma. Then she will be free to go wherever she wishes. She will be proud. She is the daughter of loyal citizens of the Soviet Union. You will stay here to die in the American strike or you can surrender and come with us to Egvekinot, where you will be tried for multiple murders under the jurisdiction of the Chukotka Autonomous District.'

Rake heard a mechanical click as Henry moved forward the safety catch.

'All this may be a technicality, of course, if your government chooses to go to war.'

The helicopter lamp illuminated Vitruk like a theater spotlight. The moon flooded the rest of the apron. Cold seeped through Rake, making him shiver.

'None of this is your responsibility, Captain.' Vitruk peeled down Carrie's mask. 'Tell him, Dr Walker. Tell him not to be such a fool.'

Carrie turned towards the hangar. Rake could tell she couldn't see him, nor did she look for him. Her eyes were steady, like he had seen them a hundred times before. This was Carrie, who knew her own mind. She was telling Rake to stop Vitruk, just like she had insisted he escape from the school gymnasium. Escape. Just do, it Rake. Whatever the stakes. She knew the cost.

There was only one way to negotiate with Vitruk, only one way he could deal with his locked mind, and that was to strip away his motive. If Vitruk wanted to be President of the Russian Federation, if he craved to be lauded in Moscow, if his end goal was to be hailed as the Russian hero who took on America, then he needed to live to see it. Rake had to cut off his lifeline, expose his weakness, then move in and kill.

Rake raised and dropped his forefinger to signal Henry. A whining stream of flame left Henry's weapon and a rocket-propelled grenade drilled through the helicopter's cockpit. Its explosion tore the fuselage apart, sending out a reddish-white inferno in a blast that threw Vitruk and Carrie to the ground. Rake ran forward, weapon drawn, heat on his face, his path obscured by black smoke. Vitruk was in vision, gone, in vision again, on the ground, a pistol held against the left side of Carrie's head.

Rake stopped, his eyes locked on Vitruk's face. Carrie looked up, her focus on Rake. A smear of soot ran down from her right eye. Blood scarred across her chin.

RACKED WITH PAIN, CARRIE felt the burning heat of the explosion and Vitruk's pistol pressed hard against her temple. His crushing weight trapped her.

'Stay still,' he ordered.

Spreading flames cupped around the aircraft. 'The fuel tank,' she gasped.

'It's safe.' Against the roar of the fire, there was a calm in his tone. She turned enough to see that the wind was blowing the flames away from what used to be the cockpit. The tail which held the fuel tank was skewed but untouched by fire. Rake stood midway between the wreckage and the hangar, stock-still, frozen mid-stride, his face etched with dread and determination.

'So, you've decided to kill us all, Ozenna,' shouted Vitruk. 'You're murdering the woman you love.'

'I can get us out of this.' Rake took a step out of cover.

'How? We're now waiting for your cruise missiles,' said Vitruk.

Rake raised his arms above his head, part peace-offering, part showing off his automatic weapon. 'Hear me out, Admiral. Please.'

'You didn't let my men hear you out before you murdered them.'

'I'm a soldier, I was doing my job. Dr Walker is a civilian—'

'So now you listen, Ozenna. In a few minutes, your bombs will tear Dr Walker's limbs from her beautiful body. They will rip through her organs and their fire will burn her alive. Or, on your word, I'll be kind and shoot her now so she will die without pain.' His finger crept inside the guard to the trigger.

Slowly, so Vitruk could see his every move, Rake squatted and put his gun on the ground. He stood up, eyes locked onto the Russian. He brought out a phone from his pocket, holding it up in full sight. 'I'll open a line to Washington.'

'To do what!' yelled Vitruk. 'Russia will never surrender.'

'To bring in a helicopter to get you out, and we'll head back to Little Diomede.'

'Then what?' Vitruk's face twisted; the hatred and blame fermenting inside him for years were finally finding a way out.

Carrie's thoughts raced. Men like Vitruk were poisoned by anger, unable to feel anything outside of themselves. One wrong word, one wrong movement, and Vitruk would kill and feel nothing. She could never change his mind. She could not over-power him. The more Rake talked, the more Vitruk's fury boiled.

'Let me make the call.' Rake edged forward half a step. 'I can—'

Vitruk fired into the air. A flash of yellow and blue flame leapt out of the chamber, and the roar of an exploding pistol cartridge crashed through Carrie's eardrum. Rake stopped, hands raised, finger curled around the phone. The warm pistol barrel rested back against Carrie's temple.

'What can you end, Ozenna?' said Vitruk. 'More American bombs on more villages. More sanctions. More killings. More bullying. More of your fucking democracy. Never again will you strip Russia of her dignity.'

'I'm moving back, OK?' Rake took a step. 'Take the weapon away from Dr Walker. Let's wind this down.'

'If you make that call, she will die.'

Rake's finger stayed away from the keypad, but unexpectedly the phone lit, casting sudden light on his face. Carrie felt Vitruk stiffen. She braced for the pain and shock of a bullet ripping through her skull.

'That was not me,' Rake said. 'It's a message to this number. It's not me. OK?'

He was pleading, showing weakness, because he cared for her. She was dead anyway. Now. Five seconds later. Five minutes. What did it matter? She was getting in the way of what Rake had to do. She needed one try to get inside Vitruk's damaged mind, something that would cut through to reach whatever it was that made anyone human, however poisoned that humanity might be. The cold would prevent any of them lasting too long. Or an air strike. Neither Rake nor Vitruk were patient men. It was now, or not at all. One go, she told herself. One chance to help Rake. To give him that second of opportunity.

Vitruk pulled her to her feet, wrenching her arm in its socket. She scrambled up with him.

Rake shouted, 'The message is from Washington. You need to—'

'I need to do nothing!' screamed Vitruk. 'Tell them they are dealing with Admiral Alexander Vitruk, the man who—'

Carrie yelled across him, 'The man who killed Larisa, his own daughter!'

Vitruk's pistol butt crashed against her head, spinning her toward the ground. The cuff bit deep into her wrist. Her vision spun. Gray-black shades of darkness turned into a sea of white. She hung off him, unable to stand, unable to fall. He raised his arm for another blow, but she had got to him. His face was creased with uncertainty. She shouted, 'You are a man who can't stop murdering children and mothers because he was so drunk his own little girl is dead!'

He hit her again, twisting her head against her neck. She had reached his blackened heart. The blow was fast and ferocious. It left her head enveloped in pain, fighting to stay conscious. Then numbness took over pain. Her vision was gray, no colors. The helicopter flames danced a dirty glaring white. Snow on the granite hills lay lifeless. The buildings were gray under a gray sky. Her hearing was gone. Or the wind was howling so loud she couldn't hear. She lost feeling except for a draining, sapping cold. The next blow would kill her. She turned her head to look further, to find Rake. Where was he? She must speak to him, tell him not to blame himself. A new pain shot through her. Not a blow. A nerve in the neck. A muscle. Something torn. What was the name? Suboccipital? No. Trapezius? She should . . . Her numbness faded. Her wrist hurt. The hard cuff. Vitruk pulling against her. It had only been a second. Maybe two. So many thoughts. So much undone. No time to live. A cold wash of hopelessness coursed through her as she waited for the last lethal blow.

A flash. A single gunshot crack. The tug at the cuff, tearing into her skin, pulling her where she couldn't go. Uncontrolled. Vitruk jerked like he was dancing. Carrie's senses rushed back. Vitruk stumbled, his legs gone, pulling her with him. The icy concrete rushed up toward her as they went down together. He hit the ground hard, and Carrie fell on top of him, arterial blood jetting from his neck warm on her skin.

Vitruk was shot. He was dying. Muscles twitching. The gush of blood became a dribble. Body warmth chilled. The face contorted in the way that unexpected death rips away confidence.

Then Rake was there, just like when she first saw him, with no other purpose except to make her safe. He didn't speak. No smile. No reunion. This was the soldier she knew from the car bomb in Kabul. Rake placed the back of his hand against her neck, feeling for a pulse. Then, focused and fast, he unpeeled the heart monitor from the Russian's wrist and attached it to Carrie's. A pulse was a pulse. Her raised heartbeat pumped a signal to the phone that would keep the missile in its silo. Her breathing slowed. She tasted cold smoke from the helicopter fire. Then Henry came into view, moving carefully, checking each step, each inch, for hidden danger.

Rake recovered Vitruk's phone. 'Hold this,' he told Carrie. They were his first words to her, not a question, but an order.

He stepped back, leaving her with Vitruk's blood-soaked body. 'This is Captain Ozenna,' Rake said into same phone that had nearly killed them both. 'The base is clear. Admiral Vitruk is dead.'

FORTY

British Ambassador's residence, Washington, DC

'The base is clear. Admiral Vitruk is dead.' Stephanie heard Ozenna's clipped, exact words. Harry was listening, along with dozens of others between the embassy and the NSA technicians at Fort Meade. Ozenna left no room for doubt. No sub-clauses. The man who would trigger the missile was dead. Phones rang, screens flashed. In short bursts of words, Ozenna described how Vitruk had a smart phone that sent his arterial pulse in a digital signal to the launch site. 'It's over,' said Stephanie, struggling to envisage it all.

A voice of authority came across the line. 'Ambassador, Congressman Lucas. Thank you. We'll take it from here.'

Harry's eyes flared with anger. 'They've cut us out.'

'Meaning—?'

'It's far from over. Holland's still going ahead.'

Stephanie's stomach clutched. 'How can he—'

She stopped mid-question. Grizlov was on the line, taut, rushed, grateful, flamboyant. 'It's over, Steph. I love you. Thank you. Thank you.'

What to say? Harry's creased and worried face told her all

she needed to know. She looked to him for guidance. Before she replied to Grizlov, another voice came across the call, ignoring Harry and Stephanie. 'Chairman Grizlov, this is the Pentagon. Is Toksong stood down, sir?'

'It is stood down. Yes,' said Grizlov.

'We need immediate confirmation of that from Admiral Vitruk.'

Stephanie interjected. 'This is Ambassador Lucas. Vitruk is confirmed dead.'

'We are not reading that, ma'am.'

'Sergey,' said Stephanie. 'Can you confirm?' Nothing. The line was gone. Stephanie slammed her hand on the table. Who ended the call? Grizlov? Supposing it was a hoax? The Pentagon was right? Vitruk a decoy? Grizlov the architect?

'Got it,' Harry said into one of his phones. He turned to Stephanie. 'Strike targets are Toksong, North Korea. Also Providenya, Zvyozdny. In all, six Russian Arctic bases.'

'Can we stop Holland?'

'I don't know.'

On the inauguration platform, a country singer from Nashville performed a familiar old song that Stephanie couldn't quite place. After that there would be a poem, then the oath of office. Not many minutes left.

Firmness in his voice, Harry spoke on two calls, mixing Russian with English and Chinese. Looking straight at Stephanie, he held up his right hand with his thumb and forefinger almost forming a circle as if to indicate he was close, but not there yet. His sentences were measured, precise. She had forgotten his Russian was so fluent. Then, he closed the thumb and forefinger and said in English. 'Yes! Moscow has handed over the Fed bomber,' he said. 'It's the guy we pinned.'

Stephanie's mind was far away from the Fed bombing. Guilt stabbed through her for almost forgetting the murders there; frustration, too. Sure. Nice one, Harry. But it won't fix the job at hand. 'What about Holland?' she said. 'That's not enough for him.' Stephanie ran her fingers through her hair.

Harry shrugged. 'No. But we need it.' He continued speaking on the phone, in Chinese now, short, precise sentences. He was a military man. For Stephanie, the diplomat, part con, part persuasion, military thinking wasn't enough. Holland needed to know that if he didn't stop, he would lose what he valued most: his reputation. His presidency would be judged not on its first hundred days, but the first hundred seconds. How to show that? Who could challenge the Commander-in-Chief? How could any politician be so stupid? How could people elect someone so dangerous? Disbelief swirled. Stephanie smashed through her raging thoughts grasping for an idea. There were a million and more people. They stretched back from the Capitol Building through the National Mall. The inauguration was being watched on televisions around the world. She spoke to Prusak, then seconds later saw him on the screen, conferring with Swain who gave permission with a barely discernible nod.

Minutes away from taking his oath, Holland touched his lapels and straightened his jacket. He drew in his cheeks, expelling a cloud of air. His eyes flitted to the teleprompter embedded in the transparent bulletproof screen between the podium and the audience. He tilted his head forward, rounding his mouth, a smile at the edge of his lips, practicing the first lines of his speech.

Something caught his eye. His eyes locked on the audience, scanning, squinting against winter sunlight, clocking Swain, Pacolli, others from the outgoing administration and settling on an empty seat where Matt Prusak had been sitting and was now gone. Holland touched his right ear: someone was relaying information to him. He shook his head. Stephanie lip-read from him a 'no.' Holland looked sharply to his right. No, he will not change course. Anger swept across his face. Holland must have guessed what Prusak was planning and aimed to pre-empt. It wasn't working. Stephanie leant against the table edge to stop the trembling in her legs.

A cable channel switched to split-screen, half on the inauguration and half on Matt Prusak, away from the stage, among the crowds in the mall, brushing his hair off his forehead, with one of the channel's reporters who announced they were breaking into the inaugural feed because the outgoing chief of staff had an announcement.

'President-elect Holland has ordered military action against Russia.' Prusak's delivery was slow and calm. 'It is illegal, unnecessary, and dangerous. In the past few minutes, the Kremlin has officially notified President Swain that any further attack on Russia will be considered an act of war and lead to a full response from Moscow.'

'But Russian troops have invaded—' began the reporter.

'Our troops have expelled them from American territory. They were a rogue force, not the Russian government,' interrupted Prusak, brusquely. 'A President needs Congressional approval to wage war. Holland doesn't have it.'

While Prusak spoke, the shot moved to Holland, his face

strained, then to Swain, an image of composed authority. The inauguration faltered. Holland stepped forward, beckoning the Chief Justice, who hesitated and didn't move, eyes fixed not on Holland, but down toward Swain, seeking guidance. The shot changed again to the National Mall. A murmur rumbled through people crowded there. A scene from the Russian airbase on Big Diomede appeared on screens around them. Most was in darkness with shapes of buildings and harsh, steep hillsides. The murmur swelled to applause as what looked like a shaky smartphone camera showed flames from a destroyed helicopter, the red-star Russian insignia smeared with soot on what was left of its tail. A body lay on the ground, illuminated by a flashlight. On the overcoat lay the identity card of Admiral Alexander Vitruk, with a photograph, his signature, and the address of his Far East Military District Headquarters in Khabarovsk. The Russian flag, lit by dim moonlight, hung shredded on a pole behind. Two men unfolded the Stars and Stripes and held it like a banner between them. Rake Ozenna's voice played over it: 'This is Captain Ozenna. The base is clear. Admiral Vitruk is dead.'

Noise from the National Mall swelled, wolf whistles, high fives, hats thrown into the air. Holland was smart enough to join the applause, even though his eyes were narrowed with determination, no expression of shared victory.

'He's not finished,' Stephanie said to Harry who didn't seem to be taking notice, wasn't even watching the screen. He remained hunched on the phone.

Holland took control, raising arms to quieten the crowd. He readied his hand, fingers outstretched for the oath, giving the

Chief Justice little choice but to step forward with the Bible. A call came in from Downing Street, asking Stephanie for developments. The Prime Minister was about to address the House of Commons? Nothing that wasn't on TV, she said, her hand gripping the phone in frustration. Holland lay his hand on the Lincoln Bible. 'I do solemnly swear that I will faithfully execute—'

Harry was off the phone, stepping toward her.

'What?' she asked, impatiently.

'Now, we wait.' His voice was flat. No encouragement. Resigned.

Yes, that was it. Energy drained from Stephanie. They had given it their best shot. If Holland wanted war, he would make war. Harry had tried and failed. Prusak, too. Stephanie, Slater, a raft of people had given it their best shot. So, how would it unravel? America destroys six Russian Arctic bases. Where would Russia strike? Hawaii? Guam? Alaska?

She half tuned back into Holland's oath. '—the Office of President of the United States, and will to the best of my ability—'

Europe would flare. Estonia. Moldova. Ukraine again. North Korea again. Syria again. It wouldn't take long. It never did. Excitedly, Harry took her hand, gripped it hard. 'Now, Steph. Watch this,' he said. As Holland spoke, a strap ran across the bottom of the screen. A joint military operation had destroyed a missile base at Toksong in North Korea. The base was now neutralized and posed no further threat.

'—preserve, protect, and defend the Constitution of the United States.'

What was going on? Four nations, China, Japan, Russia, and

the US, had moved against North Korea. Together. Stephanie could barely take it in. While Holland wanted war against Moscow, her ex-husband had been fixing up for Russian and American pilots to fly side by side with Chinese and Japanese air crew riding shotgun? Or something like that. Applause from the National Mall lifted to a crescendo smothering the voice of Prusak, still on air, trying to explain. 'Yes . . . unprecedented . . . Swain acted with friends . . . And I should add—' But the crowd drowned him out completely. Add what?

Holland began speaking. 'Thank you. Thank you. My fellow Americans, it is a humbling experience—'

She studied Holland's face, looking for signs that he was backing down. There were none.

'—our enemies must be punished for violating our freedom,' he thundered.

Sweat filmed round the hollow of Stephanie's neck. Holland's face was impassive, his tone strident and unforgiving, like that wounded animal that keeps lashing out. Her phone buzzed with a message from Prusak, in fact a photograph of the Oval Office desk, empty apart from two envelopes, one cream and compact addressed to Holland in Swain's handwriting, the traditional letter from the outgoing to the incoming President. The other, held down by a glass crystal paperweight, was a larger, pristine white envelope that carried an official logo of the Justice Department.

'What?' messaged Stephanie.

Before Prusak responded a news strap ran under Holland speaking. *President Holland subpoenaed for Grand Jury investigation on alleged breach of Logan Act.*

Stephanie threw her head back, laughing. So, Swain had done

it! Barely a hundred seconds in and Holland's presidency was as good as dead.

Holland accused of deliberately escalating the Diomede crisis.

Stephanie tuned out. It was over. She cut the line to Prusak, ignored a call from Downing Street, and found herself turning to Harry. She flung her arms around his shoulders and gave him a full-on-the-mouth lovers' kiss. What the hell! They had won!

FORTY-ONE

Little Diomede, Alaska, USA

Rake paced the edge of the helipad of Little Diomede, taking in the rush of activity around him. Nearby, Carrie sat on a rucksack, in the shadow of a slowly turning rotor blade that changed her face from dark to light and back again as she sorted through her medical bag. Boots crunched through snow, soldiers, doctors, social workers, engineers, all deployed to mop up a war zone on American soil. Floodlamps lit the village like a stage. Noise from snowmobiles and aircraft drowned conversation, which was just as well because Rake and Carrie had tried talking and it hadn't worked.

As soon as Rake had reported the Russian base clear, he rifled through Vitruk's coat to find the key and unlock Carrie's cuffs. He helped her to her feet and embraced her. He told her he loved her. Thank God! She was OK! They were safe. It was over. He talked too much and she stayed quiet. Different people. Different reactions. He wanted to hold her, carry her off like in a story. But she was stiff, holding him, then pushing him away, holding him again. Prusak, the White House Chief of Staff, called and told Rake to film Vitruk's ID; to show the American flag, which he did with Henry. Troops arrived on a Black Hawk and hoisted a bigger one on the Russian flagpole, and the helicopter flew them all back to Little Diomede where they had medical checks and debriefs.

'All that killing you did was needed,' said Carrie, trying to explain, her eyes were everywhere, except on him. 'But I don't know if I can love you with it.'

You knew, he wanted to say. You met me like that. But he didn't feel like justifying. Not to Carrie. They had been together at the start and the end. In between, they went through their own horrors, and ejecting horror takes time.

That was how they ended up, him pacing, her sitting floodlit under roaring aircraft engines, Carrie to Brooklyn, Rake staying on the island because the army needed him.

She wore a new dark green army jacket, hair tufting out of the hood. Her eyes carried a long-distance stare. Her mouth kept shaping itself as if she were about to speak, shout something to him above the noise. But he heard nothing, and his imagination may have been willing it, playing tricks. He wanted to shout out to her, but what to say. No point yelling for something that no longer exists. She was a Brooklyn East Coast liberal, he an Eskimo soldier from the Diomede. They did hostile places well together, but only a crazy person would imagine the kids and white picket fence thing could ever work. He didn't know how to keep Carrie, didn't know what would happen if he lost her. Rake had never been so afraid.

He heard Timo's voice. 'Uncle Rake, Uncle Rake, they need you.' Timo, the kid who almost got them all killed, ran up, panting with excitement, burning energy, wearing the same loose thin anorak. Carrie stood up, animated, drawing on the boy's energy. She held both his hands. 'How are you, Timo? Are you feeling better?' She lifted the hood of his jacket to feel his forehead.

'We all think you're great, Dr Walker.' Timo's voice quivered.

'Your uncle is great, too,' Carrie glanced at Rake. Warmth flashed through her eyes, then vanished.

The pilot walked across. 'We're good to go, Dr Walker.'

Rake went to help with her rucksack, but Carrie was faster and picked it up herself. She got into the helicopter, buckled up, and put on headphones. The rotor blades powered up. Rake held Timo close against the down draught. He watched to see if Carrie would say something, just a word, even a signal. But the window was dirty and the light awkward. Maybe she did and he missed it. Then, as they took off, Carrie did touch her lip with her finger and gave a short wave.

The helicopter turned into the wind and rose in the sky, getting smaller and smaller until it became a black dot lost among the flocks of birds drawn out of the hillside by its noise. Rake wasn't sure he had ever understood white people.

Timo led them up the hillside where they heard singing and the rhythm of seal-skin drums. Henry and Joan stood over two open coffins. The bodies of Don Ondola and Nikita Tuuq, recovered from the ice, lay side by side in the burial ground. They had fought. They were family. Only the governments of white men had separated them. Flames lit the faces of villagers as they honored their dead with hunting songs from the islands of the Diomedes.

ACKNOWLEDGMENTS

Many thanks to the people of Little Diomede for their hospitality during my stay including Opik Ahkinga, Frances Ozenna, Gabriel Ozenna, Robert Soolook, Andrew Milligrock, John Ahkvaluk, Joan Kaningok and Henry Soolook who guided in our helicopter. I have borrowed names and drawn on your stoicism and bravery, but all characters are fictitious. Pilot Michael Kutyba from Erickson Helicopters dodged the weather to fly us in and out. Poloumi Basu came with me capturing the people and atmosphere of the Bering Strait and the Diomedes with her superb photography. In Nome, Jim and Bernadette Stimpfle and Sue Steinacher gave time and insight and Nancy Fiskaux and her family found accommodation even when their beautiful Angel Camp by the Sea was full up. In Anchorage, thanks to Tandy Wallack of Circumpolar Expeditions and to Colonel Patrick Carpentier and Colonel Charles Butler at Joint Base Elmendorf-Richardson which is responsible for protecting the US and Canadian borders and is home to the Eskimo Scouts and to Jon Gordinier for showing us around. Hugo Gurdon, Michael Barone at the *Washington Examiner* and others guided me through the pitfalls of a fractious transition and thanks to Dan Burton, Claire Bolderson, Bob Drogin, Matthew Felling, Craig Fleener, Claudia

Milne, Cait Murphy, Larry Moffitt, Carrie Roller, Claudia Rosette, Harlan Ullman, Andrew Wilson and to the many who prefer to remain anonymous.

Only skilled hands bring a book to publication. My thanks to Martin Fletcher, Mary Sandys, Constance Walker and Don Weise for their advice and editing of the raw manuscript; to David Grossman my agent of more than twenty years, and Kate Lyall Grant at Severn House, Holly Domney at Black Thorn, Stephen Mulcahey who crafted the cover designs and their very professional teams.